DEADLY CONNECTIONS

DETECTIVE SARAH SPILLMAN MYSTERIES BOOK 1

RENÉE PAWLISH

PROLOGUE

The footsteps stopped in the hall, and the boy heard the muffled voice from the other side of the door.

"Turn out the light."

The boy slid off the futon, legs trembling. He crossed the small basement room and hit the light switch. His eyes slowly adjusted to the darkness as he darted back across the room. He didn't have to worry about running into anything. The only furniture was the futon; the only other thing in the room was a portable camping toilet in the corner.

He heard a rattling sound, and the door swung open. A rectangle of light fell on the concrete floor and a hooded figure stood in the doorway. The boy could only see dark clothes, a ghostly shadow of a face.

Death.

At least, that's how the nine-year-old's brain thought of it. "Death," the skeletal, hooded figure that he'd seen in comics his dad collected. Although the boy thought some of the comics were stupid, he liked Batman, Spiderman, and Superman. However, the comic-book character Death always scared him. So did the figure standing across the room.

He scooted farther back on the futon until his back hit the concrete wall. He bent his legs and wrapped his arms around his knees, trying to pull away.

"Are you hungry?"

He nodded. His stomach growled. He wasn't sure how long he'd been in this room, a few days, maybe. He was sure he was in a basement room because of the concrete walls and the lone little window high up on one wall, with black paint covering the panes. The room was dank and the foul odor from the portable toilet in the corner was gross.

The figure took a couple of steps into the room, then stopped and just watched him. It was the same every time. The boy sucked in a breath and shivered. It was pointless to scream or yell. He'd done that when he'd first awoken in the dark room and felt his way to the door. All the yelling, all the yanking on the door handle, and nothing had happened. No one came.

Where was Mom? Where was Dad? His lip quivered and he wanted to cry. But he'd been told not to cry. He'd been told a lot of things: to stay on the bed, not to yell, and to be a good boy. He was afraid, terrified to do anything. He didn't understand, but maybe if he obeyed, he'd get to go home.

Again, a whispered "Are you hungry?"

He nodded.

Same question each time. Then he'd get food, then he'd be told that everything would be okay, he just needed to stay quiet. After that, he'd be left alone again. And the door would be locked.

This had gone on for a few days, or so he thought. Food was just a peanut butter and jelly sandwich and water. He was hungry. He was told that if he was good, he'd get more. Each time, he had to turn out the lights and sit on the futon.

Now the figure approached and put a tray with a sandwich and a cup of water on the edge of the futon.

"You're being good?"

The boy nodded slowly.

"What do you want?"

"I want to go home," he said with a whimper.

"No. You want to stay here. If you do, I'll get you all the toys you want. Would you like that?"

He'd been asked this a few times. The first time, he'd said no, he didn't want to stay here, and after he'd said that, no food came. The second time the question was asked, he'd said yes, he wanted to stay. But now he was tired, and he wanted his mom and dad.

"You want to stay here, don't you?"

He stared at the floor. He didn't know what to say. His stomach growled. He wanted desperately to reach out for the sandwich and the cup of water, but he didn't know what would happen if he did.

"Tell me you want to stay here."

He suddenly stood up and stomped his foot, then kicked the futon. "No! I want to go home!" he shouted. "Who are you? Leave me alone!"

He ran for the door. Strong hands reached out and grabbed him.

"You will stay here."

He struggled, but the powerful hands suddenly propelled him backwards. His body slammed against the wall, his head banging against the concrete. He dropped to the floor. He hurt so bad, but he was too scared to move or cry. He could feel the rage seething from the figure standing over him.

Finally, a stepping back. "You'll learn to like it here." Then the figure turned and left the room. The door locked with a loud click.

The boy got up and rubbed his head with a shaking hand. He

stared at the door, thinking *I don't want to stay here.* He didn't know what was going to happen here, had no understanding about any of it. He knew it would be bad, though. Panic set in, and he ran across the room and flipped on the light, then dashed back to the futon. He snatched up the tray. The sandwich and cup fell to the floor. He ignored that and climbed onto the arm of the futon. He slammed the corner of the tray against the window, once, then again. The noise was loud, yet in his panic, he didn't notice. The glass broke, and he reached up to pull some of it away. Then he heard the doorknob rattle, and the voice called out for him to turn off the light. He ignored it and hit the glass with the tray again. Then the door flew open.

The boy glanced over his shoulder. "No!" he screamed.

He grabbed the sill, oblivious to the glass that cut into his hands. He jumped and was able to get his arms partway through the window.

"Come back!"

Arms grabbed him and pulled him from the window. A shard of glass slashed his arm, and he cried out in pain. Blood poured from his sliced wrist. He fought, but the arms were too strong and he was only a boy. The cut was like fire on his arm, and he felt woozy. Then he felt hands pressing hard around his wrist, trying to stop the bleeding. But the boy fell to the floor, his eyes toward the door. His breath slowed, and darkness enveloped him.

CHAPTER ONE

The mood was somber as I approached the crime-scene tape. I nodded at the uniformed officer standing guard, and he barely gave me a glance. Death always has a way of sobering people, but this was different.

"You the one who called this in?" I asked. His nameplate read "Rivera."

He nodded and drew in a stilted breath. "Yeah, we got a call, said a guy was taking out his trash, and he saw an arm in the dumpster. He grabbed his cell and called us. When we–my partner, Flatt–and I got here, we looked in the dumpster and saw the arm, just like he said. I went into the dumpster, but ..." He shook his head. "There wasn't any chance he was alive." Rivera was being careful not to look toward the dumpster. He ran a hand over his closely cropped hair. He looked to be just out of college, green around the gills in every way, including death encounters. "We called it in, got the guy who found him out of the way, and secured the area. The coroner's here."

I pointed past him. "So the scene has been disturbed?"

He shrugged. "I can't say what the guy who found the body

did, but no one's been near the dumpster since Flatt and I got here."

My gaze darted behind him. A gray-haired man in shorts, a yellow short-sleeved shirt, and sandals stood near the corner of a house, outside the crime-scene tape. He glanced at Rivera and me nervously.

"Is that the guy?" I asked.

Rivera was still avoiding the dumpster. "Yeah. His name is Clark Leblanc. He knows you'll want to talk to him, so he's been waiting around."

I nodded. "Have you seen anything suspicious?"

Rivera shook his head. "Gawkers have been coming and going, but nothing unusual to note. Flatt's been talking to them."

I didn't say anything else to him, but ducked under the tape as Rivera noted in his log that I was entering the crime-scene area. I walked toward the dumpster. It was a behemoth of a thing, dark blue, beat-up, positioned between two red-brick houses. A full white trash bag leaned against the front of the dumpster. Canvassing the ground in the crime-scene area were two men and a woman. Standing next to the dumpster in dark pants and a white shirt was Jack Jamison, the Denver Police Department's coroner. A slight breeze fluffed his steel-gray hair. He was peering into the dumpster, and he turned when he heard me approach.

"Spillman, how you doing?" His lips were pressed into a grim line.

"Bad?" I asked.

He nodded slowly, his blue eyes impassive. "Take a look." He gestured toward the top of the dumpster.

I stepped up and looked inside. A few flies buzzed around, and the pungent odor of rubbish was strong in the air, but underneath it, I smelled death. More than ten years as a homicide detective did that to you. A small figure lay sideways amongst trash and black plastic bags. His brown hair was tussled, and he wore a dark T-shirt. I resisted rubbing a hand over my face, but I wanted to. Seeing death is always hard, but when it's one so young, it's even harder. I breathed out of my mouth as I shifted, trying to get a better view of the body.

"Looks like his wrist was cut," I said.

Jack nodded. "He's got a severe slash on his left wrist. Likely that it cut the radial artery, and he probably bled out in minutes."

I glanced at the CSI crew working the crime scene. "They've taken pictures, right?"

"Yes."

I shifted again. "Look at all the dried blood on his arm." The morning sun beat down on us. I squinted at the sky. It was going to be a hot May day. "Any idea how long the body's been in there?"

He shook his head. "With the sun, and the heat in the dumpster, who knows?" I gave him a look that prompted him to give me more. "He was probably put here sometime overnight."

I moved to the corner of the dumpster so I could look at the body from a different angle. "I don't see any other blood around. Think he bled out somewhere else and was moved here?"

"That would be my guess."

I gazed around the side of the dumpster and in back, but there wasn't any sign of blood anywhere. I figured as much, but I had to check. "There's no way he crawled in here and died."

Jack shook his head again. "I don't see how."

"Let me get a better look at the body."

"Be careful."

I hefted myself up on the edge of the dumpster and gingerly shifted the body so I could see the boy's face. His mouth was partially open, his brown eyes wide, as if his last moments were filled with terror. Smudges of dirt dotted his face, and dried blood streaked down his cheek and caked his clothes. He was so cute he could've been on TV. Then it hit me. I swore.

"What?" Jack asked.

I dropped to the ground. I had smudges on my blue blouse that I swiped at, then wiped my hands together, trying to get rid of not only the grime, but the traces of death. "That's Logan Pickett."

"The kid who's been missing for a few days?" Jack scratched his jaw. "I thought he looked familiar."

"He should. He's been in the news the last couple of nights."

"I'm too damn busy to watch the news." He pointed at the dumpster again. "You need anything more here?"

"Not at the moment."

"Okay, we'll be taking the body out soon."

"When will you get to the autopsy?"

He angled his head, daring me to push him. "Geez, Spillman, I haven't even moved the kid yet. How should I know?" I dared with a glare, and he backed down. "I don't know, this afternoon? Tomorrow morning? I know you want it fast. I'll do what I can."

"Thanks." I stepped back from the dumpster and turned to the CSI team. "Hey, Dale," I said to a short, stocky man. "You have anything for me?"

He shook his head. "Nothing so far. We're getting pictures and video." He shrugged. He's about thirty, but looks ten years younger. He's good at his job, though, and he'd alert me if he found anything significant.

He turned away, and I noticed a dark-haired man with broad shoulders enter the crime scene. He walked over and fixed coal-black eyes on me. Chief Inspector Calvin Rizzo.

"Do you have an update for me?" he asked, his voice smooth and commanding. Rizzo doesn't waste time or words, but is all business, all the time. He's hard-nosed and detailed. At times he rubs me the wrong way, probably because we're alike in many respects, and I've learned to work with him, hold my tongue at times, and speak up when I feel the need.

"The boy is Logan Pickett." Rizzo is three inches taller than my five-foot-eight, and I always feel the need to stand tall so I can come close to looking him in the eye.

He didn't say anything for a moment. "Okay, you'll have to talk to the parents."

"From what I remember from the news, they're divorced. I'll see who I can reach first." He waited, and I went on. "One of the responding officers has been interviewing the neighbors to see if anyone heard or saw anything."

"Good. Spats and Moore can talk to anyone with information." Roland "Spats" Youngfield and Ernie Moore are my partners. I was expecting them to show anytime.

Rizzo gestured at the CSI team. "Have they found anything that will help us?"

"Not yet."

"All right. Keep me posted." With that, he turned and walked toward the crime-scene tape. As he went under it, two men approached. He spoke to them briefly, then held the tape up for them. They ducked under it and walked toward me.

"Rizzo says it's a missing boy?" Ernie Moore asked in a deep voice.

"Yeah, it's Logan Pickett," I said.

"Ah, hell," he said. He hefted his pants up over his gut. He's generally one to crack jokes, but not now. Not with the death of a child.

"What do you have so far?" Spats asked. He wore a tailored suit and black shoes so shiny the sun glinted off them. I'd heard he'd gotten his nickname from an old partner who said Youngfield reminded him of a gangster from the old days, the men who wore spats on their shoes. I'd never seen Spats wear them, but the nickname had stuck.

I filled them in. Both nodded as they listened and looked around.

"So not much," Spats answered his own question when I finished.

"Right," I said. "We need to talk to the officers who've been canvassing the neighborhood."

"I saw another officer nearby. I'll get him," Ernie said. He walked off in search of the other responding officer.

"Hold on, Speelmahn," Spats said. For some reason, he gives my name a Jamaican flair, even though he's from Harlem. He went over to the dumpster, and when he returned, his face was pinched. "He was killed somewhere else and moved here."

"That's what it looks like."

Ernie returned with Officer Flatt.

I got right to it. "What do you have for us?"

Flatt cleared his throat, consulted a small black notepad. "We've talked to five neighbors so far." He waved a pen in the air. "It's a Tuesday, so a lot of people have already left for work. Of those I talked to, two have some good information." He checked the notepad again. "One, Larry Blankenship, says he got up about two a.m. to go to the bathroom. He sleeps upstairs, and the bathroom window faces the alley. He saw headlights at the end of the alley."

"Did he actually see a car?"

He shrugged. "It might've been an SUV. He didn't think much of the car itself, he just thought it was pretty late for someone to be out on a weeknight."

"Anything else?" Spats asked.

"No," Flatt said. "The other one is Karen Pacheco. She's pretty old, and she has trouble sleeping. She was dozing in front of the TV, and she thought she heard a noise out back, a loud thump or something. When she went to look, she didn't see anybody." He shrugged. "That's it. The other neighbors either didn't see or hear anything, or they aren't home."

"Addresses?" I asked.

Flatt rattled off the addresses for Larry Blankenship and Karen Pacheco. I thanked him, and he went to join his partner at the crime-scene tape.

"You take Pacheco," I said to Spats. He can be exceedingly charming, and I had no doubt he could get the old lady to open up.

"I'm on Blankenship," Ernie said.

"Good. I'm going to talk to the guy who found the body," I said. "Then I have to talk to his parents before news of this gets out.

Ernie twisted up his face. "I don't envy you that."

"Yeah, it's the worst." I gestured for them to get moving. "We'll meet up later."

Both gave me a mock salute and headed for the alley entrance. I watched the CSI team for a moment. It was a new investigation, and I was being revisited by the same unease I had with each new case. I had to perform well so that no one would ever have reason to question my abilities. I couldn't afford to have anyone delving into my past, into my life before I was even a rookie cop, to discover the one mistake I'd made then that could jeopardize my career even now. I quickly dismissed the thought and walked over to Clark Leblanc, who was still waiting by the corner of a house outside the crime scene.

"Mr. Leblanc?" I said. I introduced myself.

"Call me Clark." He had a hoarse voice, full of phlegm. He cleared his throat and shifted on his feet.

"How're you doing?" I asked.

He lowered his chin and stared at the dumpster. "I won't ever get that out of my head. I've never seen a dead body, let alone a kid." His eyebrows furrowed, and he cleared his throat again.

"I'm sorry," I murmured and gave him a second. "Would you tell me exactly what happened this morning?"

"Not much. I had my usual cup of coffee. Then I cleaned out the coffee pot, dumped the coffee grounds into the bag. It was full, so I put on my sandals and brought it out here." He jerked a thumb behind him. "I live there."

I glanced past him. Through an open gate, I saw a neatly manicured backyard and the rear of a two-story house. "And then?" I prompted him.

"I, uh, went to the dumpster and was about to toss in the bag, but I looked inside to make sure there was room. That's when I saw the arm. I didn't think I saw what I saw, so I looked again. I walked to the edge of the dumpster and saw his face. I could tell he was dead." Another throat clearing. "I dropped the bag and called 911. Then I waited."

"Did you talk to anyone?"

He shook his head.

"You didn't call anyone else besides the police?" I put a little force into my question.

"No, I didn't." A tinge of indignation in his voice. "I told you exactly what happened."

"All right," I said. "Did you recognize the boy?"

"No, but I didn't get a real good look at him."

"Did you notice anything unusual in the area?"

He looked around. "No, the alley's like it always is. It's usually pretty quiet out here, sometimes people walk through, or you get the occasional car. It's not as busy as the street, though. It's not like I'm out here a lot, though. Just to take out my trash."

"Did you see or hear anything last night, someone in the alley?"

"No. I'm a heavy sleeper, except when my bladder wakes me up." He smiled. "Last night I was up, and I told the other officer I thought I saw a car, an SUV, maybe. But I didn't get a good look at it. Then I was back in bed. My head hits the pillow, and I was out until six a.m. I'm up every day at the same time." He ran a hand through his gray hair. "Although tonight may be different ..."

"That's understandable." I thanked him for his time. "We might need to talk to you again."

"That's okay by me. I gave the officer my contact information. You call anytime." He frowned, stared at the dumpster as if it were guilty of the crime. "I guess I'll go inside."

I watched him go through the gate. When it shut, I went back to check with Jamison and the CSI crew. They hadn't turned up anything noteworthy, so I left to find out more about Logan Pickett's parents.

CHAPTER TWO

Rivera barely gave me a look as I ducked under the crime-scene tape, but he noted my departure in his log. He was almost as spooked as Clark Leblanc. Rivera was young, not used to this kind of thing. I shoved back the thought that no matter how much I've led homicide investigations, a part of me never gets used to it, either.

Logan Pickett's body had been found in an alley between Monroe and Garfield streets, a little south of Sixth Avenue. A mobile command post had been set up on Garfield, and I walked over to the big van. I poked my head in the door, and looked for Chief Inspector Rizzo. He was standing by a small counter where two men were working at laptops. They were already researching everyone associated with Logan Pickett, including his parents.

Rizzo glanced over. It was early, before eight, but the command post was already warm, and he wiped sweat off his face, then handed me a piece of paper. "Here's the address for the kid's parents. The mom lives on Cook Street, a couple of blocks from here. The dad lives south, near the University of Denver." He picked up a file folder. "Mom's name is Audra Pickett. She's forty-four, a real estate agent. She works out of her home, unless she's out showing houses, so she might be home. The dad's Gary Pickett. He's an insurance agent. We're checking to see if he has a policy on the kid. Anyway, he might be at home too. If not, try his work."

"Thanks."

"You know the details on this kid?" Still looking at the report.

"I heard something on the news, they said he disappeared Saturday."

"Right. The boy had been playing outside. When Dad showed up, the kid wasn't there. No one's seen him since. Until now." He looked up at me. "Get their stories yourself. When's the autopsy?"

"I pushed Jamison. He'll try to prioritize it."

"Good. Call if you get anything," Rizzo said. "This one's going to have more heat on it, press, and the like. The little boy, you know?"

I nodded. "I'll keep you posted."

As I walked away, I saw an ambulance parked nearby. Two men were walking toward the alley with the stretcher. A few people stood at the end of the alley, watching. The gawkers wouldn't get a show. The crime-scene techs would be careful to make sure nobody saw a little boy being lifted out of the dumpster.

I headed for my gray Ford Escape, which I'd parked around the corner from the crime scene. I also own a '65 Mustang, and I love the car, have had it since high school. It's a hell of a lot of fun to drive. Only in the summer, though. The car is crap in the wintertime. Cars are so much more advanced now, that driving the Mustang felt like driving a go-kart in the winter. No control in the snow or ice. I used to drive it for work, but between how it handles and the need to drive an inconspicuous car, I finally broke down and bought another car I use for work.

The Escape is boring but serviceable. Less pizzazz, more reliability.

Time was a precious commodity in the early hours of an investigation, and I was thankful it was just a minute or two to Audra Pickett's house. The late nineteenth-century houses originally built in the area were a thing of the past, razed to make way for ones like Audra's, a two-story brick-and-siding modern structure that was sandwiched between two others of a similar style, big, newer homes built on small lots.

The real estate business is good, I thought, as I parked in front of her house. This close to the Cherry Creek Mall, housing was at a premium.

The street was void of cars, most people at work. Tonight, cars would line the blocks since most of the houses in these old neighborhoods either didn't have a garage or had small garages accessed through alleys. I got out, smoothed my slacks and tried once again to get the grime from the dumpster off my shirt. I shrugged, then walked up the sidewalk. I stepped onto a small covered porch and rang the bell.

The door opened a moment later to reveal a tall woman in jeans and a green pullover. Audra Pickett had a cell phone to her ear, and she looked at me inquisitively, but she couldn't hide the strain at the corners of her eyes.

"Yes?" She said and gestured with her other free hand at the phone. She had chewed her fingernails, a contrast to the rest of her appearance.

"I'm with the Denver Police Department," I said in a low voice, so the person on the other end of the phone wouldn't hear me.

Audra's eyebrows rose, a bit of hope there that I knew I was going to crush.

"Hey, I'm going to have to call you back," she said into the phone. Then she abruptly ended the call and stared at me. "You have news about Logan?" Before I could answer, she blurted, "What?"

"Perhaps we should go inside."

"What?" Then it dawned on her. I wasn't here for good news. "Wait. No." Her hand shook as she stepped back and held open the door. "What's going on?" Her voice had taken on a shrill tone. "Who are you, and where's the other detective I talked to?"

"Could we sit down, please?" I said.

"Tell me," she said forcefully.

I gestured where I could see the living room. She looked at me, then turned on her heel and stomped into the room. She sat on the edge of a leather chair, and I took a couch across from her. The silence was overpowering.

"What is it? What have you found out about Logan?"

"I'm with the homicide department," I began.

The hope drained from her face. "Oh God, no!" Her mouth opened and closed. No sound came out. Then, after a moment, she moaned. "What happened?"

"I'm afraid your son is dead," I said softly. "His body was found this morning in a dumpster in an alley near Garfield Street."

She burst into tears and buried her face in her hands, rocking as she moaned softly.

"No, no," she kept repeating. Then she sucked in a ragged breath and choked. As she started to cough, I stood up and went hunting for the kitchen. A faint fruity smell hung in the air as I opened cupboard doors until I found a glass. I filled it with water from the sink and went back into the living room. I handed it to her, and she took a little sip, coughed a little more, and then seemed to regain some control.

I returned to the couch and waited. This was her time, and I would let her have what she needed. I had no idea what she was really feeling, what it felt like to lose a child, and I hoped I never would. Through an open window, a bird chirped. I wanted to tell the damn thing to stop its cheery tune. Audra finally dabbed at her eyes with the back of her hands, then took a longer drink of water. With a shaky hand, she set the glass on a coffee table and looked up at me.

"Tell me everything," she said.

I drew in a breath. "We don't have much. Logan's body was found in a dumpster on the next block from your house. We're not sure on the cause of death yet."

"I don't believe it," she said quietly. "Oh, Logan." Then, "It wasn't an accident?"

I shook my head.

Her eyes widened. "I have to call Gary."

She stood up, swiped at her phone, then put it to her ear. "Gary ... stop." She walked out of the room and talked in the hallway. At one point, she sobbed. Then she raised her voice. "I don't know yet. I'll call you back."

She appeared a second later, wiping tears from her cheeks. She sat down and took a deep breath.

I waited another moment, then said, "I need to ask you some questions."

She nodded and sat straighter. "Of course."

"Logan disappeared three days ago, correct?" I said. "Saturday night."

"Yes, that's right." She worked hard to keep composed. "Saturday evening. He went outside to play, and the time flew by. The next thing I know he didn't come back inside. It's never been a problem. He and Terrell Anderson play either in our yard or theirs."

"What time was this?"

"Around six."

"Where does Terrell live?"

She pointed at the front window. "Across the street and

around the corner. Usually Terrell's mom, Latoya Anderson, or I have our eye on the boys. They know not to run off. That evening my ex-husband, Gary, was supposed to pick up Logan. I had some business to take care of, so I had Logan's bag on the porch, and he was playing in the yard. Then he hollered that he was going over to Terrell's, and I told him to be back in time for his dad to pick him up. The next thing I know, Gary is storming in the house, calling out for Logan, wondering where he is. He never knocks, just comes in like it's still his home." Fury swept across her face, then she frowned. "At first, I thought Gary was looking for a fight, but then I realized he was serious, and Logan wasn't home."

I glanced past heavy tan curtains into the yard. "It wasn't until your husband came in that you realized Logan was missing?"

"Ex-husband," she said pointedly. "And yes, that's when I knew Logan was gone."

"What happened next?"

"At first, we just figured Logan was still over at Terrell's, so I called the Andersons, but Logan wasn't there."

"And then?"

"Well," she looked away, her face scrunched up in pain. "Gary and I got in a fight."

"What exactly did you fight about?"

"He was furious that I let Logan stay in the front yard, that I wasn't watching him, and that he'd run off." She sniffled. "Logan's gone over to Terrell's plenty of times while he's waiting to be picked up, and he's always home in time. This one just happened to be different." The guilt dripped from her voice.

She gnawed at a fingernail. "The thing is, I was barely away for any time. I watch Logan when he's out in the yard, and I did until he went over to Terrell's. But the phone had rung, and I needed to check some paperwork for a client. I lost track of the time." Her voice trailed off.

She started crying again, and reached for a Kleenex on an end table. She managed to get control of herself and sniffled. "Gary was yelling at me, but we called the police and reported it. A couple of officers came out to talk to us, and they talked to Latoya and Terrell too. Latoya said Logan left their house a little before seven, and she assumed he'd come straight home. We looked all over the neighborhood, but we couldn't find Logan. He just seemed to disappear without a trace. It got dark, but we kept looking. And the next morning, we looked some more. We got the neighbors involved, and as well as some friends, but we didn't find Logan. Obviously," she tacked on.

"None of the neighbors heard or saw anything?" I knew the answer, but I wanted to see whether she would put a different spin on it now, after a few days.

"No, no one saw anything. We talked to Logan's friend, Terrell, too, and he didn't know anything, just that Logan had said he needed to go home because his dad was coming to pick him up. On a Saturday night, it's busy around here, cars coming and going. If anyone saw anything unusual, they're not saying."

"Would Logan go with a stranger?"

She shook her head vehemently. "No way, I've told him never to talk to strangers. He wouldn't do something like that."

"Even with a little persuasion?"

"No. He's a smart kid, and he listens."

"You don't know of anyone who would want to hurt him?"

"He's ... was, just a little boy." The words came out in a stutter. "Now?" she said after a long pause.

"How well do you know your neighbors?"

"Okay, I guess." She backtracked. "I know those right around me. Farther up and down the block, I just know them by name."

She looked at me with some of the saddest eyes I'd ever seen. "What else do you need?"

"May I look in his bedroom?"

"Of course."

She stood up and without a word led me upstairs and down a short hallway to a room. "I haven't touched a thing since the other night."

I stepped into the room, but she stayed in the hallway, as if crossing the threshold was somehow forbidden. I looked around. It was a big room, certainly bigger than the one I'd grown up in. I'd had to share a room with my sister until I was a teenager. Logan had plenty of space, and plenty of toys. A racecar bed sat in the corner, with red and blue sheets. A desk was set against another wall, next to it a dresser, and the wall by the door had a bookcase full of superhero figurines, books, and a few model cars.

"He made the cars with his father," Audra said.

I moved to the desk. A couple of pieces of paper were on it with a child's handwriting, some schoolwork, and a few comic books. I looked but didn't touch them. Spider-Man, Batman, and Superman.

"Gary is into comics," Audra said from the doorway. "He would spend so much time and money on those stupid things. I didn't see the point of them, still don't. But Logan loved it. I think it was a way for him to connect with his dad." Her face tightened. "Although Gary would get furious if Logan touched them, or damaged them in any way. They were so valuable to Gary. He finally bought cheap comics for Logan to play with, but even then, he got angry that Logan didn't treat them better."

"Did Gary and Logan get along?"

She shrugged. "Overall, I guess. Gary was busy with his job. He's an insurance salesman, and he has a lot of clients, puts in a lot of hours, and that would take away time from Logan. But, I guess I have to admit, Gary would try. When he wasn't busy.

And Logan, well, he's like all little kids. He just wanted some of his father's attention. It's been hard since the divorce, his shuttling between Gary and me."

"How long have you been divorced?"

"Eight months. It was the best thing for Logan. And me too." She looked away. "Gary could drink at times, especially toward the end. And we fought a lot. It was rough."

"Was he abusive?"

"Nothing like that." Still no eye contact.

"Do you have any other kids?"

"I have an older daughter, Debbie, from a previous marriage. She's going to be devastated. She loves Logan."

"Did your daughter get along with Gary?"

She shrugged. "I guess. Debbie was already twelve when I married Gary, and she didn't spend a lot of time with him." She was being evasive. "She's in college now and hardly sees Gary."

"Tell me about Logan's friends, other than Terrell."

"Oh, he has a few friends from school, but he didn't see them much because they live farther away. He has some friends on his baseball team, although he's not very good. It was important to Gary. There aren't any other kids Logan's age besides Terrell in the neighborhood." She glanced around, then stepped into the room. "Huh."

"What?"

She pointed to the desk. "There's a little Batman figurine that's missing. Logan practically wore it out." She put her hands on her hips. "Maybe he took it to Gary's house."

I looked where she did, didn't see anything. "So there's no one Logan would run off to see? No other friends?"

She shook her head.

"May I look in the closet?"

"Sure, and the dresser, if you want."

I looked in the closet first. Logan had a lot of clothes, a few pairs of shoes. Nothing hidden. The dresser had a lot of T-shirts with superheroes on them. I gave the room one final look, then looked at Audra. "I think I'm finished here."

She turned quickly, desperate to be away from her son's room. I followed her back downstairs and we stopped in the entryway.

"Oh," I said. "Did Logan have a cell phone?"

"Yes. Not until Gary and I divorced. It was so much easier for Logan to keep in touch with us when he was at the other's house. I monitored his calls, and he didn't have a data plan, so he couldn't text or use the Internet."

"Who's the carrier?"

"Verizon."

"Both you and Logan are on that plan?"

"Yes." The answers were becoming shorter.

"One final thing, for now. May I take your laptop? We'll want to check it, just routine."

"Sure, whatever you need." She glanced over her shoulder. "I don't know how much I'll be doing at the moment, and I can check email on my phone."

"We'll return it as soon as possible."

"It's no problem." She went into another room and returned with a thin laptop. "Here you go."

I took it from her. "I'm so sorry for your loss." I'd had to deliver that line before, and it never got easier.

"Thank you," she said, but it was rote. She'd gone into shock and wasn't feeling much at this point. The tears would come again, but right now she appeared numb.

I had a business card with all my contact information in my pocket. I handed it to her. "If you think of anything that might help us find Logan's killer, please call me at any time."

She took the card and stared at it. "I've got to call my family." Her thoughts were coming disconnected.

"Where do they live?"

"Maryland." Then emotion crept back into her tone. "Find whoever killed my baby."

Those words stayed with me as I walked out the door and down the sidewalk. I sat in the car for a moment to gather myself. Discussing the death with a family member was difficult. Unfortunately, I had to do it again.

CHAPTER THREE

As I walked past a silver Toyota Tacoma and up a long driveway, the screen door to the '50s ranch-style house opened.

"Are you that detective?"

The speaker was a man in his late thirties with short hair and a military bearing.

"You must be Mr. Pickett," I said.

He nodded curtly. "Yeah. Audra called me. Come on in."

Over the years, I'd grown accustomed to people handling their grief in different ways. At that moment, it seemed that Gary Pickett was working hard at concealing his grief over his son's death.

Gary whirled around and stalked into the house without holding the door open. I stepped up onto the porch and grabbed the door before it swung shut. By the time I entered the house, Gary was already down a hallway, past a closed door, headed toward the kitchen. He sat down at a round table near a long island and gestured for me to take a seat. I sat down across from him. A news program played on the TV in the family room. He grabbed his remote and shut it off.

"How did Logan die? Audra didn't tell me."

"I'm sorry for your loss," I said. He brushed that off with a glare. "She doesn't know much," I went on. "Neither do we, just yet."

The muscles in his square jaw pulsed. "I should be at work, you know. If this hadn't of happened." He tapped the table with a finger emphatically. "But I can't concentrate."

"What do you do?"

"I sell insurance. I should be at the office now, but like I said ..." His voice trailed off.

He wore khakis and a short-sleeved shirt, and had on strong cologne. I wondered if he needed to keep a routine, still getting ready for work to keep his mind off his missing son.

"What happened last Saturday night when you came to pick up Logan from Audra's house?" I asked.

Hard blue eyes bored into me. "I normally pick up Logan on Fridays, but I had a conflict, so I couldn't get him until Saturday. Did Audra tell you that?"

I shook my head.

"I was running a little late, and I called Audra to tell her that. When I drove up to her house, Logan wasn't around. I parked and went up to get him, like I usually do."

I studied him carefully. "You called Audra to tell her you were going to be late?" This I hadn't heard, either.

"Yeah, but she didn't answer. I left her a message. I also called Logan a little before that, and he said he'd be home and waiting for me."

One more thing I hadn't heard, and I made a mental note to follow up on it.

He scowled. "When I went inside, Audra was surprised. She had no idea where he was." The index finger tapped the table hard. "Did she tell you that she lets him run around outside, and she doesn't watch him?"

"She told me that at first she knew he'd be in the front yard, then that he was at his friend Terrell Anderson's house."

He snorted. "She may have said that, but she doesn't keep track of Logan. When we were married, she didn't watch him, and she doesn't now. It doesn't take much to have a kid disappear." Anger laced his tone. "She said she got distracted, but I know her. She wasn't paying attention."

"Audra told me you came into the house without knocking."

His shoulders tensed. "Yeah. I called for Logan, and he didn't answer. Audra was mad at me for walking in, but I was worried about Logan."

I didn't catch a lot of concern in his demeanor, more annoyance at his ex-wife. "What did you do when you realized he wasn't around?" I asked.

"We checked his room and the rest of the house, then went outside and searched all around for him. We couldn't find him anywhere. Audra ran over to the neighbor's, but he wasn't playing outside there, either. Then Latoya Anderson came over and we looked everywhere. We called out for Logan some more, and I drove around the neighborhood. But he was gone."

"You didn't notice anything, or anyone, suspicious?"

"Like I told the other cops Saturday night, no."

"Audra said the two of you fought a lot."

He rolled his eyes. "She told you about our divorce?" I didn't reply, and he went on. "She and I didn't get along, okay? But whatever she might've said, it's not true."

"Okay," I said noncommittally. "Did Logan have any trouble with his friend Terrell?"

"Not that I know of." He bit his lip, in anger or grief, I wasn't sure. "You have to keep your eye on kids. You can't take any chances."

I ignored the slight against his ex. "Is there any reason why Logan would run off? Any reason why he might not have wanted to visit you last weekend?"

He fixed hard eyes on me. "Why wouldn't he want to come with me? I'm his father."

I shrugged. "Just asking the question."

He shook his head. "Logan and I got along just fine. He was an okay, kid, you know? He was happy. He enjoyed coming over here."

"How often did you see him?"

"I have ... had him on Tuesday nights and every other weekend."

That didn't seem like much to me, I thought. But I didn't know how custody arrangements worked these days.

"What kinds of things did you and Logan do?"

"I don't know." He looked away, and for the first time since I'd been there, his face softened. "We would ride bikes. I fixed up an old Camaro, and he liked that. I'd take him for drives, going fast. He thought that was pretty cool. When he was younger, he and I built a couple of model cars together. Well," he held up a hand, "I mostly build them, and he watched. He seemed to have fun with it."

"He liked comics?"

"You heard that from Audra?" I nodded. "Yeah, I've collected comics since I was a kid. I have a big collection. Audra couldn't stand them, but Logan thought it was cool."

I waited to see if he'd say anything about Logan not touching his prized possessions, but he didn't. I glanced around. The kitchen was exceedingly neat, nothing on the counters, no dishes in the sink. Did that come from a military background?

"Did you let Logan read your comics?"

He shook his head. "No way. A lot of them are really valuable. You don't let a little kid mess with stuff like that." His face was stony. "I bought him some of his own, that he could rip up or wrinkle or whatever."

"And you were okay with that?"

"I don't know why he couldn't be more careful with them, but whatever."

"Logan played baseball?"

"Yes, on a rec team."

"Did he enjoy it?"

"Yeah, I guess." He glowered at me, waiting for me to go on.

"May I see Logan's room?"

"Sure."

He pushed back from his chair and stood up, his shoulders squared. I wondered if he ever relaxed. He marched downstairs to a small room off a great room with a pool table and beer signs on the walls. A small display case held a collection of knives.

"What branch did you serve in?" I asked.

"Marines."

"Thank you for your service."

He ignored that, went into the bedroom, and gestured for me to come in. "Logan slept in here."

Not his room, just where he slept, I thought.

The room was tiny, with a twin bed with white sheets and blanket against one wall, a metal desk in a corner, a small dresser, and a closet.

"Mind if I check around?" I asked.

He shook his head. "Go ahead. The other cops did that when they were here. I don't know what you'll find."

I felt his eyes on me as I looked at the bed, then under it and in the dresser, then in the closet. It didn't take me long. There was nothing in the dresser drawers, and only one child-sized plaid shirt hanging in the closet. It was a decidedly different feel than Logan's bedroom at Audra's house.

Gary looked around at the sparseness. "Logan brought his stuff with him."

Not inviting at all, I thought. *How much fun was it for Logan here?* "His stuff?"

"He'd bring clothes from his mom's house, so why would I keep anything here? And he packed the things he might want to play with for the weekend as well." His explanation was as lame as the room.

I nodded. "I'm sure it was mostly about spending time with you."

"I hope so."

"Audra thought he might've brought a little Batman figurine over here."

"I think I remember it around. I don't know where it is now."

"Nothing on the walls?" I observed.

He shrugged. "Logan didn't seem to care, and I wasn't much into decorating."

"Did he spend much time in here?"

He stared at me for a second. "I don't know, I guess. We didn't have a ton of time together, and I'd try to entertain him."

"You liked having Logan visit?"

"Sure," he said without conviction, then suddenly, "Let's go back upstairs."

I clenched my hands, then relaxed. *Good lord, he's like a board, rigid, no emotion*, I thought. I took a last look around and followed him back to the kitchen. This time, he didn't sit down. I again remained in the doorway.

"So after you searched the neighborhood, then what?"

He stood a bit straighter. "We called the police. They sent two officers over. We talked to them, and they said they'd look around." He shook his head in disgust. "Man, that was a waste of time. Logan was gone. I finally came home, and I didn't sleep a wink. The next day we looked for him more, but of course he was nowhere to be found." Anger caught in his throat. "Until now."

"When you came home, what did you do?"

He glanced away. "I watched TV."

"Alone?"

He took his time answering that. "Audra doesn't know, but I've been dating a woman. She was here."

"Did Logan know her?"

"He'd met her a time or two, but he didn't know we were dating. She never spent the night when he was here. I called her Saturday night, and she came over. I didn't want to be alone," he tacked on.

"What's her name?"

"Kristi Arnott. I suppose you'll want to talk to her."

"That's correct."

He gave me a number, and I memorized it. "Did you talk to anyone else that night?"

"No, just Kristi."

"What about last night?"

"I was home, alone."

"All night?"

"Yeah. I spent the day trying to find Logan. I was exhausted."

"You have a step-daughter?"

"Yeah. I don't see her much. She's off at college now."

I didn't even need to ask the question about his relationship with her. No love lost there.

"Logan was found in an alley on the next street up from you. Did you know the people in that area?" I asked.

"No, just seeing people as I pass by. I don't know many of the people in the old neighborhood. I work a lot, and my friends don't live in the neighborhood. I have no idea why Logan–" now he choked up a bit, "why he would be playing anywhere but Audra's or Terrell's house."

I gave him a moment. "Have you ever been in trouble with the law?" I'd been waiting to ask this, as I'd wondered if it would shut him down.

"No," he snapped. He shoved his hands in his pockets.

"Where are you from?"

"What does that matter?" Then he said, "Sacramento."

"Do you have a laptop?"

"Yeah, why?"

"May I take it? We need to check it."

"Oh, I get it." He took a couple of steps toward me. "You think I might've done something to Logan? Are you crazy? He was my son." Again, I waited. His eyes were cold. "You want it, you can get a warrant."

That I will, I thought. I met his gaze. "Is there anything else you'd like to tell me?"

He stared at me. "Find out who killed my son."

"I'm working on it."

CHAPTER FOUR

I sat in my car and stared at Gary Pickett's house. He didn't seem overly broken up about his son's death. Or he was holding back his emotions really well. Just because he wasn't acting the way I thought he should, did that mean he was responsible in some way for his son's death?

I had conflicting information from Audra and Gary. He seemed certain she didn't keep a close eye out for her son, contrary to what she'd said. She indicated he had a temper, which he denied. Who was telling the truth, or were they both lying? One thing was certain: I wasn't ready to take either of Logan's parents off my suspect list yet. I pulled out my phone and dialed Ernie.

"What're you doing?" I said when he picked up.

"I finished talking to the neighbor, Larry Blankenship, and I was heading back to the office."

"Do me a favor. I need a warrant for Gary Pickett's laptop. He didn't want to surrender it, and I want to know what's on it. I think he's hiding something."

"Not a good move on his part," he groused.

"Uh huh."

We discussed the details of the warrant, and Ernie said he'd get on it right away. I ended the call and thought for a moment. I knew I'd have to circle back to Audra and Gary, but for the moment, I had another stop to make.

I didn't have to ring the bell at Latoya Anderson's house because three women were coming out the front door as I stepped onto the porch.

"We'll see you later," a woman with mocha skin and black curly hair said from the entryway as she held open the door. I assumed this was Latoya Anderson. An inquisitive smile crossed her face at the sight of me. "May I help you?"

One of the other women hustled down the sidewalk, but the other two–one a buxom woman in jeans and a tight-fitting shirt, the other taller with dark hair and a curious look on her face–hesitated on the porch steps.

I introduced myself, and before I could say more, the dark-haired woman held up a hand. "Oh, is this about the situation this morning? A detective came to my door about an hour or so ago, asking if I had seen or heard anything last night or early this morning."

I nodded and looked at Latoya. "Could we go inside and talk?"

She hesitated, a frown spreading across her face. "What's this about?"

The taller woman turned toward us. "Is everything all right?"

"Yes, Mallory," Latoya said, although her tone indicated she wasn't too sure. "A detective was here right before you all showed up." To me, she said, "We just finished our book club. We," she pointed at the other women, "all have had kids at Roosevelt Elementary. It's not too far from here."

"Should we stay?" the woman in the jeans asked.

"Joyce ..." Latoya started to answer.

"Do you two live nearby?" I asked the other women.

Mallory shook her head.

"No," Joyce said.

"You weren't around here last night, or Saturday night?"

They both shook their heads. "Why?" they asked in unison.

"I need a few minutes with Latoya," I said. I wasn't telling them anymore. They could hear it from someone else. Both women looked at me curiously.

"I'm sure it's nothing," Latoya said. "I'll call you both later."

Joyce took a couple of steps, then tugged at Mallory's arm. "Come on."

I waited until the two reached their cars, then looked at Latoya. She stepped back and let me in. We went into a living room decorated in earth tones and sat down. A tray with remnants of finger food and four cups were on a coffee table in front of a dark couch. The rich aroma of coffee still hung in the air. Latoya gestured for me to sit in a chair by the window, and she perched on the edge of the couch.

"What's this about?" she said pointedly, then cleared her throat. "You've piqued my curiosity."

I listened for a moment. The house was quiet. "Have you talked to Audra Pickett today?"

She shook her head. "I saw her drive by when I was taking my son to school. I waved at her. I have no idea where she was headed. With our busy schedules, she and I usually only see each other periodically. You know her son is missing, right?" Then it dawned on her why I must've been there. Her face fell and a hand went to her mouth. "Oh no. Is this about Logan?"

I hated my answer, but said, "Yes." I looked at her grimly.

"I'm afraid he's dead. His body was found in a dumpster in an alley near here."

Her lip trembled. "Oh my god, no. I just can't believe it."

I waited, giving her a moment. "Did you see or hear anything around your house last night?"

Latoya shook her head. "The detective who was here earlier, Moore, I think his name was, he asked me the same thing. I was over at Audra's house until after eleven, and then I walked home. I didn't notice any unusual cars on the street, and I didn't hear anything either. It was quiet. My family was all in bed, and when I got home I went to bed too. I have to admit, I've been tired because the last couple of nights I've been over at Audra's house until late. Last night I went right to sleep."

"Did your husband see or hear anything?"

She laughed, a tiny noise. "Rob sleeps like the dead. He was barely aware that I got into bed." She stood up and went to the window. She parted sheer curtains and looked out. "How is Audra doing?" Her voice shook.

"About like you'd expect," I said. "There's no easy way to deliver this kind of news."

She turned, tears in her eyes. "Logan is ... was ... such a sweet boy. I can't believe this." She wrapped her arms around herself. "When Logan disappeared, I couldn't help but wonder what might've happened, but I just kept holding out hope that he would show up."

"I understand he was over here playing with your son right before he disappeared?"

She finally sat back down, her hands in her lap, fidgeting with a gold watch on her wrist. "Yes, we had eaten dinner and the boys had gone outside for a while, and then Terrell, that's my son, came inside and said that Logan had to go because his dad was going to pick him up. As far as I knew, that's what had happened, until Audra called me and said that Logan was missing. I ran over to their house, and my husband and I helped them search the neighborhood for Logan." She shrugged and said in a small voice, "But he was gone."

"How did Audra and Gary act?"

"They were both devastated of course. But," she stopped.

"What?"

"Audra seemed upset about Logan being gone, and so did Gary, but he seemed angrier at Audra than anything else. But that's the kind of guy he is."

I arched an eyebrow. "Meaning?"

"I hate to talk about Gary." She tilted her head. "But I guess you need to know. Gary has a temper. I don't know if Audra told you that, but that was a big reason why they divorced. Gary can be very charming, but he's ex-military and he's rigid and controlling. And boy, can he get angry. I've seen that."

"Really?" I tried for a conspiratorial tone, just one of the girls chatting.

"Oh yeah. A couple of times when I was walking near their house, I heard Gary go off on her." She pursed her lips. "They had their front window open, and he was yelling at her. She talked about it once, how the littlest things could make him furious. And he would get mad at poor Logan as well. Logan adored him, wanted his father's attention, but he also knew to be careful with his dad." She blew out a breath. "I hate to see anyone divorce, but it was the best thing for Audra, although the whole thing was contentious. Gary fought her every step of the way, tried to get custody of Logan. He didn't think she was a fit mother. I guess he told the court she has a lot of problems, but that's not true."

"What kind of problems?"

"That she wasn't around, that she drank. None of that's true."

"How close are you with Audra?"

She crossed one leg over the other. "Now, mostly seeing her

with Logan at school, that kind of thing. We don't really hang out that much anymore, it was more when our boys were younger. We'd see each other at the park or when they were playing at one of our houses. Now we talk on the phone when we get a chance. I like Audra."

"How is Audra with Logan?"

She gestured deliberately at me with a long fingernail. "She's a great mother, and she's wonderful with him. I've watched enough cop shows to know what you're thinking, but she wouldn't harm him in any way."

"And Gary?"

She took a moment to answer. "For as much as I don't have a good impression of Gary, he wouldn't hurt his boy, either."

"I understand," I said as I noted her hesitation. "I do have to look at everything."

"Yes, I suppose you do. The cop shows are like that too." She let out a little forced laugh.

"How close were Terrell and Logan?"

A beautiful smile lit her face. "Those two boys are best pals. They get along really well, and it's nice to see. Logan loves his comics, and they also like sports, Terrell especially. Logan's not as athletic as Terrell, but that doesn't stop Terrell from getting Logan to play, mostly baseball and football." She was back to speaking in the present tense, Logan's death not registering yet.

"I also heard that Logan was really into comics, in part because of his dad."

She shrugged. "Yes, Audra told me that. I don't get the whole comics thing, but he would talk about superheroes and characters from his comics a lot when he was here. He and Terrell love to watch all the superhero movies that are coming out these days. I'm not too fond of them, so I'd let my husband take them to the theater."

"How often did you see Gary with Logan?"

"Once in a while." She waved a hand in disgust. "To be honest, if Gary was around, I tried to get the boys to play here. I didn't like the way Gary treated them. It was like they were little soldiers, especially Logan. With Gary, it seemed everything was an order."

"Did Gary ever hurt Logan?"

"No, nothing like that. He just wasn't very nice."

I circled back around to the night Logan disappeared. "Saturday evening, after Logan left your house, you helped Audra and Gary look for Logan, and then what happened?"

She stared out the window for a moment. "That night seemed so long, and it wasn't even my son. I can't imagine what Audra and Gary were feeling." She held up a hand, then dropped it back in her lap. "We searched and searched, and after we had talked to the police, Gary finally went home. I stayed with Audra at her house. I just didn't feel like she should be alone, and her best friend was out of town. I must've been with her until after one or two in the morning, and then Audra finally told me to go home. I checked on her Sunday morning, and she said she'd slept, but I don't think so." She shook her head. "She had dark bags under her eyes, and you could hear it in her voice; she was exhausted. She was up all night, looking for Logan. I would be if I were in her shoes. I fixed her some breakfast, but she hardly ate anything. We went out and drove all around the neighborhood again, but didn't see Logan anywhere. I stayed with her a good bit of the day, until her friend arrived. Then I came home."

"Did you see Gary on Sunday?"

"He came over for a while and also searched the neighborhood. Then he and Audra started to fight. I finally pulled him aside and asked him to go home. He wasn't too happy with me, but he listened and left. It's funny," she said. "You asked me about how often I see Audra, and it's usually taking the kids to school or chatting as we see each other outside. I've spent more time with her in these last few days than in a long time."

"You were with Audra Saturday and last night?"

"I've been over there every day since Logan disappeared. Audra's tried to get some work done, but you can tell she can't really concentrate. I know she's been trying to keep up with her clients. You know she's in real estate?" I nodded, and she continued. "I've been over there in the evenings, trying to get her to eat, to keep her spirits up. I didn't want her to lose hope." She was quiet for a moment. "Last night I was there again until late."

"What's late?"

She thought for a second. "I guess it was almost midnight. When I came home my husband, my daughter Vonessia, and Terrell were already in bed."

"How well did your daughter know Logan?"

"Oh, Vonessia's in high school. She saw him here and there, but Terrell is the one who played with Logan."

"You haven't noticed any suspicious activity in the neighborhood, different cars, or people you don't know?"

"Not that I recall." Just then her cell phone rang. She glanced at the screen. "It's Audra." She answered and said, "Yes, I heard. A police detective is with me now. I'm so sorry."

She listened, nodded. I looked out the front window. The neighborhood seemed ideal, filled with good people who cared about each other. Then something horrific occurred to trash that ideal.

"Let me call you right back, honey. Okay, bye." She drew in a breath and blew it out loudly. "She's not doing well, I can tell."

"Is Terrell at school now?" I asked.

"Yes, of course."

"I'd like to talk to him, if that would be okay."

"Now?"

"Yes. He might have details that he doesn't realize are important."

Her jaw dropped. "Oh man, Terrell needs to hear about Logan from me. This is going to crush him." She stared at the floor and rubbed her brow. "I guess you can follow me to the school."

She slowly got up, and so did I. The dread of talking to her son showed in her sagging shoulders.

CHAPTER FIVE

Principal Gallegos, a tall Hispanic woman with long hair and thin glasses, blinked back tears when I explained why Latoya Anderson and I were there and asked to speak with Terrell.

"This is horrible. Just horrible," she finally managed to say, her voice buttery but strong. I imagined that voice was soothing for the elementary kids whom she dealt with all day. She rested her hands on her desk. "This could be very upsetting for Terrell. Might it be better to talk to him after school?"

"I'm afraid not. It's important I talk to Terrell before more time passes. He might have information critical to our investigation."

"And I want to tell him about Logan before he hears it from anyone else," Latoya said.

Outside a window behind Gallegos, kids at recess screamed and yelled. A childhood memory came to mind, and I pushed it away. Principal Gallegos took off her glasses and wiped her eyes. Then she drew in a breath, donned her glasses, and finally stood up. "I'll bring Terrell to the office across the hall, and you can speak to him there."

"Thank you," I said, hoping to encourage her helpfulness.

Latoya and I stood up and followed her through a reception area and across a tiled hallway to another office, this one labeled for the assistant principal, who wasn't around. Gallegos opened the door for us.

"You can wait in here," she said. "I'll tell Terrell his mom is here to see him."

I nodded and took a seat at a small, uncomfortable chair that was all harsh angles. If a kid sat here, he or she wouldn't want to come back. Probably the point.

Latoya leaned against the back of another chair as she nervously eyed the door. "I never imagined I would have to do something like this."

I didn't reply. I had been in schools before, had interviewed children before, when I was with the juvenile division. That had been a tough gig. I'd had too many conversations with kids who had been wounded, either physically or emotionally, who had witnessed horrible things. Kids who'd been sexually abused, tortured, and only God knew what else. Sometimes the only way to deal with it was to put the stories in a part of my brain I rarely visited. And to seek justice for the kids. No one could ever remove the horrible things they'd endured, no amount of justice did that. It had been a start, that was all. All I could do. I pushed those thoughts aside and looked at Latoya.

"He knows Logan had been missing, right? You didn't shield him from that?"

"We told him. I'm not sure he really understands that Logan," she choked up, put a hand to her mouth, "that Logan might never come back."

I didn't say anything. What could I? Logan's death was a tragedy and no words would erase that. A faint lavender smell filled the air, so different to the tension we'd brought into the room.

A moment later, Principal Gallegos returned with a tall, lanky boy with big innocent eyes. *Oh, this is going to be hard,* I thought.

He started for his mom, glanced at me, and hesitated.

"Hi," he said to Latoya. He wrinkled his nose, unaware that he had bread crumbs on his T-shirt.

"Hey, honey." She motioned at a couch. "Why don't you sit down?"

He took slow steps to the couch and sank slowly onto it as if he was somehow being punished. He put his hands in his lap, looked at me askance, then let his gaze fall to his mom. Latoya glanced to Gallegos.

"I'll be across the hall, if you need me," the principal murmured, then quietly shut the door.

Latoya sat on the couch, close to Terrell. "Honey, I have some bad news." She swiped at the crumbs with her hand and kept her voice calm, but I detected a slight warble. "Something happened to Logan, and he isn't coming home anymore."

Terrell kicked one leg back and forth. "Where is he?"

"He's in heaven."

Terrell's face froze. "He's dead?"

"Yes."

I watched him closely. Some of the innocence in his eyes drained away, never to return. He may not have fully understood everything of death, but he'd know this loss for the rest of his life.

"What happened?" he asked, his voice almost lost in the room.

"Some bad people hurt him," Latoya said. She shifted to look at me. "This lady–she's a detective with the police–wants to ask you a few questions."

Now those big eyes rested squarely on me, but he didn't say a word. The leg kept moving.

I moved my chair a tad closer and leaned in. "I'm Sarah Spillman," I said in a gentle voice. "You and Logan were buddies, right?"

"Uh huh." Barely above a whisper. He looked away. Outside the door, someone called out, and a child yelled something, the voice muffled.

"I hear you like to play sports," I went on. Nothing. "Are you good?"

"I guess."

"You can tell her," Latoya said, a tinge of pride in her voice. "He's a star on the football team."

"Oh?" I smiled. "You're not just good, you're really good."

The corners of his mouth twitched into a small smile of his own. "I'm a running back. My dad says I'm really fast."

"I'll bet you are. Can you beat other kids in a race?"

His gaze finally rested on me. "Uh huh." A little shift as he started to engage.

"How about Logan? Could you beat him?"

"Yeah. He's not very fast, even though he tries to act like he's as fast as a superhero. He'll never be as fast as them."

I rested my elbows on my knees. "Logan likes comics, right?"

He nodded. "Like Batman and Spiderman. They're okay, I guess. But Logan pretends to be them."

Just like a child, blunt, no filter.

"I read some comics," I said. "A long time ago. And I liked to read mystery novels and pretend to be the heroes in those stories." I loved trying to figure out the whodunit.

"You read comics?"

"Some, and I like sports, football especially."

"Cool."

"You played baseball with Logan too?"

"Uh huh."

"Did you play baseball with Logan last Saturday?"

"We were playing football out back."

Latoya nodded her agreement.

"And then what happened?" I went on.

Terrell thought for a second. "His dad called him and said he was going to be there in a little while, so Logan said he should go. His dad would get mad if Logan wasn't waiting for him."

I nodded knowingly. "Did Logan talk much about his mom and dad?"

He gave a halfhearted shrug.

"You can tell her what you think," Latoya said. "It's okay."

"Mrs. Pickett's nice," Terrell said.

"Logan thought his mom was cool?"

"Uh huh."

"What about his dad?"

Terrell pinched up his face. "He's not very nice. I didn't want to make him mad."

I similarly wrinkled my nose. "Yeah, it's hard when your parents get mad."

"Uh huh."

"Did Logan ever make his dad mad?"

Another shrug. "His dad likes comics too. Logan said his dad wouldn't let him touch his comics, though. He'd get mad. Maybe some other times too. Logan just said his dad would yell at him, or stuff, but he didn't always say why."

I nodded. "Did Logan like going to his dad's house?"

"I guess. Logan didn't have anyone to play with over there, and he'd get bored and call me."

Not a strong endorsement of Logan's visits to his dad.

"You're doing great." That received a tiny smile. "I'll bet you were bummed when Logan had to leave last Saturday." A nod. "When he left your house, what did you do?"

"Um. I threw the ball around, and then I went inside and played video games."

"You didn't see Logan walk to his house?"

He shook his head. "He went through the gate, and I stayed in the backyard."

"Okay, good." I nodded encouragingly. "Did you hear anything?"

His brow furrowed. "I heard a loud bang."

"From what? Do you know?"

"I don't know. Like a car."

"A car's engine, a rumbling really loud?"

He shrugged. "It was more like a bang," he repeated.

"Like a car backfiring?" I explained what that meant.

"Maybe."

I didn't know if that was significant or not, but I filed the information away.

"Did you hear anything else?"

"Uh, no. I didn't know anything had happened to Logan until my mom asked me later about it." He glanced at his mom, and she gave him another encouraging nod. "I was in my room, and she came in and asked if Logan told me he was going home or somewhere else. I told her he went home. Through the gate, like I told you."

"I see. And Logan hasn't called you since then?"

"No."

"Did you play outside last night?"

"No, I was at football practice, and when I got home, I had dinner. Then I took a shower and did my homework." Disappointment in his voice, how his evening was ruined by a shower and schoolwork.

"Have any of your friends heard from Logan since last Saturday?"

"I don't think so."

"Did Logan ever talk about running away?"

He shook his head. "Nope."

"Was he sad?"

Another head shake. "We had fun."

"Okay, good. One more thing. Did you two see any strange people around your houses lately?"

"No." He twisted up his lips. "We're careful." He glanced at his mom. "We just go between our houses."

That probably wasn't true, but he wasn't going to admit anything in front of Latoya.

"You never saw anyone that made you scared, or feel weird?"

"Nope." He scratched his arm and looked at Latoya again. He was nervous, and likely didn't have anymore to share.

"Thanks for talking to me," I said. "You really helped me."

Terrell stared at me with big eyes. "I'm not in trouble?"

"Not at all." I reached out and lightly patted his knee. "You did good."

"She's going to find out what happened to Logan," Latoya said.

"Okay." Terrell slipped off the couch. "Can I go back to class?"

"Will you be okay?" she asked.

He nodded. "I guess so."

Latoya stood up and held out her hand, but he didn't take it. Too old for that, especially in front of a stranger.

She dropped her hand. "Let me walk you back to your class," she said. Then, turning to me, "Do you need anything else?"

I stood up as well. "Not right now. I'll call or drop by if I have any more questions."

She didn't say anything else, but went out the door, Terrell close behind her.

I waited a moment, then exited the office and went out the front door. Some kids were in the playground, climbing on the jungle gym, going down the slide. Then I saw a girl on a swing. I stopped just a moment and watched her.

Then, just the flash of a memory.

I'm eight years old, on a playground swing at the school down the street. It's hot, but as I pump my legs, the swing goes higher, the air soothing cool on my face. I close my eyes, picturing my Uncle Brad. I love him, but Mom says he's not here anymore. Mom said he had a heart attack. I don't know what that really means, just that he's dead and never coming back.

I pump my legs harder. Maybe I can get to heaven and see Uncle Brad. Tears stream down my cheeks. I can never talk to him again.

I hear a voice and open my eyes. Diane is there. She grabs the swing, yells at me that I have to come home, that I was stupid to run away. The swing twists around wildly, and I fall to the ground and scrape my knees on the gravel. Diane doesn't care. She thinks because she's four years older, she can tell me what to do. She storms off, hollering that I better get home or I'll get in trouble, that Mom and Dad are looking for me. I rub my eyes and stalk after her. My knees and elbows are burning and I'm trying to wipe the blood off my legs. On the way home, I look up, looking for Uncle Brad. How can he be gone?

I shook my head at the memory. I'd just wanted a few minutes alone, a few minutes to mourn Uncle Brad. He and I had been close, and I'd adored him. He knew me, knew my little-kid struggles, knew that Diane didn't treat me very well. I could talk to him, and he understood me in a way no one else did. Diane hadn't understood that. I never liked swings after that.

I stared at the girl for a moment longer, then realized that I was rooted in place. I stretched my neck and hurried to my car. I got in and closed out the sounds of the children playing, and my childhood memory.

CHAPTER SIX

Scrubbing the wall, the soapy water cascading to the concrete floor, the sponge shredding into little bits with each stroke.

Why did the boy have to try to escape? He would've been just fine. I would have taken care of him, I would have given him everything. Didn't he know that? It's over, all the plans are ruined.

Scrub, scrub, scrub. Rinse the sponge. Scrub the walls. Scrub the floor.

There was so much blood. The blood, the blood. Like Lady Macbeth's damned spot of blood that couldn't be erased.

All traces of the boy had to disappear. That meant more cleaning, more scrubbing. No one could ever know what happened in here. No one could know about the boy.

Scrub, scrub, scrub.

No matter how much scouring, though, it couldn't erase the pain.

Scrub, scrub.

The water in the bucket had turned sudsy red. So much blood.

When the boy's wrist had been slit, he had suffered, but it couldn't be stopped. It was too deep a cut, too hard to stop the bleeding. Anger welled up. If the boy had only done as he was told! If he'd only been good, none of this would have happened.

The water was dumped into a sink, then another bucket of clean soapy water prepared.

Back into the room, more cleaning. This wasn't the way it was supposed to be.

Scrub, scrub, scrub.

A final search around the room, under the bed, everywhere. One Batman toy snatched from under the bed. Now the room was clean, no traces of the boy.

But the pain remained.

CHAPTER SEVEN

I sat down at my desk at the Denver Police Administration Building and looked across at Spats. He was typing on the computer, his tie still neatly in place, everything about him flawless. In another room, someone was on the phone, but otherwise it was quiet.

I was still thinking about my sister and that playground swing when Spats looked up.

"You okay?" he asking, bringing me back to the present.

"Yeah. What have you got so far?" I asked. A large notebook was sitting on my desk. Other detectives had been researching persons of interest, and this was what they'd compiled so far.

"I'm just typing some stuff up," he said. "Ernie is working on the search warrant for Gary's laptop now. Glad you gave that footwork to him. I don't want to be dealing with the magistrate today."

"No?"

He rubbed his temples. "I have a world class headache. Not enough sleep. My kid kept me up half the night. And that's on top of the sleepless nights with this job."

Spats has an eleven-year-old girl from a previous marriage, and a newborn boy with his girlfriend. He's trying to make this new relationship work, but it isn't easy with his erratic hours and the stress of the job.

I pointed at him. "Don't keep me in suspense. Fill me in on what you've learned."

He stopped typing and leaned back in his chair. "Whoever dumped that little boy in the dumpster knew to come in the middle of the night," he said drily. "With the exception of two people, nobody saw or heard a thing. And what they did see or hear isn't much to go on." He stopped, his words caught in his throat. "Geez, the boy wasn't much younger than my kid."

"I know," I murmured.

He cleared his throat. "What'd you learn so far?"

"I don't have a whole lot, either," I said. "I've got tension between the mother and father, sounds like a contentious divorce, but so far nothing beyond that. Except that the boy's father, Gary, is a bit of a hothead."

He nodded. "I talked to the old lady, Karen Pacheco. She was up in the middle of the night. I got a long story about her sleeping troubles." He said this with no animosity. I knew he'd handle Pacheco well. "She was dozing in front of the TV, which she does a lot of nights. She thought she heard a noise out back, a loud thump or something."

"Logan's friend, Terrell, heard something," I interrupted. "He didn't say exactly what it was, but I'm wondering if it could be a car backfiring."

"No, it wasn't that. I asked. She's a curious sort–I'd say nosy–with the goings on in the neighborhood, so she went to look. She didn't see anybody, but she saw taillights going down the alley. I pressed her a little, and she's pretty sure the car was an SUV. It was dark, though, and she was too far away to really see anything else. She also has no idea if it was a neighbor's vehicle, or a stranger in the area."

"So obviously no license plate?"

He shook his head. "No, we're not that lucky."

"What time did she think she saw the car?"

"She wasn't sure, just that she was watching an old *Cannon* episode. You remember him?" I had nothing for him but a blank stare. He smirked. "I had to look it up. It's an old show with William Conrad, a heavyset actor with a mustache. He plays a private eye."

"Never heard of it."

"Mrs. Pacheco likes it. She says Conrad was 'ruggedly handsome.' I don't know about that, I just remember him from that show *Jake and the Fatman*. My mom liked that show." I gave him a look for him to move it on. "I looked it up, and *Cannon* is on at two a.m."

"What else?"

"Mrs. Pacheco doesn't know Audra, and she didn't know the kid. Or the dad. She was as shocked as anybody about all this, pretty upset to hear about the little boy's murder. She's got a grandson about his age, she couldn't imagine anything happening to him."

"So basically, she had very little for us," I said.

He straightened his already straight tie. "That's about right. Now, there's a gentleman named Larry Blankenship. He's on the other side of the alley. Ernie talked to him. Blankenship heard a loud sound, an engine revving." He held up a hand. "Not a car backfiring. He got up to go to the bathroom around two, and he saw headlights in the alley. It might've been an SUV, but he doesn't know what color, just that it was a darker vehicle. And he didn't think to look for a license plate number. Not that he could see one, he wants us to know." He held up a finger. "Mrs.

Pacheco and Blankenship were up about the same time, so it's possible they saw the same car."

I sat back. "That's not very helpful. Did anyone hear a car backfire?"

"No."

"Do any of the neighbors have cameras outside, or camera doorbells?"

He nodded. "A couple of people did, but none showed a clear view of the alley. CSI is going through all the video. They'll have a report for us later." Now he pointed at me. "What did you find out? Details, please."

I rested my elbows on the desk and looked at him. "I talked to the parents. My gut says the mom–Audra–didn't do anything, but I do think she might've been a little careless and wasn't watching Logan last Saturday, even though she doesn't want to admit it. The dad, Gary ..." my voice trailed off.

He tipped his head to the side. "What?"

I mulled that over for a long moment. "There's something about him. I can't put my finger on it. Something doesn't seem right to me. I won't go so far as to say he's a suspect, yet. I will say that he doesn't seem to have a lot of love for his son. Maybe it's all my previous work with kids, but I just didn't like how he came across."

"Listen to your gut."

I nodded. "I always do. I got Audra's laptop, no problem. I dropped it off with Tara, and she's going to give it an initial run right away, but it'll take a while to scan the whole thing." Tara Dahl is another detective who is a tech specialist in the department, and she was doing me a favor by moving her analysis of Audra's laptop to the front of her list. "Gary, on the other hand, didn't want to surrender his laptop."

"Yeah, Ernie called me about that earlier."

"Oh right." I stifled a yawn. "Speaking of warrants, did you get one for Audra and Gary's phones? They both use Verizon, and Logan, had one, too."

"I've been waiting on the judge. Let me call over there." He picked up his phone and dialed.

"And that warrant includes pinging the phone for locations so we can find out where Audra and Gary have been recently?"

"Like Saturday night and last night? Of course."

While Spats called the judge's office, I pulled the notebook toward me. I smiled ruefully as I opened the notebook, thinking about all the work the detectives had done to gather the information. People assume the police department has access to numerous databases with information on suspects, or that a detective can just call the FBI. Unfortunately, unless a crime has occurred across state lines, the FBI is not a resource for us. And the reality is that unless a person has a criminal record, it's just as easy to go to the internet. There is so much information available online about most people, and many sites will provide thorough background checks for a fee. I opened the notebook and scanned pages. I saw the makes and models for Audra and Gary's vehicles, their license plate information, marriage and divorce records, birth information, and job information. Gary had been in the Marines, and it showed where he'd served. It also showed his honorable discharge record. Audra and Gary both had Facebook pages. I glanced at the information about Audra. She posted lots of information about herself and Logan: Pictures of him at his school, around the house, or in his baseball uniform. She was a proud mother. Gary's Facebook account had some activity, him posting pictures and making comments, but he wasn't active on other social media sites. He also hadn't purchased any kind of insurance policy on Logan. I kept reading. Audra didn't have a criminal record. Gary, on the other hand, had an arrest for disturbing the peace, a bar fight where he beat up another man.

Interesting, I thought. When I'd asked Gary whether he'd had any trouble with the law, he'd said no.

"Why did he lie to me?" I muttered under my breath. "What's he hiding?"

I turned a page. There was a list of Audra's Facebook friends. I'd have to follow up with them to see if Audra was hiding anything from me.

I felt eyes on me and looked up. Spats was staring at me. "What?" I said.

"The judge signed the warrant for the phones," he said. "I need to go pick it up."

"Good. Once you get it, don't take any crap from Verizon. Put some pressure on them to expedite the request. I want those phone records as soon as possible." Phone companies ran a lot of searches, and I didn't want my request to get delayed.

"Sure thing." He narrowed his eyes. "What were you muttering about?"

I tapped the notebook. "Gary has an arrest for disturbing the peace." I paused. "Some of the people we've heard from say he's not a nice guy, that he was at minimum verbally abusive to Audra. Does that mean he might have had something to do with Logan's death?"

"I've been thinking about that. If Gary kidnapped the kid, then how did he continue the charade of searching for him the rest of the night?"

"Maybe he drugged Logan, kept him tied up in the back seat?" I mused, then dismissed that. "I don't like that. Too risky. What if he had help?"

"Someone else kidnaps the kid, and Gary acts like the worried dad. But why?"

I lifted my shoulders. "He wanted sole custody of Logan? He's made it clear he doesn't believe Audra was a good mom."

"Then something goes wrong, maybe Gary loses his temper and kills his son?"

"Then disposes of his body in a dumpster." I pondered that. "It's cold, but I've seen worse."

"Me, too." Spats got up, touched his tie, then put on his coat. He looked immaculate. "I'll get started on those phone records. See you later."

I gave him a halfhearted wave, then yawned as I kept going through the notebook. Stacks of paper, a person's life whittled down to this. And what secrets did the pages hide? After a few minutes, I grew antsy. In my head, I heard my mother chiding me to sit still. I'd never been good at that. Not like my sister. She was a straight-A student, on the honor roll, and did everything right, at least in my parents' eyes. I, on the other hand, had a hard time conforming. Again, according to my parents. It hadn't mattered that I'd done well in school, got a degree in law enforcement, and had worked my way up to homicide detective. Some things just didn't matter. I grimaced. My family had secrets, too. I kneaded my neck for a moment and dismissed those thoughts, then called Tara.

"You want to know about that woman's computer already?" she asked. "Hey, I'm good, but not that good."

"Yes you are. Have you found anything interesting yet?"

She chuckled. "So far, nothing. The laptop has some sites about superheroes, and someone liked to play video games. Kid games," she clarified. "I don't see anything wrong with what I've found so far. No contact with anybody suspicious on social media, but again, only so far. There are visits to real estate sites, stuff like that."

"Yeah, Audra's a realtor."

"I figured," she said drily. "Other than that, nothing. You need to give me more time, though."

"Hmm," I said. "I was hoping we might see something right off the bat."

"Not this time. I'll keep working on it, and if I see anything fishy, I'll get in touch right away."

"Thanks, Tara."

I hung up and looked into the notebook again. Audra had a lot of Facebook contact with Heather Neville. Audra's best friend? I made a note to talk to her. My phone rang and I answered curtly.

"I got the warrant for Gary's laptop," Ernie said.

"That's great. And Spats is picking up the one for the phones too. Where are you?"

"The courthouse."

I could use a break. "Meet me at the Rooster & Moon in fifteen minutes. I'll get the warrant from you, and then have another talk with Gary Pickett."

"I'll see you there."

I hung up and headed out the door.

CHAPTER EIGHT

The Rooster & Moon Coffee Pub is a hip coffee shop close to the station. I like going there because they make a good cup of coffee, and it isn't the usual Starbucks or similar cookie-cutter place. At the Rooster, I can be alone with my thoughts.

And right now, I needed a cup of coffee. When I got there, Ernie hadn't arrived yet, so I ordered coffee, black, and sat down at a table near the door. I sipped the brew, feeling it give me a much-needed jolt. I held the warm mug in my hand and thought about the case.

The parents are always suspects, but Logan's murderer could've been anybody in the neighborhood, or a stranger for that matter. I needed to move fast. The more time that elapsed, the more likely it would be that we wouldn't find Logan's killer. My mind flashed to his body in the dumpster. It took a brutal person to slash his wrist, and the same cold person to dispose of his body like that. One would think that a parent couldn't do that to his or her child, but I'd seen worse. I wasn't ruling out either Audra or Gary Pickett just yet. I was still deep in thought when Ernie walked through the door, his tie askew, an unlit cigar stub clamped between his teeth. He had an envelope in his hand. He saw me and started over.

"The cigar," I said.

He glanced around, then gave an irritated shrug as he tossed the cigar in a trash can.

He walked over. "I don't understand why you like this place. It's out of the way, and I can never remember where it's at. I had to drive around the neighborhood before I found it."

"It's out of the way. That's why I like it."

He smirked at that, then tossed the envelope on the table. "Here you go." He sat down. "Hot off the presses, as they say."

I pulled out the warrant and scanned it. "Any trouble getting it?"

He shook his head. "No. When the judge heard about Gary Pickett not wanting to give up his laptop, he didn't have any problems signing the warrant. Not with Gary's son being dead."

My coffee was cooler, and I took a big gulp. "Let's see him fight me now," I muttered.

"What's next?" he asked.

"I'll handle the laptop situation with Gary," I said. "Can you look through the background information that's been gathered on Latoya Anderson? So far, I've only been able to look at Audra and Gary. I'd like to know more about Latoya and her family, see if there's anything to make us suspicious. Latoya gave Audra a solid alibi for last night, and she was also at Audra's a lot since Logan disappeared. But check on the other neighbors as well, see if anyone has suspicions of Audra. Also, Latoya's son, Terrell, mentioned hearing something, a loud bang, around the time Logan went back home. I was wondering if it could be a car backfiring. See if anyone else heard that as well. And let's make sure none of the neighbors seems fishy. It's possible one of them kidnapped and killed Logan."

"Sounds like a plan," he said. "It's a sick person who would do that to that poor little kid."

"No argument from me on that."

"When is the boy's autopsy?" he asked.

"I'm hoping that Jack will put a rush on it," I said. "It's either going to be this afternoon or in the morning."

"Let's hope that tells us a little more."

"Right. And would you follow up with the CSI team when they're finished? See if they found anything noteworthy at the crime scene. Check on the neighbor kids, too, to see if Logan was friendly with anyone else. See if any of them heard anything. Logan's friend, Terrell Anderson, thought he might've heard a car backfire. Also, see if they think that Logan was talking to anyone he shouldn't have been."

He stood up, hefted his pants up over his stomach, and gave me a curt nod. "See you back at the office."

I didn't say anything. He turned and left. I left my lukewarm coffee on the table, picked up the warrant with a smug smile, and headed out the door.

Gary's face clouded over when he opened the door and saw me. He hesitated, and I think he was tempted to tell me to go to hell, but instead he forced a smile.

"Detective Spillman. What can I do for you?" The sweet suaveness in his voice was almost too much to bear.

"I have a warrant for your laptop." I held up the envelope.

The smile vanished. He glared at me, unable to hide his contempt. "I told you I don't want to give it up. I have too much information on it that I need. I don't see why you have to take it."

I didn't even bother to shrug. "And I told you, we'll copy the hard drive and give the laptop back to you as soon as we can. You likely won't be without it more than overnight."

He held out a hand. "Let me see the warrant."

I gave him the envelope. He made a show of taking out the paper and carefully reading the warrant. He forced an exaggerated sigh. It seemed he was into melodrama at the moment. Then he handed me the paper and envelope. "I'll go get the laptop."

Before he could shut the door, I put my hand out. "I'll go with you."

He locked eyes with me, and we stared at each other for a moment. "I'm not going to do anything to it, if that's what you're wondering," he finally said.

"Then you won't mind my coming with you." I put on my own sweet smile.

He was stubborn, and he held his ground for yet another moment. Then he turned on his heel and walked into the house. I opened the door wider and stepped inside.

As he walked down the short hallway, I glanced through an open door into a master bedroom on the left. A stack of shirts and pants were folded up on the bed. He headed toward a doorway farther down the hall, but I stopped.

"Going somewhere?" I gestured toward the master bedroom.

"I have business next week."

"It's a little early to pack."

He looked at me and didn't say a word. I joined him in the doorway. He pointed to a desk in his office. "There's the laptop."

It was still on. I had him shut it down and unplug it. He handed it to me with a scowl. I took it with a grim smile. "Do you have a minute to talk?" I asked.

His back was erect as he walked back into the living room. He didn't invite me to sit down but crossed his arms and said, "What's going on?"

"You were arrested once."

"That bar brawl I got into? It wasn't anything, so why mention it?"

I couldn't tell if he was trying to bluff me, or if he thought I was really that stupid. "Want to tell me about it?"

He took a long time to answer. "It wasn't anything. A guy and I got into a bar fight. I punched him, and the bar owner called the police. I spent the night in jail. It doesn't have anything to do with Logan, that's why I didn't say anything."

"It sounds like a bigger deal to me, if the police got involved." No response. "Your wife–"

"Ex-wife," he said pointedly

"Ex-wife," I mimicked him, "says that you drank a lot, especially near the end of your relationship."

"It wasn't that bad."

"How well did you get along with her? Did you treat her well?"

"Yes," he said, then he tried to defend himself. "We'd fight sometimes, but all couples do. And I didn't drink that much. She's not a good mother, and I fought for custody of Logan. She was just trying to make me look bad. That's all there is to it."

I'd have to ask Audra for her side, I thought. "What about Logan?"

"Was I abusive to him?" he snapped. He shook his head. "Never. I had a good relationship with him, and he would've been better off living with me than her. If she's trying to tell you differently, that's not true." He jabbed a finger at me. "I know I'm a suspect, but she should be, too. She wasn't even watching out for him the night he disappeared."

He seemed to want to make a point of that. There was little compassion in what he said, and also little ownership for his actions.

"Audra also says the night Logan disappeared you started a fight with her."

"I was angry. Can you blame me?"

"Did you try to defuse the situation?"

"I did, but Audra was pissed. There wasn't anything I could do. It was all her. It's always all her."

"Tell me about your relationship again," I asked, wanting to see if he'd change his story. This time, he was a little more forthcoming.

"It wasn't that bad. I mean, sometimes we fought and it got a little heated, but it never came to blows."

I needed to check with Audra on that, too. I also made a mental note to talk to Latoya again about the Picketts' relationship. And the other neighbors. Had any of them heard Audra and Gary fighting? Had anybody seen them get violent? And had anyone witnessed Gary being abusive to Logan?

"What about Logan? You never hit him?" It was pointed, to see what he would do.

He uncrossed his arms and glared at me. "I never touched Logan, ever. You got it?"

I nodded. "Yes."

"I don't like what you're insinuating."

"And what would that be?"

"That I had something to do with Logan's death." He shoved his hands in his pockets. "I know that you look at the parents, but I didn't do anything to him."

"Then you have nothing to worry about."

"I may not have had the best marriage, but I cared about my son." His voice cracked, and I couldn't be sure how genuine it was. "I loved him. I want him back."

There was nothing I could do about that, so I stayed silent. I went on. "Why didn't you tell me about the bar brawl?"

"Because I knew what you would think. It's exactly what you *do* think, that I had something to do with my son's death," he said sullenly.

He wasn't far off. "Anything else you want to tell me?"

"You mean like have I been in other trouble with the law?" I looked at him and waited. "No, you won't find anything else."

I waited a beat, then held up the laptop. "As I said, I'll get this back to you as soon as I can."

"You won't find anything on it. I've done nothing wrong."

"Good." I smiled pleasantly. "I may need to come back and get more information, okay?"

He hesitated, then thought it best to nod. "Yeah."

"Thanks for your time."

When I left him, he was still standing in the living room, hands in his pockets, but his shoulders now slightly stooped, defeated.

CHAPTER NINE

"I've got another gift for you," I said to Tara Dahl as I walked into the room. Then I realized she had earbuds in, with her usual heavy metal blaring, and she didn't have a clue I was in the room. I tapped her on the shoulder, and she jumped. I held up Gary Pickett's laptop.

"Geez, you scared me," she said as she pulled out the earbuds. Music blasted from them, and noticing my sly, disapproving grin, she turned it down.

"You shouldn't listen to the music so loud. You know that you're going to ruin your hearing by the time you're forty."

"Hey, I've got almost fifteen years before I'm forty." She managed to hold back a snort and ran a hand through her dyed black hair, a throwback to her Goth days. "You don't appreciate great music." I laughed. "Besides," she said, "it helps to shut out the world while I work."

Tara and I had an ongoing exchange about her listening to music that was too loud, and my telling her not to, as if I were her mom. Although, for the record, I'm no more than about ten years older than she. But somebody has to watch out for her. She's too valuable not to take care of.

"What's that?"

"This, Tara, is a laptop."

"Ha ha," she said. "Whose?"

"Gary Pickett. I had to get a warrant for it, and then he surrendered it."

"Not happily?"

I nodded. "You said it." I set the laptop down, then perched on the corner of the desk. "When can you analyze this?"

Tara sat back and took off her glasses. She rubbed her eyes slowly. "You've had me busy on Audra's laptop. I just finished working on it." She saw the look on my face, then said, "I'll get it done as soon as I can."

I gestured at her monitor. "What have you found on Audra's laptop?"

"I took everything and copied it to an external hard drive, so I'm working off that. You'll be able to give the laptop back to her anytime." I arched an eyebrow at her and waited. "So far, I haven't found anything," she said in answer to my look. "Audra's got all kinds of real estate records, plenty of pictures of her and the kid, and all kinds of other stuff people store on their laptops. No porn, nothing illegal that I've found so far. Again, I just started."

"So she's a saint," I said.

Tara shrugged. "I can't speak to that, but from her laptop, so far so good."

"I want all the pictures of her and the boy," I said. "Can you send them to me?"

"Sure, you got it. What else?"

"You checked her email? Internet activity? Especially the last couple of weeks."

She nodded. "Yeah, I've got a report on that. I'll print it out and send it up to you."

"Perfect." I tapped Gary's laptop. "Same thing on this. Be thorough. I want to know what he's hiding."

"You're pretty confident he's hiding something."

It was my turn to nod. "I don't buy that he just couldn't live without the laptop." I lightly punched my gut. "This tells me otherwise."

She laughed, then put her glasses back on. "The dad's a killer?" She rubbed her face. "Wow."

I stood up. "I know. Who could do that to their child? But it's been done plenty of times before."

She turned back to the computer. "I'll talk to you soon." Her head nodded to an old tune by AC/DC.

I thanked her, grabbed Audra Pickett's laptop, and walked out of the office. I stood in the hall for a moment, leaning against the wall. It was cool against my back, soothing the tension between my shoulder blades. I hoped the information on the laptops would reveal something, a clue to what happened to Logan. I stretched, then went back to my desk and sat down. The huge notebook of information was still sitting there. I opened it again and thumbed through pages. I needed something to pop out at me. Each second that passed was lost time, time that would make it harder to find Logan's killer.

My cell phone rang. It was Harry. Harry Sousen and I have been together for over eleven years, and I love him. He's amazing. I've just never been ready for more of a commitment. I shook my head, not wanting to think about that now. Harry's the president of his own computer consulting company, and he's busy all day long, so he usually doesn't bother me during the day; plus, he knows my schedule can be chaotic. I let the call go to voice mail. Harry would have to wait until tonight.

"I've got 'em!" I jumped as Spats came walking into the room.

"I've got Audra and Gary Pickett's phone records for the last two months, plus the kid's," he said. "If we need to go back farther than that, we can."

"What about the pings for the phone locations?"

"Verizon's working on it. They said that'll take a while longer."

"How much longer?"

He gave me an impatient look. "I'll keep on them." He sat down at his desk across from me and we faced each other. I waited expectantly.

"Hang on," he said. "They've made a lot of calls." He handed me a set of pages. "That's all of Audra's records."

I took the papers from him. "What about the kid's phone?"

He shuffled pages. "Not a lot of calls, mostly to one or the other parent. He got a call from Gary Saturday afternoon."

"Telling Logan he was on his way," I said.

"I don't see any suspicious calls from the kid's phone."

I nodded and started looking through the records he'd given me. Each page had the phone number, the address, and the name of the person that Audra called or had received a call from. As I scanned through them, I recognized some of the names. Her ex, Gary. Latoya Anderson. Based on the addresses in close proximity to Audra, it showed she had placed calls to some other neighbors too. She'd called people in Maryland. I assumed these were relatives, maybe her parents, but I'd have Spats or Ernie track that down. She also called Heather Neville, the close Facebook friend. I made a note of that number. On the day of Logan's disappearance, I noticed a call from Gary to Audra. He'd told me that he'd called Audra and left a message for her; the records confirmed that. Then Audra made a call to Latoya, and a couple of other calls to numbers I didn't recognize. I circled those.

"We'll need to follow up on these calls," I said to Spats. "Some of these I don't know." I craned my neck to see the papers lying on his desk. "I think Audra called her parents to tell them about Logan. What about his parents?"

"Where's Gary from?"

"California."

"Hold on, let me look at yesterday. Ah, here's a call to a California number. Sacramento."

"Follow up with the grandparents, will you? Let's see what they have to say. And find out if they think either Audra or Gary has a drinking problem. And Gary has a girlfriend, Kristi Arnott. Talk to her." He reached for a pen and jotted on a notepad. "Your records should show Gary calling Audra last Saturday, a little before six."

He ran his pen down the page. "Yeah, for thirty seconds."

"That's right. Their stories match so far. Gary said Audra didn't answer, and he left a message."

I looked at my records again. Audra had also made a longer call around that time. That, I assumed, was the business call she had taken, the one that had kept her busy so that she wasn't paying attention to Logan. I starred that number. "Spats, I'm starring another call for you to follow up on. This should be a real estate client Audra talked to."

He noted that as well. "Sure thing."

I picked up my phone and dialed the number for Heather Neville. It went to voice mail, so I left a message identifying myself and asking her to call me back, then gave her my cell phone number. I cradled the receiver and stared at the papers on my desk.

"Hey," Spats interrupted my thoughts. "I'm looking back to the beginning of Gary's phone calls. He made several calls to the Gold Creek Gun Range. Did Gary Pickett mention owning guns?"

I rested my elbows on the desk and pictured Gary's house. "I didn't see any, just a knife collection."

"Knives? Like one that could slice a kid's wrist?"

"A good thought, right?"

He tapped the pages. "I'll look into this gun shop. Might be something there."

"Hey," I tried fruitlessly to see the pages he had. "What calls did Gary make last Saturday?"

"Let's see. He called Kristi Arnott and another number."

I narrowed my eyes. "He said he only called Kristi."

"Well, well, well. We'll need to follow up with Gary on that."

"That's right." I didn't disguise my anger. "I don't like being lied to." My desk phone rang, interrupting my ire. "Spillman."

"It's Ed Oakley. You've got the Pickett case, right? The kid who was found in the dumpster this morning?"

I sat a little straighter. "Yes. What's up?"

Oakley is another detective in the department He's from Boston, and even though he's lived in Colorado since he was a teenager, he still sounds a little Boston, his voice nasally, the trace of the accent, the occasional dropping of his r's. "I got a dead body, male, in a house here just down the block from where that kid was discovered. Something makes me think these could be connected."

"I'd bet money on that," I said. "What happened?"

"Gunshot wound in the side of the temple," he said. "On the face of it, it looks like a suicide. But ..." He didn't finish the thought.

"I want to take a look."

He laughed grimly. "That's why I called you. Figured you'd want to see this."

"I'll be right over."

He gave me the address and I scribbled it down. I thanked him and hung up. I looked at Spats, who raised an eyebrow. "What?" I told him about the body. "That's an interesting turn."

"Yeah, no kidding. Keep looking at those phone records,

okay? Oh, can you return Audra Pickett's laptop to her?" I handed it to him. "Let me know how it goes, how she seems. I'm going to take a look at this new body. I'll let you know what I find."

"You got it, Spillman."

"And I'll call Ernie. He's talking to Latoya and some of Audra's neighbors now. He'll want to know about the neighbor's death."

"Right."

I barely heard that as I was already out the door.

CHAPTER TEN

I flashed my badge at the officer standing on the front porch of an older two-story house not far from Audra Pickett's home. He logged me in with calculated boredom. I put on a pair of booties and stepped into the living room. I could smell death before I'd even taken a few steps, a faint metallic odor combined with the staleness of the house. The living room was small, with a couch and loveseat, and a TV against the wall. ESPN was on, discussing the beginning of the baseball season. Several framed photos hung on the other walls: nature scenes, the mountains, a lake. A tripod stood near the front window. I walked over and parted the curtains. Several cars were parked in front of the house. I shifted to the left, and I could see Latoya Anderson's house at the corner of the next block. I watched for a moment, then let the curtains fall back into place.

I heard voices down a hallway and also coming from upstairs. I chose the main level and followed the sound down a short hallway with more framed photos. On the right, a man with dark hair and an equally dark suit filled a doorway, his back to me. He turned as I approached.

"Spillman, how're you doing?"

Detective Ed Oakley and I had known each other for a few years. Oakley had recently been promoted to the homicide division, and he took many of the cases that I couldn't. I'd heard he was smart, and he took his job seriously, but beyond that I didn't know a lot about him.

"It ain't pretty," he said wryly. He stepped back and put a hand in his pocket. He withdrew a pair of latex gloves, which he handed to me. "You want to take a look?" He waved into the room.

I donned the gloves and stepped past him into the room. The smell of death was stronger. The room was sparse, a bed centered against one wall, nightstands on either side, a dresser in the corner, and a little table against the wall with a TV on it. Lying face-up on the bed was a blond-haired man in jeans, no shirt, bare feet. His lifeless blue eyes stared at the ceiling. Blood spatter was to his left, a Sig Sauer P220 still clutched in his right hand. I moved closer for a better look. There was a hole in his right temple, a larger one in his left. The gun had done its work.

"What's his name?" I asked.

He pulled a small notepad from his coat pocket. "Ivan Eklund. He's thirty-five, never married, no children. He doesn't have a criminal record, not even a speeding ticket. He was born in Virginia, and has lived in the Denver area for several years. Bought this house three years ago. He's a photographer."

"Who discovered him?"

"He's got a girlfriend. Rachel Connelly. She stopped by on her lunch break to see Eklund. She has a key and let herself in." He contemplated the body. "What a thing to discover. Anyway, she called 911 and waited on the porch. I talked to her, and she told me some things about him, but then I let her go home. She was a mess, as you can imagine."

I took that in as I studied the scene. "So, Eklund was sitting up, and then he blew his brains out," I said. "Is that your initial take?"

Oakley stepped into the room. "On the surface, that's what it looks like. He fell backward, and you can see some of the blood on the comforter behind him." He tilted his head. "Good gun, did the job well."

I looked where he indicated and saw exactly what he meant. A small amount of blood had spattered on the bed near Eklund's head. As Oakley had said, at first glance, it was a suicide. A faint smell mingled with the death smells, some kind of cologne. I glanced around the room. The bed was neat, as was the room. A digital alarm clock and a small lamp sat on one of the nightstands, nothing else. The dresser had nothing on it. A large framed picture of a mountain lake hung above the bed.

"Did Eklund take that?" I asked.

Oakley nodded. "He signed it."

"It's beautiful."

"I guess."

My gaze rested on the body again. It lay on a tan comforter, an expression on his face I couldn't quite read. A trace of fear, but something else. Anger?

I put my hands on my hips. "Anything to make you believe it wasn't a suicide?"

He shrugged. "Too early to tell. I'm not going to assume anything."

I nodded agreement, then pointed at Eklund's hands. "You swab them for gunshot residue?"

"Of course. I'll let you know what we find out."

"You wonder the girlfriend shot him?"

He shook his head. "And then called the police? Possible, but I doubt it. She'd be a hell of an actor to fake the emotion I saw."

The room was hot, the windows closed, the air stifling. If the house had an air conditioner, it wasn't on. I moved closer to the body, bent down, ignoring the smells coming from it. I studied Eklund's temple. "Trace gun powder there?"

"Yeah," Oakley agreed.

Eklund looked younger than his age, with a lean build and a flat stomach. Good looking. A tiny drop of blood was on his jeans. I didn't see any other wounds on his body, no signs of possible drug use. He appeared healthy.

"This whole thing stinks." I stood straight. "What's a man doing committing suicide within walking distance of a dumpster where that little boy's body was found? Unless this guy's guilty of something?"

Oakley nodded. "That's what I'm wondering, too."

"Is that Eklund's gun?"

"We're checking on it."

"Have you found anything that would lead you to believe this guy, Eklund, had something to do with Logan Pickett's death?"

He gnawed his lip. "Not so far."

"You're searching the house?"

He nodded again. "Yeah, CSI has a guy upstairs and another one in the basement."

"What do you know about Eklund?"

He glanced at the notepad again. "What we've gathered so far is that the girlfriend, Rachel, that I mentioned–there's some pictures of him and her on the refrigerator–says he stayed to himself. She says Eklund was friendly, but a bit of an introvert, and he doesn't have a lot of contact with the neighbors. He works as a photographer, both with a small company in Wheat Ridge that contracts with a lot of the schools in the metro area. His boss says Eklund was a good employee. No red flags about him. We got in touch with a sister who lives on the East Coast. She was shocked, says Eklund had been just fine, not sad or depressed. Nobody else says he was depressed, either. We're digging into his past as fast as we can, and like I said, I'll give you what we find, if you want it. There are pictures of him and the girlfriend on the fridge. He was kissing her. Quite romantic."

"Suicide note?"

He shook his head. "Not so far."

"I'm going to look around the house," I said.

"Help yourself."

I stepped by Oakley and went out the door, down the hall, and into the kitchen. There wasn't anything special about it, old cabinets that had been painted white, a little table in the corner. I looked in some of the cupboards and in the refrigerator. Nothing out of the ordinary. I didn't find any booze, nothing that would indicate he might be a heavy drinker.

As Oakley had said, a few pictures were stuck to the refrigerator door with magnets. They showed Eklund with a woman with shoulder-length blond hair. In one, they were on a boat, both tan, sunglasses, big smiles. In another, they were on a hiking trail. The third had them sitting on a couch, kissing passionately, as Oakley had said. I had no way of knowing how old the pictures were. Eklund appeared happy.

I turned from the refrigerator and moved to the sink. Out a window was a small backyard, and beyond that, an alley. I stepped outside and into the yard. It was warm, and birds chirped from a huge tree that shaded the yard. They had no concern for the death inside the house.

I walked through the grass to a gate at the far end of the yard. I peeked over the fence and down the alley to the dumpster where Logan Pickett's body had been found. The CSI team was still at work. This was their one chance at evidence, and they'd scour the alley for clues. I hoped they would have a report for me soon.

After I watched them for another minute, I judged the distance from the dumpster. Not very far from Eklund's house. I listened, heard traffic. I tried the gate handle. It stuck, and took me a moment to open. The hinges creaked as I swung the gate inward. Once in the alley, I looked around. Nothing struck me as noteworthy, so I walked back to Eklund's garage. I peeked in a window and saw a light blue Honda Pilot, a lawn mower and other gardening equipment. I craned my neck to see more, then hurried back inside the house. A door off the kitchen led to the basement, and I went downstairs. Another detective was looking around a large room.

"Find anything interesting?" I asked.

He shook his head. "The only thing out of the ordinary is he's got a room set up for photography. A black sheet for a backdrop, chairs for someone to sit on, tripods."

"Show me."

He led me down a hall to a small room and opened a door. It was as he described, dark, with a high window in the corner covered with black paper. Shelving on one wall held a variety of cameras and equipment. I moved around the room, looking for some sign that Logan Pickett might've been in here. Nothing.

"No closet?" I said.

"That's right."

I pointed past him. "Any signs Eklund might have kept that kid down here?"

"The boy found in the alley this morning?" He shook his head. "At first glance, not that I can tell. Doesn't mean he didn't."

I gazed around the main room, which had little in it except a threadbare couch and a pool table, then left the detective there and went upstairs to the second floor. There was another spare bedroom, empty, and a detective in another room that had been set up as an office. He was sitting at a desk with an open laptop.

"That's Eklund's?" I asked.

He nodded. "Yeah. It's password protected, so I can't get into it."

"Get a warrant so a tech can get into it."

"I'm already on it." He went back to searching around the desk.

More camera equipment sat on a shelf in the corner, along with photography books. "You'll be looking at what Eklund has on the cameras as well?"

He gave me a funny look. "Of course. Does this pertain to you?"

"Yeah," I said.

"We're on it, okay?"

I thanked him, then checked a small bathroom. Eklund was tidy, nothing out of place, a hand towel neatly hung on a rod, no water residue around the sink. I peeked back into the office. The detective ignored me, and I went back downstairs. Oakley was still in the bedroom.

"You'll tell me everything you find on the laptop and his cameras," I said. It wasn't a question.

Oakley nodded. "Sure thing. You really think this has something to do with the kid?"

"I don't know, but I'm not paid to believe in coincidences."

He laughed at that. "Yeah, me either. You just got that case this morning, right?"

"Yes." I blew out a long breath and glanced at my watch. "Almost lunch, although I doubt I'll have time to get anything."

"You have any other leads?"

I thought for a second. "There's something with the dad. Not sure what yet, but I'll find it." I gestured at Eklund's room. "But this ..." I didn't finish.

He gave me an appraising look. "Good luck."

"You tell me what you find soon as you can," I repeated. "And get a rush on Eklund's laptop analysis, will you? I want to know what's on it."

"I will," he said, a little irritated that I was pushing him.

"What's the girlfriend's name? Rachel?"

"Connelly. You want to talk to her?"

"Yes."

He gave me her contact information. I thanked him and headed back through the living room. ESPN was still talking baseball. I stepped outside and took off the booties and gloves. The officer gave me a curt nod, and I waved as I walked down the sidewalk.

CHAPTER ELEVEN

"I can't believe this is happening." Rachel Connolly lit a cigarette, sucked in a long drag, and blew smoke into the air. I wrinkled my nose, and she instinctively waved a hand around. "Sorry."

I shrugged it off. "No problem." On the contrary, it was. I'd have the smell on my clothes for hours. I focused on her. Detective Oakley had said she was upset, but time had left her more composed. "How long had you and Ivan been dating?"

"About a year." She wrinkled her face in a cute way, then the sadness reappeared. "He's not really my type. He's more artistic than I am, and really kind of nerdy. I'm not like that at all. I can't even draw a stick figure, and I'm a total extrovert. Not like Ivan."

She looked like money to me. Nice designer slacks, gold jewelry, diamond earrings if I didn't miss my guess. Her makeup was so artfully applied, you might not have even known she was wearing any. That was a skill I didn't have. I was adequate with what little I put on each day. Nothing more.

I sneaked a glance around. The living room was big, with tan walls and framed artwork. The couch we were sitting on was leather. The newly-built house in the Cherry Creek neighborhood had to cost close to one million in Denver's hot real estate market. The house had many artful touches, as if Rachel had used a designer to decorate. I was judging, but the house seemed much too much for a single woman.

"What do you do for work?" I asked.

"I work at a law firm downtown. We handle a lot of work for oil and gas companies, like Sundown Energy."

I'd heard of Sundown. They were a large corporation working in the oil industry across the US and Canada. A lot of money there, and she'd obviously been getting her share. I could only assume she was good at what she did.

"I hate to go over something painful again, but could you tell me how you found Ivan," I said, even though I'd heard it from Oakley.

She took another drag on the cigarette and tapped it into a fancy pottery ashtray. The house was quiet, and her voice seemed tiny in the big room. "We were supposed to get together for dinner last night, and he canceled because he had to finish some work. I'd told him that I expected a call from him this morning since he'd blown me off." She laughed hesitantly. "That was kind of a running joke between us. I tend to cancel on *him*, and he always tells me that I need to make it up to him. Which of course I do." Her face flushed a deep red at the sexual innuendo of the comment. I kept a straight face. "Anyway, he'd said that he would come early in the morning and we could have a little time together. I've been working really hard on a case, and even a little bit of time together would've been nice. Ivan didn't show, though, and at first I thought it was nothing. I got to work, and I tried to call him. He didn't answer, and I left a message." She picked up the cigarette, then put it down again without another drag. "I'd gone out with a client for an early lunch, and after that, I stopped by Ivan's house. I thought, you know, that maybe he and I could sneak in, a ..." She stopped, and her face flushed.

That was more detail than I'd gotten from Oakley. "You shared all this with the other detective?"

"Yes. Except for the part about ... you know, wanting a quickie with Ivan."

"I get it. You have a key to Ivan's house?"

She nodded, relieved that I didn't press her on their sex life. "Yes. So I called Ivan again. I thought maybe he'd gotten busy with something, and that he'd like it if I surprised him. I came in the house and called out his name, then went into the kitchen. His car keys were on a little hook by the garage door, and I figured he must be around, so I called out louder and started walking toward the bedroom." She picked up the cigarette again, and it wobbled in her trembling fingers. She took one final draw on it and crushed it out with force in the ashtray. "I thought maybe I smelled something as I headed toward his room. When I turned the corner, I saw ..." She lost her voice. She stared out the window to a freshly mown lawn. "I've never seen anyone dead," she whispered. "It was awful."

I reached out and touched her hand. "Take your time."

She sucked in some air, then said, "I might've stared at him for a moment. I'm not really sure. Then I backed up. I remember leaning against the doorjamb, not wanting to look at him, not believing it. I ran into the living room and called 911. I went out on the front porch and waited until the police arrived. They asked me some questions, and then a detective arrived, and he talked to me for a little bit, too. After that, he said I could go. I didn't go back to work. I just couldn't."

"That's understandable," I murmured.

She took a few more deeps breaths, collected herself. "What else do you want to know?"

"Did Ivan own a gun?"

"I don't know. I've never heard him mention guns, and I never saw one at his house."

"When was the last time you saw him?"

"Friday night. We went to a movie, then came back here. We talked over the weekend, but he was busy, so we didn't get together." She wagged her head in confusion. "I just don't get it. Ivan seemed fine. Why would he take his own life?"

"You didn't see any signs of his being depressed? He didn't mention any troubles?"

Another little headshake. "As far as I could tell, everything was okay. He seemed to be happy, he was making good money, and things were good with us. You know he was a photographer?"

"Yes."

"He's quite talented. That's a piece of what drew me to him. His work was good, and he was even looking forward to a photography show coming up this summer."

I thought about all of the framed photography on Eklund's walls. I hadn't looked closely enough to know whether he had taken all of them. The one hanging above his bed had caught my eye, though. I sat back. "Ivan never mentioned any issues that might lead him to something like this?"

"No." She looked across the room. "You see that photo?" I looked at a picture of a river, the running water cascading over some boulders. It was good, the light glinting off the water creating gold patterns. "Isn't that something? A simple river, yet he made it come alive."

"Yes," I said.

I was about to ask my question again, when her face pinched, puzzled. "You asked about Ivan, whether he had issues that would lead him to kill himself. I don't know, but he had been acting a little odd the last couple of weeks. He wasn't himself. Not depressed, or sad, just ... strange."

"Strange how?" I watched her intently.

She dabbed delicately at the corner of her eye with her pinky finger. "He had a picture of a boy on his camera." She looked back at me. "You know that he also takes portraits, especially of children?"

"With a company in Wheat Ridge."

"Yes, that and freelance. It's how he's supported himself through the years. That and his nature photography."

I shook my head. "I didn't know about the freelance work."

She nodded. "Yes, his nature photography is finally taking off, and he's working with a studio, along with a lot of freelance work. Graduation photos, kids and family portraits, that kind of thing. He's good at it, but he'd gotten tired of it. Anyway, I was over at his house a week or two ago maybe? I'm not sure. He was on the computer, and he didn't hear me come into his office. On the monitor was a picture of a boy, and Ivan was staring at it. The photo wasn't like Ivan's usual stuff. Not a portrait, like so many I'd seen. This one was farther away. The boy was on his bike, not looking at the camera. It was like Ivan had taken it secretly. I asked him about it, wondering if he was trying a different style. He looked surprised, then he tried to close the picture, and said it was nothing. I asked him who the little boy was, and all he would say was it was a neighbor." She gave a little shrug. "It was just odd. I've not seen him ever want to hide anything with his photography. He was proud of the pictures he took, but with that one picture of the boy, it seemed like he wasn't."

"You never found out who the boy was?"

"No."

"Did Ivan know him?"

"If he did, he wouldn't say."

I pulled out my phone, got on the internet, and googled Logan Pickett's name. I found an article that had his picture with it, and I showed Rachel. "Is this the boy?"

She took the phone from me and studied it. "Hmm, I don't

know." Then her jaw dropped. "Oh my gosh. That's the little boy who's missing, isn't it? I saw something on the news the other night."

"Yes," I said. I wasn't going to tell her yet that Logan was dead. "And you're sure Ivan never said anything else about this boy?"

She sucked in a breath. "No, I'm positive. But you know something more, don't you?" Her lawyer instincts had kicked in.

"I'm afraid I can't tell you any more," I said.

"Ivan didn't have anything to do with that boy. He wouldn't hurt anyone."

I narrowed my eyes. "How do you know?"

"Ivan's shy and sweet. Ask anyone, and you'll hear that he's kind." I'd heard that line before, from abusers and killers. It didn't hold much water. She seemed to know that. "Ivan didn't kidnap that boy."

"What do you know about Ivan's family?"

She thought for a second. "His parents live in Virginia, close to the DC area. I've heard Ivan talk to them on the phone. They seem nice. He has two younger sisters, both of them live in Virginia, too. I've never met any of them. Since I've been dating Ivan, they haven't come out here. He took a trip out there last Thanksgiving, but I didn't go."

"Has he met your family?"

"My mother. She lives here in town. My father died a couple of years ago. I have a brother, and he lives in Florida."

"Was there anything else in Ivan's behavior that you thought was strange, or different?"

She pondered that. "The other detective asked me the same thing. The only other thing that comes to mind is he said something the other day about some woman losing her child, wondering what she was going through."

My nerves tingled. "Who 'lost her child?' "

She lifted her shoulders. "When I asked, he said someone he knew. Then he changed the subject."

"When did he say that?"

"I don't know. A day or two ago?"

Was Eklund referring to Audra Pickett? I thought. Had he snatched her kid and was he wondering if Audra knew that he'd done it?

"Is there anything else Ivan said that might pertain to the missing boy?"

She shook her head. "No, sorry."

"If this wasn't suicide, do you know of any reason someone might want to kill Ivan?"

"No, I don't. Like I said, he was a nice guy, and he didn't have an enemy in the world."

I gave her a business card. "If you think of anything else that might be important, please let me know. Or let Detective Oakley know. Even the smallest thing might be important."

She picked up the card and stared at it. "I've always been on the other side of these conversations, the one digging for information. Not the one giving it." She stared at the floor. "I can't believe he would have done this." Her voice was small.

When I left, she was still sitting on the couch, staring out the window.

CHAPTER TWELVE

"Did someone give you a laptop for Ivan Eklund?"

I was leaning in the doorway of the tech room, and Tara jumped.

"Don't scare me like that." She frowned and turned down her music, then pointed at her monitor. "I'm still working on Gary Pickett's laptop. What's the rush on this other one?" She pushed her glasses up. "Wait a minute. Who's Ivan Eklund?"

"He died this morning, appears to be a suicide, but I'm not jumping to conclusions yet."

"And?"

"He happens to live near where Logan Pickett's body was found. Oakley said they'd be bringing Eklund's laptop in, and I told him to get a rush on the analysis."

She swore under her breath. "Wow." She reached for her coffee. "Someone on Oakley's team dropped off a laptop, but they didn't say that case might be related to yours."

"Did you find any photos on Gary's laptop?"

"A few, mostly of the little boy. Also some military pictures, some of Gary back in his Marine uniform." She turned back to her monitor. "You know this guy, Gary Pickett? His internet searches are pretty interesting."

"Interesting?"

"He's on a lot of political sites, far-right places. I checked a couple of them, and they have some pretty radical agendas."

I moved closer and caught a whiff of her lavender perfume. "What are you talking about?" This was not what I expected.

She pulled up a document and pointed at it. "He's been looking at a lot of sites that write about conspiracy theories and New World Order stuff. And he's been on 4chan."

"What's that?"

"It's an internet forum site where the users can post things anonymously. It was popular with anime, and then with gamers. It's also been used for activist and political movements, because of its anonymity."

"Lovely."

"If you ever want some light reading ..." She took a sip of coffee. "There's been a lot of controversy surrounding 4chan, including cyberbullying claims, celebrity photos leaked on the site, and child pornography being posted there."

"Did Gary post anything there?"

"Not that I can find. He doesn't have any porn of any kind on his laptop." She set her cup down and looked at her monitor. "He's also been looking up some Colorado militia groups."

"I've heard of a few. I don't know much about them, other than that some are being monitored closely by the feds. I came across a group once on a murder investigation a few years ago. Turns out the militia group didn't have anything to do with the murder. The group was harmless as far as I could tell, but there was some riffraff among them."

She nodded. "Yeah, some just want to protect their rights. Others, I wouldn't want to be within a mile of them. If you want any more info on militia groups, there's a Professor Wilder at

DU you should talk to. He's a good guy, and a wealth of knowledge."

I cocked an eyebrow at her. "Someone at the University of Denver is an expert on militias?"

Tara smiled. "It came up on another case." She swiveled in her chair and looked at me. "Gary also has some emails back and forth with a guy named John Merrick."

"Who's that?"

"From the emails, I can tell he owns Gold Creek Gun Range."

"Gary's been calling the gun range."

"Uh-huh. From some work on other cases, I've heard rumors that Merrick might be involved in a militia group. Nothing special on the emails, though, just 'meet me here' or some info on guns. I'll have them on the report. Oh, on one email Gary says something about keeping it a secret, and that no one needed to find out."

"Secret about what?"

"It doesn't say."

"Hmm." I filed that away. "Gary is a former Marine. It would make sense that he would go to a gun store. He's certainly an interesting character."

"But is he a murderer?" Tara asked drily.

"Good question."

"So far I haven't found anything illegal on his laptop. But I thought you'd want to know about the right-wing stuff."

I leaned down and stared at the monitor. "That may be enough reason for his not wanting us to have his laptop, but keep looking. I'll bet he has something on here, something else he doesn't want us to find." I read through some of the information she had on him. "What are you trying to hide?" I muttered as I gazed at the screen. Then I stood straight and stretched. "What about emails since Logan died?"

"Yeah, I checked that first. Gary's emails about that are pretty straightforward, just telling people about how his son was dead. Not a lot of emotion in it, if you ask me, but then I'm no psychologist."

"Make sure I get those."

"I will." Tara tapped another small laptop on the other side of her desk. "You're going to have to decide. You want me to finish with Gary Pickett's laptop, or do you want me to start on Eklund's?"

I gave her a wry smile. "Both."

She let out an exasperated sigh. "I'll get somebody else to help me with it. You guys always need it yesterday." There wasn't malice in the statement. She knew how critical time was. "I'm getting lunch first."

"I wish I could," I said, then pointed at Eklund's laptop. "Whoever analyzes his laptop needs to look for photos he might've deleted, specifically of kids. Eklund took at least a couple of photos of Logan Pickett around the time Logan disappeared. I want to know if he has more of the kid, or any other kids, for that matter."

She gulped. "Not another pedophile?"

I held up my hands. "That's what I want to find out."

"Lovely."

I gave her a "What's this world coming to" look and left.

"What have you got?" Spats said when I walked up to my desk.

I sat down and heard the sigh of the chair cushion, and I felt the same sigh in myself. "Have you heard of Ivan Eklund?"

He shook his head. "That's the dead guy?"

"Yes. He lived a few houses down from where Logan Pickett's body was found. Shot himself in the temple." I raked a hand through my hair. "Seems a little fishy, don't you think? A dead guy's discovered right near where the boy's body was found?"

Spats stared at me. "You're serious? When you left here, I didn't believe it."

I leaned back. "So far, the house is clean, at least that's what Oakley says. I walked around, too, and I didn't see any signs that would indicate Eklund had kept Logan in the house. However ..." I thought for a second.

"What? Don't keep me in suspense."

"I talked to Ivan's girlfriend, Rachel Connelly. Nice woman. She's got money. Ivan was a photographer." Spats waited for me to connect the dots. "Apparently, Eklund's up-and-coming. He takes lots of nature photography; it was all over the house. He's good, too."

"And?"

I leaned forward, the chair sighing again, accentuating my next words. "He also takes portraits, graduation pictures, family photos, that kind of thing."

Spats leaned forward as well. "And pictures of little kids?"

I nodded. "Supposedly he's taken pictures of Logan Pickett as well."

Spats rubbed his eyes. "Porn?"

"Not that the girlfriend knows, but I'm not willing to shut the door on that yet. Tara's going to work on Eklund's laptop soon. I told her to speed it up." I tapped my desk for emphasis. "I want to know what this guy was doing."

"Me too."

"And get this. Gary Pickett has been spending a lot of time checking out militia groups on the internet."

"Not usual, but not illegal."

"True. I suspect he wanted to keep that hidden, and that's why he didn't want to surrender his laptop. He mentioned something in some emails about keeping 'it' a secret, and that no one needed to find out. I want to know what that secret is. I'm going to look into Gary some more."

"Gary would've been better off saying what he had on the laptop and just giving it to you. Resisting only makes him look more suspicious."

I nodded again. "What have you found out about Gary and that gun shop? I found out the owner's name is John Merrick. We'll need to have a talk with Merrick, but I want to go in prepped."

"I'm working on it, Speelmahn." He held up a finger. "I got a hold of Logan's grandparents. Audra's mother–Lucy–was pleasant enough, but got choked up when discussing Logan. She'd been holding out hope that he'd be found, of course. When Audra called and said Logan was dead, Lucy said it was the worst news imaginable. We talked for a while, and in the conversation, she mentioned that she didn't like Gary."

"Oh?"

"Yeah, she was pretty forthcoming with that. She said she never understood why Audra married him, that he was nice at first, but he was verbally abusive to Audra, that he ordered her and the daughter around. Lucy didn't outright say that Gary might've kidnapped and killed his son, but there was a trace of suspicion in her voice."

"Bitter and angry at Gary? Looking for a scapegoat, someone to blame for her grandson's death?"

"Maybe. Or maybe he did it."

"Did she say anything about Audra having a drinking problem?"

"I asked about that in a few ways, and nope, at least as far as her mom knows, Audra doesn't drink much at all. Lucy also said that the divorce was pretty contentious."

"What about Gary's parents?"

"I talked to his father, Ken. Of course he's sad about Logan, and he didn't understand why Audra hadn't kept a better eye on Logan. Overall, Ken thought Audra was a good mother, and he was a bit sorry they'd divorced. He also agreed that it was a bad divorce, but he thought Gary should've gotten custody of Logan. He's proud of Gary, says that he had a tough time when he got out of the Marines, but he's really turned it around."

"A different view of Gary, depending on who you talk to."

"Yes."

"Did he think either one has a drinking problem?"

"No. And I called the real estate client that Audra talked to on Saturday, and she said they'd had a nice talk." Spats held up some papers on his desk. "Other than that, it doesn't appear that Audra made any unusual calls lately. I've been looking over her internet searches, too, and I don't see any red flags."

Just then, Ernie ambled into the office. "I've got something," he announced, then sank into his chair.

"Spill it," Spats said.

"I've been following up on Audra Pickett's neighbors, on some of the interviews that were taken right after Logan was kidnapped. To a person, they can't believe something like this would happen in their neighborhood. And the ones who've heard about that man who killed himself are even more stunned. From their perspective, Audra was a good mom, and a bunch weren't too fond of Gary. He complained about Audra a lot, said she wasn't good with Logan, but none of the neighbors saw that."

"Did any of them hear Audra and Gary fighting, or either one drinking too much?"

"One of the next-door neighbors sometimes heard fights, but no one knew anything about drinking problems."

"Has anyone heard a car that backfired around the time Logan disappeared, or the night he was murdered?"

He shook his head. "Negative."

I frowned. "Too bad. That's probably a dead end."

"Get to the good stuff," Spats urged.

Ernie grunted. "Hold your horses." He gave a small smile. "You're not going to believe this. There's another kid in the neighborhood who saw something the night that Logan was kidnapped."

I sat up. "Who?"

"One of the neighbors told me about a Mrs. Frawley, who's got a daughter, Bev, a teenager who's developmentally delayed. Mrs. Frawley told the neighbor that her daughter had been talking about Logan."

"Where do the Frawleys live?"

"Down the street from Audra."

"You talked to Mrs. Frawley?"

"Sure." Ernie shrugged. "Mrs. Frawley was a little hesitant to talk. She's protective of her daughter. She says her daughter is scared, and she's not sure it would be a good idea for us to talk to her. I pushed Mrs. Frawley a bit, and she said maybe later, that her daughter was at an appointment. We should go talk to Bev. Get her before she forgets anything."

I stood up. "I'll go talk to her."

Ernie held up a hand. "I need to go. I've already got the mom warmed up. You'll have a hard time if you go alone."

"Fair enough." I beckoned to him. "Let's go."

He sighed. "I just sat down." He groaned dramatically as he heaved himself to his feet, then followed me out the door.

CHAPTER THIRTEEN

"Hello, Detective Moore," a slender woman with brown hair said as she let us into her foyer. She held out her hand to me. "I'm Donna Frawley."

I shook her hand and introduced myself.

"Mrs. Frawley," Ernie said deferentially. "We'd like to speak to your daughter."

"We'll be as careful as possible," I tacked on.

She hesitated. "Okay, but please don't upset her. I heard that Ivan killed himself, but Bev doesn't know."

"We won't say a word about that," I assured her.

She finally relented. "Bev's in the family room."

Mrs. Frawley led us down the hall to a large room with a TV, couches, and a chair. Sitting in a large school desk–the kind that was a combo chair and desk–was a frail girl with blonde hair. She had a pencil in her hand, and she was writing on a big notepad, her brow furrowed with concentration. She looked up when we entered the room. She had the deepest blue eyes I'd ever seen, and they couldn't hide the fear at the strangers in her midst.

"It's okay, Bev. These two people want to ask you a few questions." That didn't seem to allay Bev's fear. She glanced away, the pencil still in her hand, the eraser end shaking.

Mrs. Frawley gestured for us to move into the room. I took a seat on the couch and let Ernie take the lead. A pleasant cinnamon odor drifted in from the kitchen, and I saw a rack of cookies on the counter.

"I didn't do anything," Bev said in a small voice, then repeated, "I didn't do anything." She used the pencil to push some crayons that sat near the notepad.

"It's okay, honey. You're not in any trouble. When we get finished, you can have a cookie." Bev didn't acknowledge that. Mrs. Frawley played nervously with her hair, then glanced at me. "I was afraid this might happen," she whispered. "She doesn't need the disruptions. I try to keep her on a routine."

Before I could say anything, Ernie moved carefully toward Bev, and I don't know how he did it, but he managed to make his big frame seem smaller. While he was still a fair distance from the desk, he got down on one knee. He reached for a toy doll with red hair that was on the floor near the desk. Bev sucked in a breath, and Ernie let his hand fall to his side.

"That's a neat doll," he said, his voice calm. "Does she have a name?"

Mrs. Frawley and I kept quiet, and let Ernie talk to Bev.

She scrunched up her nose. "Alice."

"May I hold her?"

Bev glanced at him, her chin tucked into her chest. Then she gave a small nod. She had to be fourteen or fifteen, and yet she was so childlike.

Ernie picked it up. "She's got a pretty dress on," he said as he turned the doll around in his hand. "What color is this?"

"That's not a dress," Bev corrected him. "That's a skirt."

Mrs. Frawley covered her mouth with her hand and

murmured to me, "I taught her the difference between a skirt and a dress."

If Ernie heard her, he didn't act like it. He nodded thoughtfully at Bev. "Now that you mention it, you're right about that. It's a skirt, and I see that she has a pretty flowered shirt."

"You can comb her hair too."

"Can you show me?"

Ernie held out the doll. Bev hesitated, then set her pencil down and took the doll. "You take it like this, and you do this," she said as she picked up a small plastic comb from the floor and ran it through the doll's hair. "See, now she's got pretty hair, like mine." Mrs. Frawley smiled again.

Ernie rubbed his chin. "You did a great job. She's beautiful. Do you have other dolls?"

She nodded shyly. "I have two others."

"That's pretty cool," he said. "I have a daughter who likes these kinds of dolls."

That got Bev's attention. She tipped her head shyly and blinked at him. "You like dolls?" she asked.

Ernie nodded as he sat down cross-legged on the floor, closer to her. "I know a lot about dolls. I know that you can dress them, and wash and comb their hair. I know some of them cry, and you can give some of them milk with a bottle."

"You can do this with them," Bev reached out for the doll and Ernie handed it to her. "See, you can take a hat and put it on her head."

Ernie looked as if he'd never seen that. "That is really neat. Hey, may I take your picture with that? I want to show my daughter."

Mrs. Frawley hesitated, and I put a hand out to stop her. I mouthed for her to wait a moment, then whispered, "He's just trying to make her feel more comfortable."

Ernie was on a roll. I didn't know he was this good with kids, all his gruffness gone. Bev glanced at her mother.

"It's okay," Mrs. Frawley said, then gave me a look that said Ernie had better know what he was doing.

Ernie pulled out his cell phone, focused on her, and leaned back. "Hold the doll up and give me a good smile."

She did as instructed and threw him a big crooked smile. Ernie pretended as if he had snapped her picture, but I could tell he didn't actually take it. So did Mrs. Frawley, and she visibly relaxed.

"He takes my picture too." Bev said.

"Who does?" Ernie kept his voice casual, an even tone.

"That man down the street. Ivan. He's my friend."

"That's right," Mrs. Frawley quickly explained. "Ivan Eklund. He took portraits of the kids at the school, and I hired him to do some of our family."

"Oh yeah?" Ernie smiled at Bev. "He took your picture?"

She pointed to the fireplace mantel, with a framed photo of her sitting on the front porch. "He took that."

He craned his neck to see. "May I take a closer look at it?"

Bev nodded, pleased that he wanted to. He got up with more agility than I'd seen in him in a while. He hefted up his pants and picked up the photo.

"This is really nice. You've got a beautiful smile."

Bev gave him another crooked smile, just like in the photo. "Thanks," she said shyly. "My friend Ivan took that. He takes lots of pictures of me."

"Not that many," Mrs. Frawley blurted out before I could stop her. I didn't want her to interrupt Bev's flow.

Bev shook her head at her mother. "Ivan takes lots of pictures of me," her voice was emphatic. "He takes pictures of the other kids in the neighborhood too."

"Oh," Ernie said, his tone still level. I glared at Mrs. Frawley so that she would remain quiet. Her eyes were wide in surprise, but she seemed to get that we needed information from her daughter. He put the picture back and moved toward the desk. "Who else besides you?" he asked.

She concentrated hard. "I know that boy Terrell, and Logan. And some other kids, but I don't know their names. They're mean to me. Except not Logan and Terrell. They're nice to me."

Mrs. Frawley wiped at her eyes, but kept quiet.

"When did you see Logan?" Ernie was still casual, his tone warm and inviting.

"The other day. The night sponge was on TV."

"SpongeBob Squarepants," Mrs. Frawley whispered.

Ernie must've heard that. "Were you outside that afternoon?" he asked Bev.

She nodded. "I was sitting on the front porch." She glanced at her mom. "It was okay, right?"

"Yes, of course," Mrs. Frawley said. "You asked me if it was okay, and I said yes."

Bev looked back at Ernie. "My mom said it was okay," she repeated. "Logan ran from Terrell's house down the street."

"Did you see Logan go to his house?"

"No, but I saw Ivan."

I felt myself tense, but Ernie kept at the questioning in his easy manner.

"Where was he?"

Bev glanced toward the hallway, as if she were looking out front. "He was sitting in his car." Again she pointed, as if she were outside. "He was at the corner. I saw him for a minute. Then I came inside."

"Where did Logan go?"

"I don't know."

"What kind of car was it?" Then Ernie realized she probably wouldn't know that. "What color was it?"

"Blue. It's a pretty color."

"Blue, like this?" He picked up a dark blue crayon from her desk.

She shook her head. "Like that." She pointed to an abstract painting on the wall that had lighter blue streaks in it.

I wondered if Terrell had seen the same blue car. I knew he'd described a loud bang that could've been a car backfiring. Could it have been Ivan's?

Ernie seemed to be thinking the same thing. "Did the car make a sound, like a loud bang?"

She shook her head. "I didn't hear the car. I just saw Ivan at the corner. He was taking pictures of the boys. He likes to take pictures of us kids." She pointed at the mantel again. "He took that picture of me."

Ernie nodded. He got down on his knee. "You don't remember anything else about Ivan's car?"

She wrapped her arms around herself. "I've never been in Ivan's car. Mommy told me never to get in anyone's car, even if I know them."

He nodded encouragingly. "That's good. You want to be safe. Did you ever feel scared around Ivan?"

"No, he's my friend. He takes my picture."

Ernie glanced at me. I sensed what he did. We were losing Bev. We'd probably gotten all we were going to from her.

"Ivan was friends with the other kids, right?" he went on. Bev stared at him. "Did Ivan play with the kids?" He danced carefully around the issue.

"I don't know. I saw him take pictures."

"Did you talk to Terrell or Logan about Ivan?"

She drug her foot along the carpet carefully. "I don't think so. He took pictures, that's all." She pursed her lips. "I have to finish my work." She picked up her pencil again and began drawing on the notepad.

"Thank you so much for talking to me," Ernie said. He smiled as warmly as possible and stood up. Bev concentrated on the paper.

"That's right, honey, you finish your drawing," Mrs. Frawley said. "I'm going to talk to these people, okay? Then you can have a cookie."

Mrs. Frawley gestured, and we followed her into the hallway, where she could still watch her daughter and talk to us.

"Have you heard of Ivan taking pictures of the kids from afar like that?" I asked in a low voice.

She shook her head. "Ivan takes portraits. You saw the one of Bev. That's all I'm aware of, and I don't recall any of the neighbors saying that he did anything else, either. It's news to me that he might've been watching the kids." She shuddered. "Was he a pedophile?" She glanced at her daughter. "Oh my gosh."

"We don't know that yet," I said. "He doesn't have any record." It probably wouldn't help to say that. I knew the rumor of Eklund being a pedophile would spread through the neighborhood like wildfire.

"Did Ivan kill Logan?" Mrs. Frawley asked.

"We don't have any evidence of that," I replied.

"I can't believe it," Mrs. Frawley said. "Ivan was the nicest man. He was kind to my daughter, and from what I hear, to the other kids too."

Of course, I thought but didn't say. That's how you reel the kids in.

We thanked Mrs. Frawley for her time, and Ernie and I headed outside.

CHAPTER FOURTEEN

"Follow up with Oakley on his investigation," I said to Ernie as we walked to our cars. "I want to see Eklund's phone records. We need to track down who he was talking to, and I want to know more about him in general, what the neighbors thought of him, what he was like. Oakley should have a report."

"All right." He jerked a thumb toward the Frawley house. "What'd you think?"

I opened my car door, then pushed stray hair out of my face. "Eklund drove a blue car."

"That's what went through my mind when Bev said she saw a blue car."

"What might've Eklund been doing to the kids in the neighborhood?"

He nodded. "Taking pictures of kids, being nice to them. It's a perfect way to build trust, and then take advantage of them."

"Exactly."

He pulled a cigar from his coat pocket and studied the end of it. "I'll see what I can dig up on him."

"I'll see you back at the office, but I'm going to pop by the ME office, see if Jack's working on Logan's autopsy."

Ernie jammed the unlit cigar in his mouth and left without another word. As I started the car and pulled into the street, Spats called.

"Hey, Harry called me. He said he left you a message."

I swore. "What's he doing calling you?" I said it, but I knew. Harry needed something from me quickly, and I wasn't responding. Before Spats could retort, I said, "I haven't had time to call him back. I'll do it now."

"I'm just the messenger."

"I'll take care of it. Get on Merrick."

"I'm going to get some lunch, return Audra's laptop, and then I will." He knew my gruffness was a way to cover for my own mistake. I was thankful he didn't call me out.

The office of the medical examiner is in an industrial area in the crook of Interstate 25 and Sixth Avenue. It doesn't have easy access from either highway, and I had to weave my way through side streets to get there. I was tempted to get a late lunch, but I wanted to wait until after I'd gone to the morgue. I did call Harry on my way.

"Sarah, I left you a message." His tone was pure frustration, unusual for him. It wasn't often that he was that irritated with me.

"I'm sorry, it's been a busy morning."

"They're always busy." He was in a mood.

"What's going on?"

"We're supposed to go to that benefit tonight. It's been on our calendar for months, and I paid a lot for the tickets. You said when you left this morning that you'd let me know how your day was going, and if you could make it."

I'd completely forgotten we'd talked about the benefit. I hadn't wanted to go in the first place, but I'd let him talk me into it. I was mad at myself for not just saying no when he suggested we go, and even more irritated because in not wanting to go, I was being selfish. Harry does a lot of things that I want to do; I should be more willing to do some of the things he wants to. This benefit would help the homeless, which was great. I just didn't want to hobnob with a bunch of his well-to-do executive friends. By his tone, I could tell that he expected me to be by his side tonight. I frowned as I stared out the windshield. My cases recently had been difficult, taking time away from him and from our lives together. He wasn't going to be pleased now.

"I'm not sure I can make it. I–"

Before I could say more, he interrupted. "Sarah, I know you've been busy, but you seemed as if you *would* make it. You told me–"

"I can't help it," I said, my turn to interrupt. "I've got a dead child, found in the dumpster, and I've got to work the investigation now, before any leads go cold."

Silence filled the line between us, a chasm I knew had been building. I had been preoccupied lately, and I needed to address that. But not right now.

"Oh man." He let out a big sigh. "Okay, I guess. Call me later and let me know whether you can make it." He hesitated, then said, "I'll ... talk to you later."

He ended the call before I could say anything else. I'm sure he was torn, knowing I was looking into the death of a child. But he also wanted me.

By now, I'd parked at a long nondescript building that was the ME office. I went inside, and as I made my way to Jack Jamison's corner office, a vaguely chemical smell assaulted my nostrils.

I hoped Jack had been able to get to Logan Pickett right away. I'd been to plenty of autopsies over the years, and it's something you never got used to. In death, bodies smell, and it's an unpleasant thing that never leaves you. Right now, I wished I could've been somewhere else.

Jack was sitting at his desk when I came around the corner. I popped my head in. He had more in his office than I ever would, pictures of his family on his desk, a picture of fall aspen hung on one wall, a bookcase on the opposite, full of professional books and manuals. He glanced up when he saw me and gestured toward a chair across from his desk.

"Have a seat." He pushed some papers aside, then made a note on one of them. "I pushed that boy's autopsy to the front of the line. It's finished, and I'll have a full report for you later today. It takes time to compile everything, and I don't like being rushed."

I didn't have time for a long conversation, but he was going to give me the details however he wanted to. I sat down and waited. Through the open door, I heard voices, then silence.

Jack scratched his jaw and consulted some notes. Then he finally picked up a file folder. "It's already been a day. We're backed up."

I knew that was my cue. "I appreciate you getting to this one. We need to find out what happened to Logan, and fast."

"Yes, I know. I handled this one myself." He opened the folder and picked up a sheet of paper. "This is what I have. I didn't find any signs of poisons, or any drugs in his system. I'm running a full toxicology, but that will take a while. However, on my initial assessment, he was clean. I didn't see any signs of needle marks that would indicate he'd been injected with anything. He experienced trauma from the slit to the wrist, which is the cause of death. He bled out. My guess would be he died within a few hours before being put in the dumpster." I knew there was more, and I also knew from experience to hold my questions. "He had bruises on both wrists, consistent with someone grabbing him. Besides that, he had a few other bruises on his legs and lower back, probably got them within days of his death. He didn't have anything in his stomach, either." He paused, and I knew I could ask some questions.

"The bruises, would they be consistent with his being abused by someone?"

He thought about that as he stared at the paper. "Possibly. Could I say for certain he'd been abused? No. I can make no determination on how those bruises came about, no clear pattern to indicate a weapon or a hand. I didn't see any old wounds, although his left forearm had been broken, and two fingers in his right hand. I don't know if that would've been from abuse, though."

"I'll ask the mother about it."

"That's a good place to start."

"No sign of head trauma or anything like that?"

He shook his head. "Like I said, the bruises, and the slit on the wrist, that's all."

"Anything that could tell you for certain this is a homicide?"

He blew a long breath out. "You know I can't make that type of determination. This could have been an accident, or someone could have done this to him. That's up to you to figure out."

"Any way to determine what caused the cut?"

"It was a clean cut. Hard to say if it was glass, or a knife. Certainly not a dull knife," he mused, almost to himself. "It's possible the wound was self-inflicted."

"A nine-year-old boy slits his wrist? I find that hard to believe, but I guess it could happen."

"A lot of kids these days are being bullied, and they're doing desperate things to escape it. Some even suicide." I thought back to my childhood. It hadn't always been easy, but I'd never thought to kill myself. "If Logan did that to himself," he posed the question, "who dumped his body in a dumpster instead of telling someone about it?"

I raised eyebrows at him. "Yeah, that's why we're pretty sure this wasn't."

He put the paper back in the file and looked at me. "I'll email you the full report as soon as I finish it." He pushed back his chair and got up. "I've got plenty more to do this afternoon. I'll leave the detecting up to you."

I rose as well, and as I turned to the door, I said, "You have another case I'm interested in. Ivan Eklund. A possible suicide."

He followed me into the hallway. "Oh, Eklund. What's your interest in him?"

"He lives right down the street from the dumpster were Logan Pickett's body was found."

He stopped and looked at me with exasperation. "I suppose you want a rush on that one too?"

"I figured Oakley would've already asked you to."

"Maybe he told someone else." He ran a hand through his steel-gray hair. "Going to be one of those days. Only they *all* seem like one of those days. What is this world coming to?"

"I was thinking the same thing earlier." I smiled. "You'll get to Eklund soon. I have faith."

"Faith, huh? I guess we need a little more of that right now. I'll see what the schedule is, and if Eklund can be moved up, I'll do it." Before I could thank him, he held up a hand. "Don't get your hopes up. Soon *might* be today, but I'd expect tomorrow."

I started to push him, and he shook his head. "We'll get on it as soon as we can."

He pulled his door shut, gave me a little wave, then turned and headed in the other direction. When he disappeared around the corner, I left.

CHAPTER FIFTEEN

No one was around when I got back to my desk. I had stopped at a fast food joint on the way back to the office, so I set down the bag with my Wendy's lunch and flopped into my chair. I stretched and let out a satisfying groan, then dug into the bag for my hamburger. My mouth watered as I bit into it. It wasn't healthy, but it was damn good. I took a few minutes to eat the rest of the burger, and munched on some French fries. I sipped some soda, then wiped my hands with a napkin. I pushed my fries to the side.

Another notebook had been left on my desk. I opened it up and as I nibbled on the fries, I began scanning pages, all about Gary Pickett, which was good. I wanted to know everything about the man that I could. The notebook was full. The techs had had plenty of time to dig into him. And it was enlightening.

Gary was from Sacramento, and had one younger sister. His parents were still married, and they still owned the house Gary had grown up in. He'd been an average student, and had played on the football and baseball teams in high school. He'd worked odd jobs after he graduated, then had joined the Marines at age twenty. He enlisted for four years, and he had done one tour in Iraq. He'd risen to the rank of Lance Corporal, which was the third-lowest among enlisted ranks. A side note said that enlisted Marines that are never promoted to a higher rank are known as "Terminal Lances." *Had Gary shown no interest in promotion, or was he not good enough?* I wondered.

I ate a few fries and kept reading. Gary was an expert marksman, and his record was impeccable, no trouble while he'd been in. On the other hand, his service wasn't particularly distinctive. He had been stationed in San Diego, and had come to Denver at the end of his service. I flipped pages and found his marriage license. He'd married Audra in San Diego while he was still in the Marines.

"There has to be someone who can tell me what you were really like in the Marines," I muttered to myself. His file said that he had a Facebook profile, and I got on the internet and looked it up. I couldn't see everything because he had some privacy settings in place, but I was able to scroll through and see some posts. He had a lot with pictures of him in the mountains, hiking or cycling, and some with him fishing. None with him and Logan. Then I came across one of him where he had tagged John Merrick. I went to John Merrick's Facebook profile, but his settings were locked down, and I couldn't see anything. I went back to Gary's page and studied the photo of him and Merrick. I couldn't say for sure, but it looked as if they were in front of Merrick's gun store. They appeared smiling and friendly.

I looked through more of his photos and came upon a picture of Gary with another man, both in uniform. His friend–Elroy Burke–had been tagged in the photo. I wondered what Gary was like as a Marine. On the surface, he'd been a model soldier, if not outstanding. But were there any cracks in that image? I got on my computer and found some information about Elroy Burke. He was living in Washington, DC, working at a consulting firm, and

I was able to find a phone number for him. I called it, was routed twice, and then a sharp male voice answered. "Elroy Burke's office. May I help you?"

I identified myself. "I need to speak to Mr. Burke please. It's an urgent matter."

"He isn't here right now. May I have him call you back?" All business.

"That'll be fine." I gave him my name and number, and hung up.

I stared at the phone for a second, then went back to reading through the notebook. The techs doing the research had been thorough.

I sipped more Coke, ate the rest of my fries, and turned pages. Once out of the military, Gary had started working with another agent at a State Farm insurance office in Lakewood, and then he opened up his own office. His tax records showed he made around eighty thousand per year, a decent salary for an insurance agent, and he didn't have any negative work history. He didn't belong to any professional organizations, and he had no credit card debt.

His divorce agreement showed that he wasn't paying any maintenance to Audra, but he was paying child support to her, and he was on time every month. He had received a chunk of change from Audra, most likely his half of the value of the house they'd bought together, and he turned around and bought a new house. He owned a newer Toyota Tacoma truck, and the Camaro that he'd said he was restoring. He had several thousand dollars in savings, he had stock investments in a 401k, and an IRA. He paid his bills on time and had a good credit score. On paper at least, Gary looked fiscally sound. The only chink in his armor was that he'd had three speeding tickets over the last few years. He had no other criminal history.

"Am I missing something?" I asked myself as I stared at a

picture of his driver's license photo. I shook my head. "You lied to me, and that makes me suspicious."

I was about to see if I could find other social media accounts for him when my desk phone rang.

"Spillman."

"This is Elroy Burke," a deep male voice said. "You called me?" The tone was brisk, someone who was accustomed to telling people what to do, rather than being on the receiving end of questions.

"Thank you for returning my call," I said. I went for a sympathizing tone, conveying that I knew how busy he was, and that I was grateful for his taking time to talk to me. I identified myself, then said, "I understand that you were in the Marines with a gentleman named Gary Pickett?"

"Gary? Yeah, I remember him. We were buddies. He's someone you'd want to go into battle with. What's this about?"

I wanted Burke to keep talking, so I explained only that I was working on a possible murder, and that Gary's name came up.

"How unfortunate," Burke said. "I'm not sure how Gary might be involved in your investigation, but I can assure you he was a good Marine."

"I looked at Gary's Marine service. He never advanced beyond Lance Corporal."

"Yes, that's true. Some guys don't want a career in the Marines. Gary might have initially, but after he came back from Iraq, he'd lost interest. If you ask me, his experience there gave him a different perspective. It happens." He cleared his throat, a deep, husky sound. "What's this call about? Is Gary in some kind of trouble? Because I would think twice about that. With the exception of one minor incident when we were in California, he didn't give anyone any trouble."

"One incident?"

"It was nothing, really," he brushed it off. "Maybe I shouldn't talk about this."

I put on some pressure. "I'm in the middle of a murder investigation. It's imperative I learn as much about Gary as I can."

"Is Gary a suspect?"

"I can't divulge that," I said.

A long silence stretched through the phone line. I heard him take a deep breath.

"You could be helping him."

"When he came back from his tour, he got into an argument with his wife," he said. "Things got a little out of hand, they had a big fight, and his wife called my wife. I went over there to diffuse the situation."

"Were the police called?"

"I was able to smooth it over without calling anyone. It really wasn't a big thing, and Logan was okay in the long run, so we never reported it to anyone."

I took a gamble. "*Logan was okay?*"

"He'd fallen down and broken his arm. Gary assured me it was an accident, and Audra said the same thing." His sigh was loud. "I know it sounds bad, but Gary was a good friend. I know that sometimes guys have trouble when they return from a tour overseas, and I didn't want to see his career end in any trouble. I worked with him after that, talked to him, and things seemed to be okay. He finished his enlistment, and I heard that he was out of the Marines and doing well. Is that not the case?"

"As far as I know, he's done well for himself, selling insurance." I wasn't going to tell him about Logan. He could find that out another way. "So other than this little altercation, you didn't have any other trouble with Gary? He never had other domestic disputes with his wife?"

"Not that I'm aware of, and he would've told me. There was

that one incident, and I chalked it up to just a bad time after he returned from Iraq. Nothing more than that."

It was obvious he wanted me to believe him. I found myself wondering if he'd covered up other domestic disputes for Gary.

"How was Gary in the field, with other guys? Did he have a temper, anything like that?"

"No, he had good leadership skills. He would've made a good commanding officer, but he didn't want that. I can understand. It's not for everyone."

"His fellow Marines liked him?"

"For the most part. Not everyone hits it off with each other, but Gary had a way about him. He could get people to follow him, a natural-born leader."

"Did he ever get into any bar fights, things like that?"

"Well," he laughed. "We could get a little out of hand, letting off steam. But nothing that got him in trouble with the law."

Burke obviously had a soft spot for Gary, I thought drily.

"I hope Gary isn't in any kind of trouble," he said, curious now.

"Nothing like that." I thanked him for his time and hung up before he could start asking me questions.

I sat back. So Logan's left arm had been broken at the same time that Audra and Gary had gotten in a fight. Had it been an accident, as Burke had said? I stared across the room, mulling that over. There was more to Gary than met the eye. He'd lied to me, in more ways than one. And what about Audra? It seemed she had possibly lied to me too. Or she was guilty at least of not sharing everything, such as the fight she'd had with Gary, and Logan's being hurt. But why? I wanted to know more about that fight, and I wanted to know what had really happened to Logan. Audra might tell me that. I needed to follow up with her on a few things too.

I downed the last of my Coke and wiped my hands on the napkin. Just then, my cell phone rang.

"Harry," I said, a tad too impatiently. "I don't have–"

"Just let me speak, hon, okay?"

He didn't call me "hon" very often. "Okay." I was hesitant, waiting for what was next.

"You know that this benefit is important to me." I started to protest, but he quickly stopped me. "No, let me finish. Please." I bit my lip and stayed silent. "Like I said, you know I really want to go to this dinner. And you caught me off-guard because I thought you were between cases, that things were slower, and you'd be free. But," he sucked in a breath. "Look, this is a little kid. It's way more important to find out what happened to him than to go to this dinner. What I'm saying is I get it, okay? I may not always have the right thing to say right in the moment, but if you give me time, I can come around."

I stared at the wall across from me. I felt my heart ache, as much with love for Harry as for how much he put up with. He was a guy, and he wanted my attention, and a lot of times he didn't get it. What he did get was a fiercely independent woman who had her own issues, and her own reasons for keeping walls up sometimes. And he put up with all of it. I sighed and put my head down.

"Sarah?"

"Thanks for understanding." It was all I could manage at that moment.

He heard something in my tone, though. My resolve fading. "You hang in there."

"I will."

"I love you, Sarah."

"I love you too."

"If I don't hear from you, I'll just go by myself. There's lots of friends at our table. If you can make it, let me know. If not, I'll see you at home."

"Thanks for understanding," I repeated.

He told me again that he loved me and ended the call. I let out a big sigh. Harry is a wonderful man, and at times I feel he deserves better than me. I know he'd love to be married. He'd proposed a few times over the years, but I kept putting him off. I'd considered it, and I didn't like what I'd concluded about myself. What if I couldn't make a marriage work? What if I failed? How would that look, especially to Diane, the perfect sister? I let out a bitter laugh.

It took a long time before I lifted my head, and I was glad Spats and Ernie weren't around. I wiped my eyes, then pocketed my phone and left.

CHAPTER SIXTEEN

Audra was surprised to see me. "Detective, what can I do for you?" Her eyes drooped with weariness.

"A few things have come up that I'd like to discuss with you," I said. "Do you have a little time?"

She blinked, then stepped back and let me into the house. Instead of going into the living room, she gestured toward the back of the house. "I was just fixing another cup of coffee. I'm so tired, and yet on edge, if that makes sense. Would you like anything?" Weariness dragged through her voice.

"I'll take a cup of coffee," I said as I followed her into the kitchen.

It was as I expected for the type of home: rich cherry cabinets, granite countertops, and stainless steel appliances. Lots of pictures of Logan were stuck to the refrigerator; he aged before my eyes, from a tiny baby to a growing boy. Such a cute kid, such a tragedy. She took a coffee mug from the cupboard, filled it with coffee, and glanced at me. "Sugar, cream?"

"Just black, thank you."

She handed the cup to me. A small wave of the hand was the

indication for me to sit at a barstool at the kitchen island, and she stood leaning against the counter and gulped her coffee. "That detective brought my laptop back. Thanks. I doubt you found anything useful on it."

I dodged that question with one of my own. "How are you holding up?"

She stared with puffy eyes into her cup. "As well as can be expected, I guess. Some of the time, I don't feel anything at all. Other times, I can barely move." She looked up at me. "What have you found out?"

I took a sip of coffee and listened to a lawnmower engine that drifted in through an open window. I gauged my words carefully. "I've been looking into Gary a bit more, and I have a few questions."

She tried to hold her mug steady, but her hands shook slightly. "Oh?"

"You don't like to talk about him."

She set the mug down with a clink. "Yeah, Gary and I don't get along. I'm sure you've been asking questions about us, and you've heard that."

"That's correct. We have to look at everyone, including Gary." And you, I left unsaid. "At first I thought that he had a pretty clean past, but I had an interesting conversation with a former friend of his, from their Marines days."

She glanced away. "I know what you're going to say." I waited. "You found out about the fight we had, back in San Diego." I raised my cup, sipped, and waited. "I guess I should've told you about it, but I was ashamed. I can't believe that Gary and I fought like we did, and I can't believe what happened to Logan."

"What exactly happened to Logan?"

She buried her face in her hands, let out a little sob, then seemed to get control of herself. "Gary had come home from work, and he was in a foul mood. He was in a foul mood a lot then. Going over to Iraq changed him. He wasn't the same guy." Then she waved that away. "Well, he was, at least from the standpoint of his violent tendencies. I'd seen him explode like that from the time when we dated, and then just as quickly his anger would pass. I hate to admit it, but I ignored it. He was so fun, so exciting, when I first met him. Unlike the guys that I usually dated, and my first husband, for that matter. I'd always gone for the guys that were smart, steady, and quite frankly, boring. Gary is younger than I am, and he lived on the wild side. He liked to race motorcycles, he drove fast, he lived on the edge. The Marines kept him in order, at least to a certain degree. Then he did a tour in Iraq, and when he came back, he was different. He didn't seem quite as loyal to the Marines, he didn't think everything that our country was doing was right, and he'd rant and rave about that. Especially when he was drinking. He was ready for his service to end, and he wanted to get into the real world. That was different as well. When I first met him, he was buckling down and maybe trying to rise in the ranks. After Iraq, he gave up on that, but he would never share why. But something happened overseas that affected him, and he wouldn't talk about it. Anyway," she gave me a wan look, "you want to know about the night we fought."

"Yes."

"Gary came home, and he'd been drinking. As I recall, I made some crack about politics, and he blew up. He said I didn't know what I was talking about, that I needed to really look at things, and that his eyes had been opened. I didn't know what he meant, and told him that. One thing led to another, and the next thing I know, we're screaming and yelling at each other. He backed me against the wall, and he slapped me. I fell to the floor, and that's when I heard Logan yell at him. Gary whirled around, and he grabbed Logan so hard, it snapped his arm." She opened her mouth to speak, but nothing came out. Then she took another drink and set the mug down. "Logan was so little. He screamed in pain, and Gary let him go. I swooped in and grabbed Logan, and by then Gary had backed off. I called Gary's friend Roy Burke, and he came over. Elroy smoothed things over, and I took Logan to the hospital. I told them Logan had fallen off his chair. I was furious with Gary, but he was so apologetic, so kind, and he promised never to do anything like that again." She glanced away. "Things were okay for a while. Gary finished his service, he got out of the Marines, and we moved to Denver. He had some connections here, and he got a job in insurance. He's smart, and he's done well for himself. But his explosive temper never went away, and I finally got tired of it. So I divorced him."

"Logan had broken fingers too."

"Yeah, that was in a bike accident. He crashed. I felt so bad about that."

With her tone, and the look in her eyes, I believed that. "What kinds of things would set Gary off?"

"The government. Politics. He got more and more interested in conspiracy theories, and he hated it if I tried to point out where the theories were wrong." She rolled her eyes. "Have you read any of that stuff? Some of it's downright nutty. Gary bought into a lot of it, though. He was getting pretty anti-government."

"And you didn't tell me this before ..." I let my voice trail off.

"It's embarrassing, to say that you were with someone like that."

"It happens to the best of us."

She stared out the back window. The lawnmower had stopped, replaced with an accusing silence. "I should've seen that Gary wasn't right for me, long before I married him."

"Which leads me to wondering, would Gary attempt to kidnap Logan?"

She shook her head slowly. "I don't know about that."

"Others have said that Gary thought you were not a good mother."

"Yeah, I heard that." Anger in her tone. "During the custody battle, he said I made up stuff about his drinking because he didn't want me to win the custody battle. He would often tell me he could do a better job of raising Logan on his own." She sniffed disgustedly. "I guess that could be a subtle threat–that he'd take Logan from me, but it never occurred to me that he'd actually do it. Until just now. Do you think he'd really do that?"

I locked eyes with her. "Do *you*?"

She mulled that over. "I don't want to believe he'd go this far, but..." She began to pace. "How would he do it?" Then she frowned. "I can't see Gary ... killing Logan." She barely got the last couple of words out.

I shrugged. "Maybe that part was an accident. Something went wrong, and ..."

"Gary came to pick Logan up. He could've just left with Logan and never returned."

"But then you'd know he was the kidnapper."

"I suppose. But why come here to pick up Logan if he knew Logan was already gone?"

"He looks innocent that way."

"Then who would have taken Logan?"

"An accomplice."

"Who?" she repeated.

"A friend, a relative?"

"I don't know anyone who would help Gary."

"Did you know Gary called Logan Saturday afternoon?"

She shook her head. "Why?"

"To tell Logan he was coming over soon."

"Maybe Gary mentioned it, I don't remember." She bit her lip. "I don't believe this," she muttered. "Logan was the only good thing that came out of my marriage to Gary, and now he's gone."

"Does Gary own a lot of guns?"

"He had a few around, always locked up. He was careful about that."

"Would he go to a gun range?"

"No, not that I know of."

Interesting, I thought. "He never mentioned Gold Creek Gun Range?"

She shook her head. "Not that I remember."

"Have you heard the name John Merrick?"

Her brow furrowed. "That name doesn't sound familiar. Is that a friend of Gary's?"

"I'm not sure."

She reached for her mug, then thought better of it. "Too much coffee." She put her hands on the counter. "I just can't believe Gary would do something like this." She looked at me expectantly.

"Gary mentioned that he called you before he came to pick up Logan, and you didn't answer. He left a message."

"Did I not tell you that? I probably put it out of my mind because he was angry. Like he always is."

Was that just an innocent oversight? I thought. "What'd he say?"

"The usual, why wasn't I answering, would Logan be ready, I better not delay him because he couldn't wait around. It's like that every time he picks up Logan."

Her phone rang. She picked it up and glanced at the screen. "It's my mother."

I got up. "I won't take any more of your time now. Thanks for the coffee."

"If you need anything, just call me." She led me to the front door, and as she did, she answered the phone.

CHAPTER SEVENTEEN

I sat in my car for a moment, staring out the windshield. Gary had a lot to explain. If he had something to do with his son's kidnapping and murder, I was going to find out.

I put the car in gear and peeled away from the curb, the screech of tires echoing my mood. In no time, I was back on Gary's front porch, hoping to catch him by surprise. I jammed my hand on the doorbell and waited.

Nothing.

I pressed the doorbell again, this time holding it. I heard chimes from within, but no one answered. I knocked purposefully on the door, hard enough to hurt my knuckles. Still no answer. Now I didn't have a choice but to call him. I dialed his number and after one ring it went to voicemail. "Gary, it's Detective Spillman. I need to talk to you. Please call me back."

Right to the point. I wondered whether he was screening calls, knowing the number might be the police. *Well,* I thought as I walked back to my car. *He won't be able to avoid me forever.*

I sat behind the wheel for a minute, the heat of the day warming up the car. I felt weary myself, and I yawned and stretched. Then my phone rang. I quickly looked at the screen, ready to take on Gary, but it was Ernie.

"What do you have for me?" I asked.

"A couple of things. First, I talked to Tara, and she's got someone else working on Ivan Eklund's laptop. He found some pictures of the boy with his mom. Thought you might want to see them."

"Yeah, I do." I gave Gary Pickett's house one final look, then started the car. "I'll head back now." I glanced up. White wispy clouds were overhead, not enough to help deter the heat. It was an unusually warm day for May. "Okay, thanks."

"The other thing is, the techs have been looking at Eklund's cameras. There are a lot of photos to go through, including some from last Saturday, when Logan was kidnapped."

"I definitely want to see that. I'm on my way."

"You're gonna love this," Ernie said as I walked up to my desk. He pointed his unlit cigar at his monitor, then popped the cigar back into the corner of his mouth and talked around it. "They gave me a whole bunch of stuff, a dump of all that was on Eklund's cameras. I've put it all on a flash drive for you." He reached to the side of his laptop and pulled out a USB drive, then handed it to me. "Take a look at Saturday's."

I took the drive from him, sat down at my desk. I fired up my own laptop as I jerked my head toward Spats's desk. "What's he doing?"

"He went to get something to eat, and he's following up on Eklund's phone records, and on that guy, John Merrick."

I nodded and quickly filled him in on my conversation with Audra Pickett as I put the drive into the port, then took my mouse and clicked on the USB drive to open it up.

Ernie glanced at me. "You got Saturday's pictures up?"

I gave him an impatient stare. "Hold on."

It took me a second to scroll through the photos, and then I found pictures dated last Saturday. I started through them. "Some nature photos," I said. There were some that showed stunning red-rock formations tilted at a sixty-degree angle. "I recognize those rocks. Looks like Roxborough Park."

"Yeah, he's got talent, doesn't he?" This was quite the compliment from Ernie, who rarely gave them out.

"Harry and I like to hike there. I say 'like to,' but I can't remember the last time we actually went down there."

"I hear that. The job, you know?"

I nodded, thinking about the benefit that I wasn't going to make tonight. I should call Harry and tell him that, but a tiny part of me held out hope that I could pull away from work and meet him there, even if it was for just a bit.

"Look for photos later in the afternoon."

I clicked through photos, then checked the dates on them in Explorer. "There aren't any. Just the rock formation pictures from the morning, then nothing until Monday."

"Yeah." Ernie shifted and his chair creaked. "What do you think? Did Bev get it wrong? Maybe Ivan wasn't taking pictures of the neighborhood kids Saturday evening."

"I don't know about that. She seemed pretty sure of herself, but maybe..."

"I know what you're thinking, maybe she's not reliable, maybe not too clear some days? Can we count on what she said to be accurate? Did she get it wrong?"

"Or was Ivan just using the zoom lens to focus better on the kids? Or did he delete the photos he took during that timeframe?" I kept scrolling through pictures. "He's got some photos of the moon on Monday night. And nothing Tuesday."

"Go back a few days."

I checked the dates of the photos and then clicked on one from three days before to Logan Pickett's kidnapping. "More nature photography."

Ernie gave a scrolling motion with his hand, for me to keep looking.

I did as I was told, and then saw what he must've seen. "There's Logan."

A picture of Logan popped up on my screen. I recognized Latoya Anderson's house in the background.

"Did you talk to Latoya Anderson?" I asked.

"Yeah. I did a background check too. I don't see any issues there, no reason to be suspicious of her or her husband. I talked to her as well. She said Audra and Gary fought some, about the same information you heard. She's spent a lot of time at Audra's house since Logan disappeared. She didn't know anything about Eklund, either."

"Did she see his car around?"

"I didn't have that info when I talked to her."

"Right." I rifled through some papers and found Latoya's number. I called, but she didn't answer. I left a message for her to call me back, then went back to the photo. Logan wore tan shorts and a T-shirt with Batman on it. There were several photos of him as he walked back from Terrell's house to his own. In a few of them, there were two women walking down the block nearby. Neighbors, I assumed. Then one of Logan walking up his sidewalk. I went through that series of photos again, looking for anything suspicious. I didn't find anything.

"What did you see?" I asked Ernie.

"I've looked through all the photos from around the time Logan was kidnapped. Nothing suspicious. Just a kid walking home. But why would Ivan be taking those photos?"

"Good question."

"There's more like those, from a few days earlier."

I shook my head. "Do we have a pedophile on our hands?"

I checked farther back in the photos, and sure enough, there was another series of photos of Logan, this time riding his bike with Terrell. They both had on shorts and T-shirts, and bike helmets that seemed too big for them. They were both smiling, with their oversized, adult teeth dominating their little-boy faces.

"I don't see anything suspicious here, no car, not that we know of one. But still." I thought for a moment. "There aren't any of other kids in the neighborhood, other than some formal studio portraits. Was Bev wrong about that too? Or did she see Eklund watching the kids and assume he was taking pictures of them?"

"I don't know." He took the cigar out of his mouth and dropped it into an ashtray on the corner of his desk. "You mentioned Ivan being a pedophile, but here's the thing. I talked to Tara about Eklund's internet searches, and so far, she hasn't found anything on the computer. Eklund didn't visit any porn sites, or any online sites that deal in child porn. He didn't have dirty pics of *any* kind on his laptop, let alone kids."

"Did the laptop show signs of anything being deleted recently?"

He shrugged. "Tara didn't think so. They're running a scan to recover deleted files. It's possible he got rid of photos like that and cleared his browsing history, but we won't know the results for a while. I hate to say it, but I kinda doubt they'll find anything. It looks like, if Ivan is a pedophile, he didn't dabble in that on his laptop."

"Or maybe he was just getting into that kind of behavior?"

Ernie shrugged.

I turned back to my monitor and scrolled through the photos of Logan again. "There aren't pictures of other kids like this, from afar. All the other photos are portraits."

"Yep."

I stopped at another one of Logan on his bike. "In this one, he looks like he's looking at a car, or maybe waving at someone?"

Ernie got up and came over. "Hmm, you're right. Can you tell who?"

We both stared at the screen. I zoomed in so we could study the surrounding area, but all we saw was the front grill of a red vehicle.

"What kind of car has that kind of grill, with the edges kind of flared under the headlights?" I asked. "Can you get on that?"

"Sure."

I went through the other photos of Logan on his bike. In those, he had ridden farther down the street, and there was no sign of the red vehicle.

"Huh," Ernie said. He tapped the screen. "I've gone through all the photos on this drive. There are a lot of portraits, kids at the school, or family photos, that kind of thing."

"That fits. Ivan made a living doing that. The nature photography was something he'd done on the side, and that was only beginning to pay off, according to his girlfriend."

"But if Eklund was innocent, why was he taking so many pictures like that of Logan?"

"Did we have a budding pedophile on our hands? Maybe Logan was his first target, and it went bad."

"I still think if that was true, he would've had some pictures on his laptop. At least a few."

"Or maybe his phone?"

Ernie nodded. "Has Oakley gotten those records?"

"Last I heard, he was working on the warrant."

I picked up my soda glass and shook it. Empty. I set it down in frustration. "What else did they find on the laptop?"

Ernie pulled out his swivel chair, sat down, and the chair groaned. He glanced at a piece of paper. "Besides the photos, he had some good software to manipulate the photos, and editing software. Other than that, not a lot, some tax information, banking stuff, that kind of thing. Also, plenty of invoices for his portrait business, all neatly labeled. I didn't see one for Audra Pickett. I called her right before you got back and asked if she'd ever hired Eklund to take pictures of Logan, but she said she hadn't." He frowned. "The techs will go over the stuff on his laptop more, but at first blush, there's nothing suspicious."

"Except a bunch of pictures of the dead boy."

"Yeah, I'll give you that."

I put my elbows on the desk, rested my chin on my hands. "I have a theory, that Gary kidnapped Logan, but used an accomplice, so he'd look innocent. Could Eklund have been that guy?"

Ernie was staring at his screen. "I guess that's possible. Or Eklund took the kid, had his fun with him, and then disposed of him."

"So he took pictures of Logan Saturday evening, just as Bev said, then he took the boy. But then he realized the pictures would be damning evidence, so he got rid of them. But ..." I thought aloud, "why not get rid of *all* the pictures of Logan, not just the ones from the evening of the kidnapping?"

Ernie opened his mouth to answer, then shrugged. "Don't know," he finally muttered.

I went through the photos one more time, but I didn't see anything else of note.

Ernie picked up his cigar again and resumed chewing on it. "Gary Pickett's been lying to you as well."

"That's right. Why would he do that, if he's innocent?"

"Good question."

"Has the CSI team finished? Did you hear from them on what they found where Logan's body was discovered?"

"That's a dead end so far. Nothing of note."

I thought for a second. "You keep looking at Eklund. His family, friends. Everything."

"I will. And I've got more neighbors to talk to. I'll work on that too."

"I still need to follow up on John Merrick, the gun shop owner that Gary's been in touch with."

Before I could say more, Spats waltzed into the room, still looking as fresh as he had this morning, with a smile on his clean-shaven face.

CHAPTER EIGHTEEN

"What's with you?" Ernie asked Spats.

Spats looked at us, his eyes full of excitement. "You're not going to believe this. I've got something on Gary Pickett."

I looked at him expectantly. "What's that?"

Ernie looked expectantly at Spats.

"We know Gary's been calling the Gold Creek Gun Range, right?" Spats said.

"Spill it," Ernie said, sounding like Spats had earlier.

Spats gave us a sly smile. "He's also been calling the owner, John Merrick. Not at the store, but on Merrick's cell. You want to know the last time?"

"Saturday night?" Ernie said.

I leaned my elbows on the desk and looked at him. "And last night?"

"Ding, ding." Spats gave a grim smile, then sat down at his desk. "Gary calls the shop, and Merrick, quite a bit."

"Which wouldn't be any big deal," I said. "He's ex-military.

I'm sure he still has a penchant for guns, or he likes the gun range. But then why lie to me about calling Merrick those nights?"

"And why resist giving his laptop to you?" Ernie said.

"I don't like the guy." I sat back in my chair. "He rubs me the wrong way."

"You want to be careful, though. You don't want to assume." Spats said.

"I'm not doing that. Eklund is high on my radar as well, and whatever happened with him, I want to know."

"Before I forget," Spats said, "I called Kristi Arnott too."

"Gary's girlfriend?" Ernie asked.

"Right, but she didn't answer. I left a message."

"Too bad," I said. "I'd like to know what she thinks of Gary, and if she can corroborate his whereabouts Saturday night." I looked at Spats. "Has Verizon gotten the phone locations for Audra and Gary?"

"Not yet. I'll bug them again. And I followed up on the call Audra received at the time Logan went missing. It's legit. She was talking to a man about a real estate transaction." Spats glanced at Ernie. "When is Tara going to be done with Eklund's laptop?"

"Hopefully soon." Ernie grunted. "I want to know if he scrubbed his computer, took off dirty pics."

"He feels guilty about taking Logan's picture, but he doesn't want people to think he's a pedophile, so he gets rid of the pics before he offs himself?" Spats asked.

Ernie pursed his lips. "It could happen."

"While you're looking at him, I'm going to pay a visit to this gun shop," I announced. I turned to Spats. "What can you tell me about the shop?"

"It's been open for several years, and it's successful. The owner, John Merrick, makes a lot of calls to Gary Pickett."

"Business transactions?" Ernie asked.

"Would you conduct business late at night, or early in the morning?" Spats replied.

"Just friends?" I mused.

"It's worth looking into." Spats consulted some notes. "Here's what I have on Merrick. He's fifty-two, and he's owned Gold Creek Gun Range for twenty years. Before that he was an electrician. He's a former Marine, like Gary, and he had an undistinguished military career."

"Just like Gary," I murmured.

"Right. He owns a house in Golden, pretty nice place from the pictures I saw. He was arrested for drunk-and-disorderly right after he got out of the Marines; other than that, his record is clean, except for a speeding ticket five years ago. He pays his taxes, he's a member of the NRA. And," he drew the word out. "I think he's a member of Colorado Citizens Militia."

I nodded. "Tara mentioned he might be a member."

"Uh huh." He flipped pages. "It took a little poking to find that. He's not shouting it publicly. I can't say for certain, but he's on some documentation I found for the group."

"I've never heard of them," Ernie said.

"They've got a Facebook page. The About section says," Spats glanced at his notes, " 'We promote patriotism and maintain the strength of the United States Constitution.' The posts are mostly pro-gun stuff, and some things that border on racist."

"Tara gave me the name of a professor at DU." I rooted around in my desk and found my note. "Wilder. I need to call him, see if he can tell me more about this group."

"You need to be careful with this guy," Spats said.

I shrugged that off as I dialed Wilder's number. "He's not doing anything that'll get his gun license revoked. Where is this gun shop?" Then I held up a finger. "Wilder's voicemail." I left a message, asking him to call me as soon as he could, then cradled the phone.

Spats held up a piece of paper. "It's way the hell out west, near the foothills." He tossed the paper across the desk to me.

I thought about that. "That's a ways for Gary to go. Isn't there a closer gun range to his house?"

"I looked at that too. There's a gun shop in Wheat Ridge, a couple in Aurora, and if he was looking to buy a newer gun, or ammo, he could go to a sporting goods store. Could be he likes the gun range at Gold Creek. And if he's friends with Merrick, that's another reason to go there."

"That's one thing I'll try to find out." I grabbed the notebooks with the research on Audra and Gary Pickett, and stood up. "I'll let you know how it goes."

Spats turned to his computer. "I'll keep digging for more information on Merrick, see if he has a bigger connection with Gary than we know."

Ernie stared at me. "Be careful," he echoed Spats' warning.

"I will," I called over my shoulder as I headed for the door.

As Spats had said, Gold Creek Gun Range was way the hell out west, nestled in the foothills near the suburb of Golden. Pine and aspen trees surrounded a long building that had a view of Interstate C470, where rush-hour traffic was growing.

I parked next to a blue Mercedes, and as I got out, I heard the popping of guns going off somewhere behind the building. I glanced toward a wood fence with a gate at one end of the lot. I couldn't see behind it. The sun was lower in the sky, and it was still warm, but I donned a light jacket to hide the gun on my hip. Less threatening that way. I walked into the building and looked around. The interior was cool, with a long room with rifles hanging from two walls, and third and fourth walls full of accessories. A long counter was at the back, and a bearded man with a

John Deere baseball cap gazed at me with alert eyes. Nearby was another man who was helping a customer. A Ted Nugent song played from a stereo behind the counter. The bearded man put his hands on the glass countertop and stared at me as I approached.

"Can I help you?"

"Are you John Merrick?" I asked.

"That's me. Who wants to know?"

I walked over and flashed him my badge "I'd like to ask you a few questions."

I usually got cooperation when I've gone to gun shops because the owners didn't want any trouble with law enforcement or they'd lose their gun dealer's license. And cops buy guns, so gun shop owners don't tend to want to alienate good customers. In this case, Merrick's eyes were cool.

"What's this about?" he asked. "I haven't done anything wrong."

"I didn't say you did."

"You interested in a gun?" His voice was low and curt.

"Not at the moment, thank you. I have an investigation going right now, and I thought you might be able to help me."

He glanced at the other worker and his customer. Both were listening. Merrick slowly responded. "How's that?"

"I don't know if you heard, a little boy named Logan Pickett went missing the other day."

"I saw that on the news."

"I need some help, if you don't mind. I understand you know Gary Pickett, Logan's father."

His eyes didn't waver. "What's that to you?"

"You're friends with him, right? No crime in that."

"Yeah, I've known Gary for a while now." It was obvious he was choosing his words carefully. "He's a good guy. We were both Marines."

I scanned the store. "It's a nice place. Mind if I see your target practice area?" If I kept things casual, he might talk more. And I needed to get us away from prying ears.

He didn't move, seeming to resist the idea, then thought better of it. "Sure, right this way."

Merrick came around the counter, and I followed him down to one end of the store where he went through a door and down a long hallway. I heard gunshots more clearly.

We stepped through a doorway and into an indoor gun range with several lanes, each with electronically controlled rail-based target retrieval systems for target practice. A big man was standing in the first lane, firing at a target about twenty yards away. He finished, gave us a nod, and went back into the main building. Merrick gestured for me to follow him, and we went to a lane at the far end.

"Gary liked to be here, on the end. There's not much to see."

"How good a shot is Gary?" I asked, even though I knew the answer.

"He was an expert marksman in the Marines, and he hasn't lost his touch." The last sentence held a veiled threat, as if I should be careful of Gary.

"I heard that." I surveyed the lane. "It's a nice set-up." Then I said, "Did you hear his son was murdered? I'm looking into that."

"I didn't have anything to do with it."

"I didn't say you did," I said. "I thought you might be able to help me." Nothing from him. If he wanted me not to be suspicious, he was going about it the wrong way. "How often does Gary come in here?"

He pulled at his beard. "I don't know, sometimes. I'm not always here, so I can't tell you that. And I don't keep a log of everyone who comes and goes."

"Has Gary purchased guns here?"

"He likes to use the range," he dodged the question.

"If customers have to pay to use the range, you would have records of those charges."

"Yeah?"

It was a challenge. If I wanted those records, I was going to have to get a warrant. And right now I knew I didn't have enough to do that.

I wasn't getting much from him, so I addressed the main reason I was there. "Gary's called your cell phone too. Do all your customers have your cell phone number?"

He stared at me. "Maybe."

"Gary called you Saturday night?"

"Not that I recall."

"Huh," I said thoughtfully. "I have the phone records. He called you Saturday, and again last night."

"He may have called, but I didn't talk to him. I thought that's what you meant."

"When was the last time you did talk to Gary?"

"I don't remember."

"You call each other a lot."

"About guns, or times for the range."

"Ah, I see." He was lying to me. "You don't talk about anything else? Has Gary said anything about trouble with his ex, or issues with Logan?"

"No."

My cell phone rang. I glanced at the number, and it took me a second before I recognized who it was. Heather Neville. I'd have to call her back. "Have you heard of Colorado Citizens Militia?" I continued with Merrick.

He took a moment, again gauging his words carefully. "I've heard of them. You hang around a gun shop, you hear things like that."

"Things like what?"

Now he crossed his arms, defensive. "Nothing much. I guess those groups want to protect their rights."

"Is Gary part of that group?"

"You'd have to ask him that."

"So no rumors about that?"

He shook his head. "That's not something he would share."

"Are you a part of Colorado Citizens Militia?"

"No."

"Huh," I repeated. "I thought I heard you were."

"You heard wrong."

"I must have." I returned to Gary. "What types of guns is Gary interested in?"

"A variety of them."

"Did he buy a lot of guns from you?"

"A few, here and there." He'd now told me that Gary had bought guns here. He realized his mistake and tried to cover it. "He likes to use the range, keep his skills sharp. No crime in that."

"That's true. Did Logan ever come here with Gary?"

"He was here a time or two for target practice. The kid wasn't any good, and Gary would get frustrated. Logan was scared of guns."

"Frustrated how?"

He ignored that. "I don't know what you're going to find. Gary's a good guy, and he's real upset about his kid."

"So you've talked to Gary since Saturday night?"

"I don't remember when it was."

"What about last night?"

"Yeah, we talked for a minute."

"What about?"

"The ballgame, okay?" He glared at me. "As far as I know, private conversations are still private."

I nodded. "I'm just trying to find out what happened to his son."

"Yeah, that's too bad. But I can't help you."

He didn't sound too broken up about Logan. "Were you here last night?"

"Yeah, for a while. Then I went to get something to eat and I went home."

I kept him talking. "You're sure you can't tell me anything about Logan's murder?"

"I don't talk about my customers."

"I get the impression Gary's more than a customer."

"Maybe. And I don't know anything about his kid."

"Might anyone else here be able to tell me more about Gary?"

His eyes narrowed. "No."

I didn't think he'd say yes, which was why I waited until now to push him about his association with Gary. Merrick continued to stare at me, and it was clear he wasn't going to say more.

As if he'd heard that, he said, "I need to get back to the store."

He pointed toward the door, and we walked back into the main room. The customer was gone, and Merrick's employee gave me a long look as I headed for the exit. Then I stopped.

"Oh, one more thing." I locked eyes with Merrick. "Where were you Saturday night?"

"I was here until about five, then I went bowling. Ask for Bill. He knows me, and he'll tell you I was there until after ten."

"What bowling alley?"

"Brunswick. On Kipling." Merrick then glanced at his employee, who shrugged.

"Yeah," the other man said. "He said he went bowling after he left here."

Merrick smiled triumphantly. "See?"

He was lying, I was sure of it. "That's great," I said. "I'll check it out."

"You do that," he dared me.

"And last night?"

"I was here." He looked to his employee again.

"Yeah, he was here," the man said.

"And after that?"

"I went home."

"Who was there?"

"Just me. I watched TV and went to bed. I need to help other customers now." He glared at me. "I'm not in any trouble."

Not yet, I thought. *What are you and Gary covering up?*

I looked carefully around the store. No one was around. I didn't take offense at the dismissal, though. "Thanks for your time," I said pleasantly as I opened the door. Merrick didn't reply.

As I walked to my car, I puzzled over Merrick. People who have nothing to hide cooperate, and based on my conversation with Merrick, he definitely had something to hide. I'd stirred the pot a bit, and he was smart enough to know I'd caught him lying.

The question was, what would he do next?

CHAPTER NINETEEN

I stood near the doorway to Gold Creek Gun Range for a moment. I can't say that I was entirely surprised that Merrick had lied to me, but I had been hoping against hope that he might help more than he did. What was he hiding? I stepped aside to let a man in jeans and a leather jacket walk through the door. Merrick's angry voice drifted outside.

"This wasn't what I was expecting. I..."

I couldn't hear the rest. I grabbed the door handle and let the door ease closed until it was just cracked. Then I listened. Merrick was furious.

"Yeah, you need to think better."

I heard other voices, and some of what Merrick said was drowned out. Had he said something about meeting "him" somewhere? I let the door close as quietly as possible and hurried back to my car. I drove down the road, parked behind a sedan, rolled down the window, and watched the front of the store.

What would Merrick do next? I glanced at my phone, then got on Facebook. I went through Merrick's posts again, but didn't find anything that helped my investigation. Then, out of the corner of my eye, I sensed movement. I looked up and saw Merrick coming out the front door of Gold Creek, his phone plastered to his ear. Even at this distance, I could see anger etched on his face. He stomped to a big black Ram truck at the far end of the lot, got in, and peeled out of the parking lot. He drove north, and I followed.

He got on Sixth Avenue and drove east, and I was easily able to see his big monstrosity of a truck up ahead while keeping cars between us. He was speeding, and I hoped neither he nor I would get pulled over before I could find out where he was going.

We crossed over Interstate 25 and stopped at the light at Kalamath Street. When the light turned green, I quickly switched lanes, wary that the next light might change before I could get through it. I kept the truck in sight, and barely made it through yet another light. Then my luck ran out. The truck blasted through a yellow light that was red by the time I got to the intersection. I swore. Then my luck returned when the truck had to slow as it approached Broadway, a one-way street. Merrick turned right, and I sped up and weaved around another car in order to make the light myself. The truck was farther ahead, and it turned left into a Thai restaurant parking lot. I cut across two lanes of traffic and pulled into a parking place on Broadway where I could see Merrick's truck. He got out but didn't go into the restaurant. Instead, he leaned against the side of the truck and lit a cigarette, then smoked and looked around. I didn't think he could see me. After a minute, a silver Toyota Tacoma pulled in and parked across from him. I thought I had seen it before, and then knew I had when Gary Pickett got out. I'd seen the Tacoma in his driveway.

Gary crossed the lot and stopped by Merrick's truck. Then he and Merrick got into an animated conversation, both pointing and yelling. This didn't seem to be just something about guns. The two knew each other, which was contrary to what Merrick had told me.

I thought they would stop arguing when a white SUV pulled into the lot, but to my surprise, a big man with dark hair and a handlebar mustache got out of the SUV and approached Gary and Merrick. The three of them resumed the conversation in earnest. Whatever they were discussing, none of them was happy. Gary kept pointing at Merrick, and Merrick threw his cigarette on the ground in frustration. The new man pointed at Gary. Shifting blame?

Finally, the big man gestured as if telling the others to calm down, and he put a hand on Gary's shoulder. They seemed to make some kind of peace, and then the big man shook Gary's hand, said something to Merrick, and got back in his car. He drove out of the parking lot in the opposite direction from me. I was too far away to get his license plate number. I shifted my attention back to Gary and Merrick. They seemed to be calmer, and with a shrug, Gary pointed at the restaurant. Merrick nodded, and they both went inside. It was after six, and I was starting to get hungry myself. Thai food sounded good just then. While I waited for the two to come out of the restaurant, I called Spats, a good distraction from my hunger.

"Hey," I said without preamble when he answered. "In your investigation, have you come across anyone driving a white SUV?"

"Not anybody that I talked to." I heard papers shuffling. "I can look through all this stuff. You need an answer right now?"

"No, but if you hear of anyone who does, make sure to let me know."

"Sure thing. What's this about?"

"I talked to Merrick." I gave him the rundown of my conversation at the gun range. "Both he and Gary have been lying to me, and I'm trying to figure out what they're up to."

"I'll see what else I can find on Merrick."

I ended the call and watched the restaurant. Then I remembered Heather Neville had called me back. I tried her, and got voice mail again. I swore under my breath, and left another message asking her to return my call. I pocketed my phone and turned my attention back to the restaurant.

Half an hour later, Gary and Merrick came back out. Whatever tension had been there before, it was gone. Gary gave Merrick a friendly wave, hopped in his truck, and drove away. I had a choice to make: follow him, or continue to tail Merrick. I decided I could follow up with Gary later. I watched Merrick get in his truck and turn onto Broadway. I let several cars get between us, and then pulled out.

Merrick circled around the block, got onto Lincoln Avenue, which led him back to Eighth Avenue. He was heading back west. If he knew I was tailing him, he didn't act like it. He drove fast, but not with an intent to lose a tail. He went to a storage facility on Wadsworth Boulevard in Lakewood, was in a unit for a few minutes, then headed south. He turned east on Mississippi Avenue and soon stopped at a farm supply store. I parked in a large gas station lot and watched. Merrick went into the store, then emerged a bit later and backed his truck up to a large garage door. A store employee helped Merrick load several white bags into the truck. As he did so, I spotted yellow markers on the bags. I was pretty sure it was fertilizer. When they finished, Merrick shook the guy's hand, then got in the truck and drove back to the gun range. He parked his truck in the same spot as before and disappeared inside the shop. I parked down the road and watched. He didn't come back out.

I didn't know what Merrick and Gary had talked about at the

restaurant, or who the other man was, but one thing I did know. Both Gary Pickett and John Merrick were lying to me, and they were hiding something. What, if anything, did their lies have to do with Logan?

CHAPTER TWENTY

John Merrick had said that he was at Brunswick Bowling on Saturday, that he had left there after working at the gun range. I had doubt that Merrick's employee was telling the truth when he'd agreed that Merrick had gone to the bowling alley Saturday after work. All that proved was that Merrick might've lied to his employee. I could still check the bowling alley. Brunswick Zone was on Kipling, a few miles south of Sixth Avenue. I pulled into the road and headed toward Sixth. As I was driving there, I called Spats.

"How did it go with Merrick?" he asked.

"He's dirty," I said, then gave him a rundown of what I'd been doing since I left the office. "I'm not sure what he's covering up, but he's lying to me. He told me that he barely knows Gary Pickett. That's a lie. I want to know what's up with him. Do me a favor. Get twenty-four hour surveillance on Merrick, so we can keeps tabs on him. I'm going now to check his alibi for Saturday night."

"I'll get a team on it right away."

I disconnected, and as I put my phone away, I saw the time.

After seven. I groaned, not realizing how late it had gotten. By now Harry was at the benefit, without me. I hoped he was having a good time, and that he wasn't too disappointed I hadn't made it. He'd been understanding with me, and I needed to make it up to him. Sometimes, as much as I love the job, it gets in the way.

Brunswick Zone is in a large building on Kentucky Avenue, next to a Mexican restaurant that I used to enjoy going to. I hadn't been in the area in a while, and it had since closed, replaced with what seemed to be an identical Mexican restaurant with a slightly different name. I parked and went inside Brunswick.

There's something about bowling alleys that I love, the sounds of the balls hitting the floor, the pins clattering loudly as they're knocked down, the noisy sounds of people reveling as they play. Bowling alleys these days don't allow smoking, but I remembered going with my parents. When I was a kid, my dad used to smoke, and he'd sit back on the bench and give us kids tips while he smoked and talked to my mother. I'm a good bowler, and it is one thing that I do better than my sister Diane. Uncle Brad would sometimes join us, and he was our coach as well. No matter how much Uncle Brad tried to give her pointers, Diane just never learned how to bowl well. Thinking about that, I laughed, just a little smugly.

Brunswick Zone has several lanes, and at the moment most of them were full, probably bowling league night. I walked past the lanes, listening to people laughing as they bowled. For an instant, I wished I were at a lane myself, waiting my turn while Harry bowled. Then my focus returned to the task at hand. I approached a counter where a man in a blue shirt was helping a woman with shoe rental. "Bill" was stitched onto his left pocket.

Perfect. The man I wanted. I waited until he finished with the woman, then approached.

"What size?" he asked in a hurried tone. It was busy, and he was keeping things moving, grabbing another pair of returned shoes and spraying the insides. I took out my badge and showed it to him. He raised his eyebrows and made eye contact. "What do you need?" he asked. "I'm not in any trouble?" There was no humor in his joke. He smiled as he put the shoes into a cubicle behind him, then turned back to me.

"Not at all. I'm hoping you can help me out, though."

He waved to a teenager standing nearby to help with the rentals, then jerked his head as he moved farther down the counter, away from listening ears. His eyes were wary. "What's up?"

I didn't waste any time. "I had a conversation with a man named John Merrick, and he said you could confirm he was here last Saturday night, around six or so."

"John, yes." He was quick to answer. "He was here then. He's in a bowling league, and they're here most Saturday nights."

"That's a definite yes for last Saturday?" I pressed.

The teenager–his shirt read "Chris"–was grabbing a pair of shoes, and he glanced back and forth between Bill and me. Then he shook his head. "No, don't you remember? John wasn't here last Saturday."

Bill licked his lower lip and glared at Chris. "No, John was here last Saturday." His words were firm and pointed.

Chris didn't get it. "No, Bill, I remember. Freddie," he said to me, "he's one of John's friends, he was talking about how he'd had a really good game, bowled nine strikes, and John wasn't here to see it." He looked at Bill for confirmation.

"No that's not right," Bill said. "That happened a week ago, not this last Saturday."

Chris saw something in Bill's face and hesitated. "Oh, yeah."

He was cautious now. "That's right. It wasn't last Saturday. It must've been a week ago." To me, "Sorry, my mistake." He quickly moved away to help somebody with a shoe rental.

Bill turned back to me. He pasted a smile on his face. "Yes, it was a week ago that John wasn't here. He *was* here this last Saturday. He got here about six, and he left after ten."

I gave him a long look and shrugged. "Okay, if you say so."

"I do." He gave me another unfriendly smile. "While you're here, would you like to bowl? On the house?"

I returned an icy grin. "No thanks. I might be back, and I hope you'll be just as helpful."

He didn't say anything to that. We locked eyes for a moment, both of us knowing he was lying. But I couldn't prove a thing.

"I've got to get back to work." He joined Chris, who seemed nervous.

With that, I returned to my car and sat for a minute. Bill was lying to me. His answers were too quick, almost rehearsed, as if Merrick had called him right before I showed up to tell him what to say. I was stuck, though. I couldn't force anything with him right now. If it came down to it, and Bill had to testify in a court of law, we'd see whether he would lie then.

I was hungry, so I stopped at the Mexican restaurant for a quick bite. It wasn't as good as the old place, but at that moment, it hit the spot. As I was walking back to my car, my cell phone rang, and I answered with a terse "Hello."

"I've got a little more information on Merrick for you," Spats said.

"What's that?"

"He rented an SUV last Saturday morning. He had it for twenty-four hours and returned it Sunday morning. And he rented a different SUV Tuesday evening and returned it the next morning."

"What color was it?" I asked.

He consulted his notes. "Blue."

"It fits the time frame of the kidnapping and Logan's murder." I thought about that. "The big man he met at the restaurant drove a white SUV." I snapped my fingers. "Mr. Blankenship thought he might have seen an SUV in the alley the night Logan's body was dropped in the dumpster."

"That's right." I could hear him checking his notes again. "Merrick also rented an SUV a month ago, and a month before that."

I mulled that over. "Was Merrick or this big man involved in Logan's death?" I speculated. "Did one of them drive into the alley behind Eklund's house and drop Logan's body into the dumpster?"

"It's possible, but what's a motive?"

"Maybe they're buddies with Gary Pickett and were helping him get his son away from Audra."

"Then something happened, Logan died, and they had to get rid of the body?" Spats finished my thought.

"I wonder what Merrick's up to," I mused. "He rents an SUV to kidnap Logan, then rents another to dump the body?"

"You'll want to talk to Merrick again and ask him about that."

"Oh, I intend to, but I want to see what he does overnight. You got a tail on him?"

"Yeah, I sent someone to the gun range right after we talked. Merrick was still there, and the tail's on him. Merrick left the gun range a few minutes ago, then to a McDonalds. Then he stopped at a bar near Golden, and he's still there now."

I stared out the windshield. "I'm beat, and I need to smooth things over with Harry. I'm going home, but I've got the notebooks with me, and I'll spend some time looking through them."

"Sounds good. I'm going to keep poking at Merrick, see what else I can find."

"Oh, did Kristi Arnott call you back?"

"Nope. I tried her again, still no answer."

"She's avoiding you?"

He snickered. "She can't dodge me forever. I'll track her down tomorrow."

"Sounds good. I'll see you in the morning."

I ended the call and drove out of the parking lot. I got on Kipling and headed toward Sixth Avenue, and at nine o'clock, I pulled into my driveway. Harry and I live on Grape Street in an older neighborhood east of downtown. He and I had bought the place ten years ago, when housing was cheaper, and we've done a lot of renovating on it. I love that it's set back from the street, and that it has a big yard. And I love its warmth and comfort. However, tonight it was gloomy and quiet when I went inside. I called out, but got no answer.

I went straight to the bar near the kitchen, poured Scotch, and sat down in the dark in the living room. I took a long drink, and the silence enveloped me. Everything from the day suddenly hit me. A little boy was dead, discarded in a dumpster like so much trash. Who could do that to someone so young, so innocent? I took another drink, coughed on it, and set the glass down on the coffee table. My shoulders sagged, and I allowed myself a moment to cry. Then I put my fists to my eyes and stopped. I wasn't going to let someone get away with this. I was still in that position when I heard the garage door open and close. A light went on in the kitchen.

"Sarah?"

Harry has a smooth voice, and at that moment it soothed me like nothing else could have. He poked his head into the living room, and I turned to look at him. He's several inches taller than me, with a solid build. He frowned at me. He looked good in a dark suit and tie.

"How was the benefit?"

He came over and sat down on the couch. "My guess is it was

better than your evening." He took my hand, kissed it. "Want to talk about it?"

I shook my head. "Maybe when it's all over."

He knew he didn't need to say anything, and any irritation he'd felt earlier in the day had vanished. We sat there for a moment, then he reached for the glass.

"Scotch?"

I nodded. He stared at the glass for a moment, then took a little sip. "Better than what they served tonight."

I laughed. "I'm sorry I missed it."

"Don't be." He contemplated me for a minute. "You going to be okay?"

"Yes." I drew in a breath and stood up. "Come with me."

He stood up, and we went into the bedroom. We made love, and he was more tender than usual, sensing, I suppose, that I was in a vulnerable place. I enjoyed the feel of his touch, his soft kisses, but more I relished his caresses afterward. He held me in his arms a long time, and I fell into a dreamless sleep.

CHAPTER TWENTY-ONE

The pain came in waves. An agony almost as bad as the initial loss, that horrible aching feeling, as if the world were caving in. Having the boy was supposed to help, was supposed to fill that gaping hole, that indescribable sense of loss. Losing this boy was almost like the first time, and facing that again was unbearable.

The room smelled of cleanser and bleach, and no traces of the boy were around. And yet, a boy should be here. This had not turned out the way it was supposed to. Anger flared, a raging fire that had to be quickly tamped down. No, not now.

Calm finally returned, then pondering of what to do.

There could be a replacement for the loss. Then they'd feel better. A replacement would make the sadness go away.

Why not another one? They wouldn't be here that much longer. It could all be worked out. The plans didn't have to be ruined.

Why not?

CHAPTER TWENTY-TWO

"How long have you been up?" Harry asked as he came into the kitchen.

I had my arm propped up on the table, my head resting on my hand. "Not too long."

In reality, I'd been up since the middle of the night. Harry had slept peacefully while I'd stared at the ceiling. I'd finally gotten up, rather than wake him with my tossing and turning. I'd taken the notebooks with the information on Audra and Gary Pickett, tiptoed into the kitchen, and pored over them. I read pages and pages on them, internet searches, phone records. I'd looked at countless pictures of Logan that Audra had on her laptop. None of it pointed me to a killer. I hadn't realized the sun had come up.

Harry bent down, put his arms around me, and kissed me. "I hope you find what you're looking for."

I nodded, and he gave my shoulders a squeeze. He nuzzled my neck. "Mind if I turn on the TV?"

"Go ahead."

He switched on a small TV on the corner of the counter, found a news channel, and then went to make coffee. The aroma filled the room, and I gratefully took a cup from him. In the background, the weatherman said it was going to be a warm day. I sipped coffee and flipped pages. Gary had a big interest in right-wing political issues and militia groups, but so far, we hadn't found more than that. The information was starting to run together, the names and places becoming one. I rubbed my eyes to clear my head.

Harry leaned against the counter, sipped his coffee, and watched the news for a minute. Then he quickly fixed a couple of bagels and cream cheese and handed one to me. "Make sure you eat this."

I glanced up at him and smiled. "Always looking out for me."

"Somebody has to."

He ate his, gulped the last of his coffee, and put his cup down. "I'm going to take a shower. I need to get to work early today."

I nodded. "I'll get ready when you're finished."

While he went to shower, I ate the bagel, begrudgingly admitting to myself that it did taste good. By the time I popped the last bite in my mouth, he was dressed and headed out the door. I showered and put on blue slacks and a cotton short-sleeved shirt for the warm day ahead. I clipped my badge to my belt and put on my holster with my Glock. The last thing I did was to try to rub away the dark circles under my eyes, then gave up and went back into the kitchen. I stared at the notebooks. They seemed to be mocking me that I couldn't find a valuable nugget to help in my investigation. I took out my cell phone. Gary Pickett still hadn't called me back. That pissed me off, but now I knew how to get him to return my call. With a small, wicked smile that gave me too much satisfaction, I shoved the phone back in my pocket, grabbed the notebooks, and left.

I was at work before eight. I stopped at Tara Dahl's office, and she was already at her desk. She sipped something from a Starbucks cup, then gestured with her free hand for me to come in. She stared at the cup, then set it down on a coaster. "I should quit buying Starbucks. I'm saving to buy a condo."

"I'm glad I bought my house when I did. The real estate market is expensive right now."

She nodded. "How are you this morning?"

"I'll be better if you have good news for me."

"I don't know about that, but here." She tapped the laptop sitting on her desk. "This is Gary Pickett's. You can take it back to him."

"Good. How is the analysis on it going?"

"I'll have an in-depth profile of his internet searches a little bit later. I can tell that he's tried to clear his history, but we'll get it figured out. With the right kind of tools, I can find out a lot."

"And I want it all."

She laughed. I thanked her and took the laptop. Now I had what I needed to get Gary to talk to me. I went upstairs to my desk and sat down. Spats was just getting off the phone.

"Morning, Speelmahn," he said. "I just touched base with the surveillance guys. Merrick stayed at that bar last night until about ten. One of the detectives went into the bar. He said Merrick was sitting at the bar with a big man. He didn't do anything else the rest of the night, just went home."

"Did the other guy have dark hair and a handlebar mustache?"

"Yeah. You heard of him?"

"I don't know his name. He's the man who met Gary Pickett and Merrick yesterday at that Thai restaurant." I ran a hand across my face. "I'd like to know who he is."

"I'll see what I can find out."

"Good," I said. "What's Merrick up to this morning?"

"He left his house and went to the gun range." He eyed the laptop. "Gary's?"

I smiled. "Yep. I don't think he'll avoid me now." He laughed as I picked up my cell phone and dialed Gary. Of course he didn't answer. "Mr. Pickett, this is Detective Spillman. I have your laptop, and I'd like to return it to you. Please give me a call so I can arrange this." I ended the call and looked at Spats with a grin. "Let's see how long it takes him to call me now."

"I'll bet no more than a few minutes. Who wouldn't want their laptop back?"

Sixty seconds later, my cell phone rang. Spats gave me a cocky grin.

"Spillman."

"It's Gary Pickett," he said, his tone abrupt. "It's about time you got my laptop for me."

I ignored that. "We're really busy at the moment. Could you come down to the station, and we'll go over what we did with the laptop." That would get him out of his comfort zone. That, and if he was out of sorts, might cause him to let slip something he hadn't intended to.

He swore. "I guess if that's the only way I can get it back."

"Great," I said pleasantly. "When you get here, ask for me." I gave him the address, then had to repeat it.

"I'll be there in a little bit." He disconnected.

Spats was still grinning. "Now you can talk to him."

"Yep."

Spats stood up. "I'm going to see if I can find Kristi Arnott. She's dodging me, so maybe I can find her at her workplace."

"Good. And if you get a chance, follow up on Audra's Facebook friends. If you can talk to any of them, see if they can shed light on what happened to Logan."

"You got it."

I waved him off, then worked on a report, and soon my desk phone rang. "Spillman."

It was the front desk. "I've got a guy here, Gary Pickett. He says you have his laptop."

"I'll be right down."

I grabbed the laptop and almost crashed into Ernie as I headed out of the room.

"Hey," he said. "I'm talking to some of Eklund's friends today, see if I can find anyone who believes he might be a perv."

"Sounds good. I'm going to stir the pot with Gary Pickett."

He smirked. "I saw him when I came in. He doesn't look too happy."

"Neither am I."

I heard Ernie's laugh as I went to the stairs. When I entered the lobby, Gary was seated in a chair. His fierce glare didn't match the feel of his smooth slacks and starched white shirt. He saw me and held out his hand. "My laptop?"

"Could you come with me for a moment?" I asked. "I'd like to go over a few things you told me." His jaw tensed and he muttered something under his breath. "What's that?"

"Can we make this quick?" he snapped.

"I'll see what I can do," I replied.

I motioned for him to come with me and took him to a nondescript room. He took a chair at a table. I sat across from him. The room smelled of disinfectant. He glanced around, but there was nothing else to see except gray walls.

"There are a few things I'd like to discuss with you," I said.

He hesitated. "What's that?"

"You told me about your arrest–"

"Yeah, I *did* tell you. It was a stupid bar fight, and the guy was giving me a hard time. I punched him." His shoulders lifted up. "So what? He deserved it. It wasn't a big deal."

I let that linger for a second, then said, "I also found out that you and Audra had quite a fight when you were still in San Diego, while you were in the Marines. The military police showed up at your house, and Logan's arm was broken. Your Marine buddy, Roy, helped defuse the situation so you wouldn't get in trouble."

He sat back and crossed his arms, clearly annoyed that I'd talked to his pal. I waited, then said, "Care to explain?"

He took his time, then was careful with his choice of words. "I'd been stressed after coming back from Iraq. Surely you can understand that. Anyway, Audra knows how to press my buttons, and she did that night. I'd been drinking a little, and maybe I got a bit out of hand. It wasn't that bad. We got into a big argument. Her fault, by the way. Money was tight, and she was spending it left and right. It put a lot of pressure on me, and our marriage. And yeah, I went out and had a few after a long day, and we argued about money. She came after me with a knife. I had to overpower her to get it away from her. In the struggle I accidentally hit her on the side of the face. But when Roy got there, it was all cool. That's all there is to it."

"What about Logan's broken arm? In the report, Audra says that you hurt him as well."

He shook his head. "When we first started arguing, he got knocked off his chair. That was Audra's fault too. She was so mad at me and she got up fast and bumped his chair. He was crying, of course, making a big deal about it. And he kept crying the whole time Roy was there. I tried to get him to shut up, but he wouldn't." There was little compassion in what he said, and little ownership for his actions. "As far as Logan breaking his arm, that was an accident. No big deal."

Apparently a lot of things were no big deal to him. "Logan broke his arm from falling out of a chair?"

"Yes."

"Had Logan been hurt other times?"

"No. And Audra hasn't been hurt either."

"Logan had two broken fingers as well."

"He fell off his bike. It was an accident."

That matched what Audra had told me, and the way he looked me squarely in the eye, I believed him. I went on. "She said you seemed more on edge after you came back from Iraq, that you showed quite an interest in the government, and politics. You talked a lot about conspiracy theories, that kind of thing."

"Everybody's entitled to their opinions. I wasn't happy after my service. I got things together out here, though. I got good training in the insurance business, I have a good job, and even though I got divorced, things were finally going well for me. But *this* ... losing Logan ... Oh my god, I guess nothing will ever be okay now." He put a fist to his mouth and stifled a sob.

I waited a second, then said, "I'm sorry that this happened. I know this is hard."

He wiped his eyes, then glared at me, the muscles in his jaw tightening again.

"How well do you know John Merrick?" I asked.

Something flickered in his eyes. "He owns a gun range. I see him there."

"You call him rather frequently."

"You've been looking at my phone records?"

I tipped my head at him. "What do you think?"

He swore. "You guys are unbelievable."

"We also checked your emails. In one of them, you talk about a secret."

"That doesn't have anything to do with my son," he retorted. "Somebody killed my son, and you're looking at me?"

"Convince me that I shouldn't be." He didn't respond. "Have you heard of the Colorado Citizens Militia?"

He glanced away. "No."

I tapped his laptop. "Huh. I could've sworn you'd done some internet searches on them. I'll bet you've visited their Facebook page too."

His eyes went to the laptop, then back to me. "Maybe I have. I do a lot of stuff on the internet."

"Where were you the night Logan was killed?"

"I told you, I searched for Logan, and then I was with my girlfriend."

"And you talked to Merrick. You seem pretty chummy with him. Not just a customer."

"We talk once in a while."

"From what I've seen, it's rather more frequently than that."

"So what? It doesn't have anything to do with Logan's death."

"You saw him yesterday at a Thai restaurant on Broadway."

He gulped, managed to gather himself. "So?"

"You know a big man with a handlebar mustache. What's his name?"

"None of your business." He gestured at the laptop. "I've answered your questions. Why don't you find what happened to my son, not interrogate me like *I'm* the criminal. Give me my laptop."

Protesting a little too much? I thought. "Did you tell your girlfriend Kristi not to talk to us?"

"No," he said a little too quickly. The lies kept coming.

"Do you know Ivan Eklund?"

"No," he barked. "I'm out of here. Give me my laptop."

I counted to ten, letting him get good and uncomfortable. He finally raised his eyebrows.

"Well?"

"Here you go." I slid it across the table.

He grabbed it and stood up. He frowned at me, whirled around, and headed out the door. I got up quickly and escorted him to the lobby. He went out the entrance without giving me another look.

CHAPTER TWENTY-THREE

When I got back to my desk, I called Audra Pickett. "Quick question," I said when she answered.

"Okay. What progress have you made?"

"Still investigating. I talked to Gary."

"Oh boy," she said. A TV was on in the background, then she cut the sound. "What did he tell you now?"

"We discussed that fight you two had in San Diego. You know what I'm referring to, I assume. He says you came after him with a knife, and that he had to overpower you to get it from you." She made a sharp noise. I went on. "In the struggle, he accidentally hit you, and Logan fell off his chair, and that's how he broke his arm." I paused. She still didn't say anything. "What's true?"

"Man, this dredging up the past is not fun." She cleared her throat. "Yeah, he hit me on the side of the face, but I didn't bump Logan off his chair. Think about it, do you believe a kid would break his arm falling out of a chair?"

"It's possible," I said, even though I tended to agree with Audra.

"That's typical Gary, making it everyone else's fault. It didn't happen like he said, and I get that you probably think we're both lying. All I can do is reiterate that Logan saw us fighting, he went at Gary, and Gary grabbed him, and that's when Logan's arm snapped." Her voice cracked. "I wish you would believe me."

I didn't answer that. "I'm sorry I have to bring up these things. I'm just trying to get to the truth."

"I know you are. It's upsetting, but you call with any questions. I want to find out who killed Logan, okay?"

"Thanks for your time." I disconnected and stared at the phone.

"Hey sunshine. Not even going to say 'hi' to me?" Ernie said from his desk.

"Knock it off," I said. "What's up?"

He shook his head and laughed gruffly. "How did your interview with Gary go? Based on your tone, I'm going to say not so good."

I tossed my phone down in disgust. "The guy's a narcissist if I ever saw one. Everything is everybody else's fault, not his, and he's lying through his teeth. He's hiding something. Whether he killed his son or not, I still don't know. But he's dirty."

He leaned to the side, making eye contact with me. "I've got something for you. I talked to Oakley. He's done some follow-up on Ivan Eklund's photography business. Eklund worked out of a studio off Santa Fe and Ninth. You know, that area that has the First Friday Art Walks?"

Ernie never ceased to surprise me. He didn't strike me as the type who would care about art, and I sure didn't know he knew anything about the Santa Fe Art Walk, a big event held the first Friday of each month in Denver's art district. Several blocks of Santa Fe are closed to traffic, and people wander in and out of art studios and galleries, and buy food from several food trucks. Who knew that Ernie might be a part of that scene?

"It'd be worth going over there and talk to the woman who runs the studio, see what she thinks of Eklund."

My phone rang. "It's that professor." I held up a finger for Ernie to hold on while I answered it.

"I'm curious about this," Ernie whispered.

I shook my head at him impatiently and swiped to answer the phone. "Professor Wilder, thanks for returning my call."

"No problem at all." Wilder had a smooth voice, deeper than I'd imagined. "What can I help you with?"

"Tara Dahl, in my department, suggested I talk to you. I need a quick education about right-wing political groups and militia groups in Colorado."

"Those can be two different things," he said with a small laugh, "and I have a reputation, I see. I'm happy to help. I have a class soon, and then a quick appointment, but after that I should be free for a couple of hours. Could you come down to the school?"

I glanced at the time on my computer. "If I came in about ninety minutes, would that work?"

"Perfect." He told me where his office was on the campus and ended the call. I looked at Ernie. "He'll talk to me."

"I want to know what he says."

I nodded. "What's the name of that art gallery? I'll stop there on my way to DU."

"Colorado Fine Photography." He gave me the address.

"I'll catch up with you later."

Colorado Fine Photography is in an old building one block off of Santa Fe. The traffic was humming as I walked inside, but once the door closed, I was surrounded by soft instrumental music and the sound of running water from a small fountain in the corner. I glanced around. Several large framed photographs and paintings were on the walls, all nature scenes, some naturalistic and others veering toward true abstraction. In my opinion, all of them were beautiful.

An older woman with long straight hair pulled into a ponytail came around the small desk in the far corner and smiled at me brightly. "Welcome," she said. She looked chic in a white pantsuit. "Feel free to look around. Is there anything in particular you're looking for?"

I shook my head as I approached. "I'm not here about art. If you don't mind, I'd like to ask you a few questions about Ivan Eklund." I showed her my badge.

"Oh, I was so sorry to hear about Ivan." She frowned. "He was such a nice young man, so talented. I heard from Ivan's girlfriend, Rachel." She held out a hand. "Forgive my manners. I'm Charlotte Hall. I run the studio. Ivan was supposed to come in last night to drop off some photos, and he didn't show up. I called his house, and then Rachel called me later and told me that Ivan had committed suicide." Her face puckered up, and tears welled up in her eyes. "Excuse me." She went to the desk for a Kleenex and wiped her eyes. "I admit, I was shocked."

"You were close to Ivan?"

"We were friends."

"What was Ivan like?"

"Oh." A dreamy look entered her eyes as she stared past me. "He was special." She gestured to encompass the walls and the variety of framed artwork. "He had a great eye, knew how to frame a scene. Here, let me show you." She moved around a partition wall where a large framed photograph hung. Gold-leaved aspen cascaded down a mountainside. A lake in the foreground reflected back the aspen in a beautiful way.

"See how he captures the light here? It's just visually stunning. I haven't seen talent like his since John Fielder." John

Fielder is the premier Colorado photographer, known for his landscape photography. "I'm in awe of that kind of talent." She smiled sadly. "It's such a shame that Ivan won't be around to share more of his talent with the world."

"Yes, I can see that." I gave her a moment before continuing. "I also understand that he did portraits–kids, families, that kind of thing."

"Yes, that's true. He was very good at that too, but it was mostly to pay the bills." She gave a slight shrug. "The life of an artist is never easy. It's hard to make money at this, so artists have to support themselves in other ways. Ivan started out doing portraits at a K-mart. It wasn't his passion, obviously. His passion was his nature photography." Her eyes went back to the artwork on the walls.

"I understand Ivan worked in a lot of schools, taking portraits of kids."

She nodded. "Yes, I saw a lot of those. I'm sure I'm biased, but I thought even those were so good. If there was a way to get a shy child to smile, he could do it. He'd capture their personalities in a way few others could."

"Did he take pictures of kids from afar, action shots, that kind of thing? Or was it just portraits?"

She pursed her lips. "I'm not aware of him doing anything with people other than portraits, posed pictures. Any portraits were for money, to support himself. Other than that, he was working on nature photography. Let me show you another." Before I could protest, she walked me farther down the wall to another mountain scene.

"See this one here? How he's captured the gloom of the evening? It's just wonderful. I could stare at this one for a long time."

She did continue to look at the photo. I had more questions.

"Was Ivan ever in any kind of trouble?"

"No, he wasn't." Still looking at the photo.

"Was he ever inappropriate with kids?"

Her eyes swung sharply back to me. "What do you mean? Are you talking about abuse?"

"That's what I'm wondering. Did you ever hear of anything like that?"

She shook her head vehemently. "No, never. That was not Ivan. When I saw him with children, he was great with them, kind and compassionate. He would never do something inappropriate." She seemed very sure in her answer.

"You saw Ivan taking portraits of children?"

"A few times," she said slowly. "You know, Ivan asked me, totally out of the blue the other day what it might feel like to lose my child. It was so bizarre. I have two sons, grown now. I asked him what he meant, and he wanted to know how I'd have felt if one of my sons had died when they were younger."

"What was your answer?"

Her eyes lost their warmth. "I told him it would be devastating, and if that had happened to me, I don't know that I could've gone on."

"Why did he ask that?"

She shrugged. "He didn't say."

"Did Ivan talk about any troubles recently, was he depressed?"

"No, that's the thing. Lately he'd been really upbeat. He was finally about to turn the corner and make some real money with his photography. He was happy about that." Her hands twisted, her consternation showing. "That's what I don't understand. I mean, I get that we don't know everything about a person, but his suicide just seems so strange."

"Had he talked about anyone new, someone he was concerned about? Was anything suspicious going on with him?"

She mulled that over. "Now that you mention it, for about the last week or so before he died, he was asking me about right-wing political groups, and politics in general. He was asking what would make a person think that they needed to go to extremes to protect themselves against the government. It struck me as odd because Ivan never seemed political about anything. And yet he suddenly seemed to show an interest in the government and what was going on."

"Was he angry about the government, anything like that?"

"No, just a lot of questions about how right-wing political groups differ from others, and did I know anyone in any groups. I don't, by the way."

"Did Ivan ever mention a man named Gary Pickett, or a John Merrick?" I asked, wondering if Eklund might've had some connection to Gary, might've known him somehow, and had gone after his son.

Charlotte again thought. "No, I don't recognize either of those names."

"Did Ivan own any guns?" I asked, now wondering whether she might be aware of some connection between Eklund and John Merrick, even if she didn't recognize the name.

Her hands went to her chest. "Not that I'm aware of. Ivan was a very peaceful man. I'm not sure he would've ever wanted to shoot a gun, let alone own one."

"How much do you know about Ivan's past?"

"Not a lot. He grew up on the East Coast, in Virginia, close to the DC area. He has two sisters. He lived with a friend for quite a while until he was able to buy a house. I know that because Ivan said he liked living alone, that when he had a roommate, he didn't have the privacy he wanted."

"Privacy for what?"

She gave me a funny look. "I don't know. Whatever one wants privacy for."

Like abusing little kids? I thought but didn't say.

"Sounds like you know Ivan's girlfriend Rachel?"

"Yes. She's nice, although I'm not sure she was right for him."

"Why do you say that?"

She pursed her lips. "Just a hunch. She was so different from him. But I guess opposites attract." She closed her eyes for a second. "Rachel said a detective who talked to her indicated that Ivan had killed himself, but she just had to wonder about that. Both she and I really can't believe Ivan would take his own life. However, that would mean someone murdered him. I hope, if that's the case, that you find out who did that to him."

"Why would someone want to murder him?"

She shrugged. "I can't answer that. I'm not aware of any trouble Ivan might have been in, or of anyone hating him. I don't know anyone that would want to do that to him."

That left me with little else to go on. "I appreciate you meeting with me," I said. I handed her a business card as I headed for the door. "If you think of anything that might be important, please give me a call."

She took the card. "Sarah, that's a nice name. My aunt was named Sarah."

I smiled. "Thanks for your time."

She nodded and turned back toward the mountain scene that Ivan had taken. I left her like that. I didn't know what else to ask at the moment, and if I needed to, I could always talk to her again.

CHAPTER TWENTY-FOUR

I got caught in traffic on Interstate 25, which delayed me. When I finally turned south off I-25, toward the University of Denver, I was running late. DU is a small, private school near I-25 and University Boulevard. Coincidentally, fairly close to where Gary Pickett lives. Professor Wilder's office is in Sturm Hall, on the school's main campus. I found a parking place on a side street. It was a beautiful morning, and I enjoyed the sun's warmth as I passed lush lawns on my way to the building.

I got to Wilder's office a little after our agreed-upon time. His office door was closed, and I knocked, but no one answered. I paced the floor, and a few minutes later, a stocky man with long graying hair and glasses walked down the hall.

"You must be Detective Spillman," he said with a smile. He shifted books from one hand to the other, then unlocked his door and stepped into a small office. "Come in."

I followed him in and took a seat at an oak chair across from a similar oak desk. He scooted around the desk, plopped the books onto a stack of others, then sat down and looked at me. "I'm sorry

I was late, it seems at the end of every class, students have questions."

"No problem, I appreciate your time." I glanced around. Although the space was small, it felt inviting, with several bookcases filled with books, some pictures of historical places like Machu Picchu and Stonehenge, and knickknacks on a windowsill.

"You've got questions about Denver's right-wing and militia groups," he began. "Now that is an interesting subject. One you wouldn't think we have to deal with, but we do." He sat back and laced his fingers. "How much do you know about these types of groups?"

"Not a lot, I'm afraid."

"That's quite all right. If you don't mind, I'll give you a little bit of background." I nodded, and he went on. "First, we have right-wing political groups, those opposed to socialism and social democracy. They range in how extreme they are, and how much they resort to violence. Then you have militia groups. These groups have been around since revolutionary times. Over our history, they've not been uncommon. They usually stay on the fringes, and they haven't caused," he tipped his head to the side, "too many problems. However, we've heard more about them after Timothy McVeigh and the Oklahoma City bombing. You've heard of that?" I nodded again, and he smiled. "You'd be surprised how many younger people haven't. Anyway, McVeigh was erroneously thought to be a member of a militia group in Michigan. Turns out he wasn't in any extremist groups at all. You had the Justus Township incident in Montana. There was a decline in groups for a while in the late 1990s and early in this century, but with the global financial crisis in 2007, and then the election of Barack Obama in 2008, modern militias surged again. Right now, there are more than five hundred groups across the United States, more than double what they were in 2008.

There's the 3 Percent Militia, the Oath Keepers, and on and on. These groups tend to call themselves patriot groups. They have a wide range of ideas and objectives, but at their core is a dissatisfaction with government and a fear of a tyrannical government. As such, they think the way to protect their rights is through armed force." It was a good introduction, and I felt as if I were in class. "Now, in Colorado, we've seen a rise in militia groups. There's the Colorado Front Range Militia, 3 Percent Defense Militia, the Northern Colorado Militia. Have you heard of any of these?"

I shook my head. "No, not in my investigations. I'm sure other officers have, but I haven't had a reason to learn about them. Before now."

"Perfectly understandable. As you can imagine, some of these groups don't necessarily want to make themselves known, until they get pushed to the brink. Then you might have trouble."

"Are you familiar with the Colorado Citizens Militia?"

"That's a newer group, some would say they're only a right-wing political group. But, as their name says, they are a militia. They lean toward nationalism and object to what they see as control by elitist liberals. And, they don't like the power of large corporations."

"Are they violent?"

"I don't know of any official acts of violence. That's not to say that they couldn't have done things under the radar."

"Speaking of violence, what would push a group that far?"

He shrugged. "It depends on political leanings at the time, or if they're acting against what they see the other political party or its organizations doing."

"What type of individual is drawn to these groups?"

"There's a blurring of lines between militias and Christian fundamentalists, those who think the Apocalypse may be at hand, and they're preparing for that. Militia members believe the government is getting out of hand. Frequently, they include law enforcement personnel or ex-cops. A lot of veterans returning from Iraq and Afghanistan join, and they bring their military training. And it's generally men who join. Obviously they're going to want guns and be strong supporters of the Second Amendment."

Some of this matched what I knew about Gary Pickett. "Do any of these groups indoctrinate their children into the militia?"

He leaned forward, hands on the desk. "Not as such, but I'm sure family members hear some things about a particular group's activities."

"What about criminal backgrounds?"

"Depends on the man. And speaking of criminality, there is that element in some groups. Of course, some militias denounce breaking the law or using violence, but others definitely cross that line. The crimes are usually related to weapons or explosives, and the more serious crimes are often about plotting to blow up a building."

"Do you know of groups that resort to crime for money? Or that might kidnap children for some reason?"

A frown formed. "Some militia groups have been condemned for detaining migrants at the border until border security arrived, but that's the extent that I'm aware of." He tipped his head, curious. "I hope this doesn't mean we have an issue with one of these groups? I haven't heard about anything yet."

"I don't know that."

"I suppose you could have a group that resorts to criminal activity in order to profit, but that would be something new to me. These groups aren't about money; they're radically ideological about what they see as a dangerous infringement on their rights."

"What about racism?"

"Yes, that's a part of it, at least for some militia groups. Some group leaders condemn racism, but that doesn't mean the individuals within a group aren't racist. However, there have been problems of late with attacks on Muslim groups."

"Whoever is perceived as the latest threat gets targeted."

"Yes," he agreed sadly.

"How did you develop your knowledge on militias?"

"It started out as something I covered in a history class on late-century political trends. Then it led to a whole course on the history of right and left wing groups and militias. Through my own research, I've come into contact with law enforcement, and I've even had members of these political groups and militias talk to me. It's been eye-opening, to say the least."

"I'll bet."

"If you're interested, call Special Agent Mike Crozier at the FBI. I've gotten to know him over the years. He keeps tabs on some of these groups, and he shares with me what he can."

"That'd be great."

He rummaged in a drawer for a notebook, then grabbed a piece of paper and wrote down a number. As he handed me the paper, he glanced at a clock on the wall. "I have office hours now, and I'm afraid we may be interrupted by some of my students."

I was politely being dismissed, just as he would one of his students I imagined. I stood up and thanked him for his time. "It's been very educational." I handed him a business card. "If you think of anything that might be helpful in my investigation, I'd appreciate a call."

"Sure." He stood up, leaned over his desk, and took the card. "It's been a pleasure. And if you hear more about the Colorado Citizens Militia, I'd appreciate hearing about it."

"Absolutely." I walked out the door, mulling over what I'd learned.

CHAPTER TWENTY-FIVE

When I got back to my desk, Ernie was on the phone. I sat down and logged onto my computer.

"Yeah, that's right," Ernie was saying. "If something else occurs to you, give me a call, okay? Thanks." He hung up, then swiveled his chair around to face me.

I checked my email, then pumped my fist. Tara had sent a report of Gary Pickett's internet history.

He cocked an eyebrow. "I can see the look in your eye. What have you got?"

I began scanning his internet searches. "There it is," I said excitedly. "Gary has been looking at the Colorado Citizens Militia, a local militia group here in Colorado. Now we have the proof." I sat back and looked at Ernie. "I got quite the education from Professor Wilder. I had no idea how many of these groups are around, or how they operate. It's crazy." I kept my eyes on my monitor as I talked. "We knew Gary has an interest in militia groups, I just didn't know for sure if it was *this* one."

"What'd the professor tell you?"

I gave him the scoop, then told him about my conversation

with Charlotte Hall at the gallery. "And Charlotte said that lately Eklund had been interested in politics and right-wing groups. I'd be willing to bet there's a connection between Gary Pickett and Eklund. I asked Gary if he knew Eklund, and he denied it. Was he lying?"

He sat back and chewed on his cigar. "You think Ivan Eklund is involved in the same militia group as Gary Pickett?"

"Don't forget John Merrick." I took a pencil and fiddled with it. "It's possible. Except that Eklund was talking about right-wing groups, not necessarily militia groups. And I don't know whether any of them are actually involved in a militia group, per se."

"True."

"Hang on," I said, then pulled out the paper with Mike Crozier's number on it. "Wilder gave me the name of an FBI agent who has tracked some of these militia groups. Let's see what this guy has to say." I grabbed my desk phone and dialed. When a man's deep clipped voice answered, I identified myself. "Professor Wilder at DU suggested I give you a call."

"He's a good man and knows his stuff."

"Yes he does. I was wondering if you have any information on the Colorado Citizens Militia."

"This pertains to an investigation of yours?"

"It seems to." I told him about Logan Pickett, then everything I had so far on Gary Pickett and John Merrick.

"That is interesting, and I'm afraid I might disappoint you. I don't have a lot of information on the Colorado Citizens Militia. We've been keeping tabs on that group now for over a year, but so far, they seem to be lying low. They've got a website, which I'm sure you've already looked at, with some basic information, but unlike many other groups, they don't have much of a social media presence. I haven't heard of anyone in the group itself plotting anything criminal, although some of the individual members have been arrested for burglaries, DUIs, and other misdemeanors. At this point, I'm not aware of any rogue members doing something illegal. Are you?"

"I'm not sure," I said. "Do you know of a member in the Colorado Citizens Militia who has dark hair and a handlebar mustache? He's a big, burly man."

"He doesn't sound familiar. I've not personally met any of the guys in the group, though."

"I'll have to keep looking then."

"You better make it fast, unless you want to go out of state."

"What's that mean?"

"From what I hear, the group may be relocating soon."

My ears perked up. "Where?"

"Idaho is the rumor. I guess Colorado's not to their liking anymore."

"Interesting." I thanked him for his time and hung up. I looked at Ernie. "The Colorado Citizens Militia might be heading out of state." He tipped his head at me. I thought back through conversations I'd had with Audra and Gary Pickett. "Audra said Gary didn't think she was a good mother, and I got the sense she thought Gary might've been capable of taking Logan from her. If Gary is part of this militia group, and the group is leaving the state, maybe he plans to relocate with the group. That'd be a reason for him to kidnap Logan, if he wanted his son with him instead of Audra."

"That's just what I was thinking." Ernie pointed at me with the cigar. "Have you eliminated the mother?"

"I won't do that for sure until I know who the killer is. But–" I thought for a second, picturing Audra in my mind. Her grief and pain seemed so visceral. "I don't see her killing Logan. She had Latoya Anderson around her house, both the night of his kidnapping, and each day since then. We know from the autopsy that Logan likely died within hours of being found. It would be hard for her to keep him hidden from Latoya that whole time. I'm not saying it's impossible, but it would've been difficult to keep his body from being discovered."

"She could've drugged him."

"True, but we won't know what Logan might've had in his system until we get the toxicology report back. Have you talked to the CSI team?"

"Yeah. From what I can tell, there isn't a thing in that alley that helps us."

"Too bad." The pencil was back in my hand as I mulled things over. "Let's go back to Gary Pickett. He and Merrick both seem to have a connection to the same militia group. What does that have to do with the murdered boy? Did Merrick kidnap Logan for Gary?"

"What about Eklund? Did he take the boy, and Gary found out, and the militia group killed Eklund?"

"Interesting theory," I said. "Eklund kidnapped Logan, had his fun with him, then killed him?"

"Right." Ernie didn't say anything else.

I grimaced and tossed the pencil down. Ernie stared thoughtfully at his laptop as I continued scrolling through Gary's internet searches. Then I sat back, frustrated. "What is Gary holding back?"

"Huh?"

"Gary is lying through his teeth. He's downplaying the fact that he broke Logan's arm back in California, while he was in the Marines, and that he and Audra had a domestic dispute. And he won't say a word about this militia group. If he knows something about his son's disappearance, wouldn't he tell us? Unless he's involved somehow, or the militia group doesn't want him to talk to us."

"Why would they care, unless they're involved too?"

"Exactly," I said. I tapped a finger on my desk. "If Gary

kidnapped Logan, he *had* to have had help. He's also smart enough to know he needs an alibi."

"Who is the girlfriend, Kristi Arnott?"

I nodded and looked at my phone. "Spats should call me if he talks to her."

"If someone else does the dirty work and snatches Logan, Gary looks innocent. He's there helping look for his son."

"Right."

"What if Eklund isn't a pedophile? How else might he fit into this?"

I mulled that over. "Maybe Gary masterminded the whole thing. What if he knows Eklund too, and he got Merrick and Eklund to work together to kidnap Logan, then Eklund kept Logan at his house."

"What about Eklund's girlfriend? If she was around his house, how does he keep the kid quiet?"

I went back over my conversation with Rachel Connelly. "The last time she'd seen Ivan was Friday, and they went to her house. She did say he'd been busy over the weekend."

"He didn't want her there because he had the kid with him?"

"That's a possibility."

"And as we've said before, something went bad, they kill the kid and put him in the dumpster behind Eklund's house," Ernie said, then pinched his face. "It's a stretch."

"Stranger things have happened." I let out a heavy sigh.

"You're leaving out one thing. If Eklund was helping Gary, why does Eklund commit suicide?" Thought lines formed on his brow. "What, he's feeling guilty about the kid, so he offs himself?"

I shook my head. "My feeling is he didn't commit suicide. We're waiting on the autopsy, but I'd doubt that they find gunshot residue on his hands."

"He was set up?"

I shrugged. "That's a working theory of mine. We need more on Eklund."

"I'm getting what I can from his neighbors."

"When were you going to tell me that?"

He smirked at me. "You've been doing all the talking." I threw the pencil at him. "Don't get your hopes up," he said as he dodged it. "A lot of them are impatient with me, since they already talked to Oakley's team. When I try to tell them I'm looking at his death from a different angle, they don't seem to care. Anyway, the most intriguing thing I heard was from a neighbor who lives a few blocks away. She saw Eklund arguing with a woman."

"When was this?"

"The neighbor wasn't sure, but she thought about a week ago. She said Eklund and the woman were standing in his yard. He was pointing at the woman, and he seemed pretty angry. She said that wasn't like Eklund, that he was always very nice."

"Who was the woman?"

"The neighbor didn't know."

"Description?" While he told me, I checked my email.

"She was taller with dark hair. The neighbor didn't recognize her."

"That sounds a little like Audra."

"Could be."

"Tara sent me a file on Eklund's internet history too. Do you have time to look this over? I'm going to work the Gary angle more."

"Yeah. I need a break from talking to neighbors."

"I'm emailing it to you now. See if you can find a connection with him and the Colorado Citizens Militia as well."

"Sure thing." He opened the file. "I'll search 'militia.' And there you go."

"What?"

"You found something already?"

Ernie nodded. "Yeah, Ivan visited a site about militia groups a week ago. Coincidence?"

I gave him a sideways smile. "We don't believe in coincidences."

"Yeah, but we don't have anything to show that any one of the three killed the kid, remember?"

I put my head in my hands for a second. "No, we don't." I narrowed my eyes. "I think it's time to shake some trees and see what falls out." He gave me a funny look. "It's time to talk to Merrick again."

"You need to be careful with him. He's smart enough to know you're on to him, and he could be dangerous."

"Merrick and Gary are both lying to me. I don't like it when people lie to me."

"Yeah, I know, but I should go with you. Both of those men could be dangerous."

My phone rang before I could answer. "It's Heather Neville." I swiped at the screen and greeted her. "Thanks for returning my call."

"I'm sorry we've been playing telephone tag." She had a higher voice, sounding a little rushed. "I travel a good bit, and I'm in meetings a lot. And I'm afraid I have another one shortly, and then I've got to head to Golden."

"I just need a moment of your time."

"I'm already late. Can you meet me at Caribou Coffee at Colorado Mills? Say, in thirty minutes? I'll have a little time then." I agreed. "I'll have a black computer bag, and I'm in a gray suit. I'll see you soon." With that, she ended the call.

I turned to Ernie. "Heather can meet me in half an hour. Then I'll talk to Merrick."

Ernie grimaced, not happy that I wasn't listening to him.

"You know I don't usually worry about you, but maybe I should go with you."

Ernie and I have been partners for a long time, and sometimes he worries about me. At times I didn't mind, but now was not one of them. I could take care of myself. He looked at me askance. He wasn't going to let this go.

"Nothing's going to happen."

"You're probably right," he said. "Call it a gut feeling I have."

"I'll talk to Heather," I said. "Then if you want, meet me at the gun range and we'll talk to Merrick together. Would that make you happy?"

He smiled. "Yeah, it would."

I grabbed my keys and headed for the door.

CHAPTER TWENTY-SIX

I arrived at Caribou Coffee with enough time to purchase a cup of coffee and a bagel. I ate the bagel, a late lunch that was a repeat of breakfast and not entirely satisfying, but I didn't have time for more. I sipped some coffee while I waited for Heather Neville. The pick-me-up was good. I had just finished when a woman in a smart gray business suit strolled through the door, her heels clicking on the tile floor. A black computer bag was tucked under one arm. Her gaze darted around the room, then fell on me. She walked over and sat down across from me, all business.

"You're Detective Spillman?"

I nodded. "Thanks for meeting me."

"I'm sorry I couldn't meet sooner. My schedule is crazy."

"What do you do?"

"I provide support for a proprietary software system. We work with accountants and small businesses. I travel to company sites, both here in Denver and the western US."

"Sounds interesting."

"Trust me, it's not." She pointed at my cup. "Do you mind if I get something?"

"Go right ahead."

She left her computer bag with me, went up to the counter, and returned a few minutes later with a drink topped with whipped cream drizzled with caramel. "I'll pay for this with extra time at the gym, but it's worth it." She drank a bit, then wiped her upper lip delicately with a napkin. "You want to talk to me about Audra, right?"

"You two are friends?"

"Best friends." She set her glass down and tugged at her suit jacket, trying to pull it tighter around herself. "It's such a scary thing, having your kid disappear like that." She threw her fingers up. "Poof. And he was gone. Then when Audra called me and said Logan had been killed, I couldn't believe it." Her voice cracked, then she quickly controlled her emotion. "I can't lose it when I have to meet a client soon."

"Do you have kids of your own?"

She glanced toward the line of people waiting to order, then back at me. "A daughter a few years younger than Logan. If something happened to her ..." She left the rest unsaid. "Audra's devastated, of course. I was out of town over the weekend, and I'm glad Latoya was there for her."

"How long have you and Audra been friends?"

"We met in college, then both moved around the country, and then we both happened to settle here."

"You've seen Audra with Logan?"

"A lot. We try to get our kids together to play. It can be tough with our schedules, so I'd say it's not as often lately."

"Audra's a good mother?"

"The best. Gary, on the other hand ..." I widened my eyes and waited. "You must have heard stuff about him."

"Some," I said nonchalantly.

"He's an ass. Audra's a smart woman, but I have no idea what she saw in him. I told her he was bad news. She was head over heels in love, though. Or lust." She laughed at her own joke. "That's what it was. Sex. Once that grew old, they had nothing left. And Gary became abusive. I was glad when she left him."

"Abusive how?"

She hesitated. "I'm not sure if he ever hit her, but he was verbally abusive, yelling at Audra, picking fights. He was demeaning to her. It really took a toll on her self-esteem."

"How was he toward Logan?"

"He ordered that little boy around. It was awful to see. And get this." She leaned in. "Gary thought he'd be a better parent than Audra. Can you believe that?"

I didn't answer. "He's made a lot of accusations about Audra, that she isn't a good parent, that if there were problems in the marriage, they were her fault."

She dismissed that with a flick of her hand. "None of that's true. Like I said, Gary was abusive to her, and he hurt Logan on at least one occasion." I tipped my head to the side, and she went on. "He broke Logan's arm when Audra and Gary had a fight."

"I heard that." I got to the crux of the issue. "I don't think Gary could've kidnapped Logan Saturday night. He was around, looking for Logan. But he could've orchestrated it. Was he capable of that?"

"Sure. If he wanted Logan for himself, he'd do whatever it took."

"Have you heard of John Merrick or Ivan Eklund?"

She thought about that, then shook her head. "I don't think so." She drew in a breath. "Audra recently gave me a picture of Logan in his baseball uniform. Oh," she said with an ache, "his brown hair was sticking out from under his cap." She laughed, then tears appeared in her eyes. "That cap was too big. He wasn't very good, but he could pull off the uniform." She tried to smile.

"Yes, I saw that picture."

Her face clouded. "If you find out who did this, let me get my hands on them first, okay?"

She checked her phone. "I need to leave for another appointment. Again, I'm sorry I took so long to get back to you." She stood up and grabbed her coffee. "I need this for the road." She tucked the computer bag under her arm. "I'm not sure if I helped or not, but if you need anything from me, call me. I'll do what I can. You've got to find whoever did that to poor Logan."

I thanked her, and she headed out the door, heels clicking a purposeful beat.

CHAPTER TWENTY-SEVEN

After Heather Neville left, I pulled out my phone and called Ernie. I expected him to answer, but it went to voice mail.

"Hey, why aren't you answering?" I said, letting my impatience show. "Call me back. I want to talk to Merrick now."

I disconnected and took a sip of my coffee. Cold. I gulped it down anyway, tapped my foot and stared at my phone. I was wasting time. I could talk to Merrick on my own. I waited one more minute, then stood up and marched out the door.

It didn't take me long to drive from Caribou Coffee to Gold Creek Gun Range. I parked down the road from the shop, not wanting Merrick to know I was around. I watched the shop for a minute. One car, a beat-up Toyota 4x4, was parked at the far end of the lot, and Merrick's big black Ram truck sat near the shop entrance. I rolled down my window and listened. No sounds of guns from the outdoor range. I watched for another minute, and then a familiar white SUV drove into the lot, and the stocky man with the handlebar mustache, the guy I'd seen at the Thai restaurant, got out. He went inside the shop, came back out, and drove to the wood fence at the end of the lot. Someone on the other side opened the gate, and the SUV drove through. The gate closed. I pulled out my phone and called the detective who was on surveillance.

"King," he barked into the phone.

"It's Spillman," I said. "You're on surveillance at the gun range, correct?"

"Since this morning. Nothing's happened so far. I took over for the detective at his house. Merrick was at his house overnight, left at nine, went to a Burger King drive-through, and then he showed up at the shop a little before ten. That's his Ram truck parked down in front, and he hasn't left since. Not much happening now."

"Okay. I'm parked down the road now."

"I thought I saw you."

"Uh-huh." I made a quick decision "I'm headed into the shop." *Screw Ernie,* I thought. I wasn't waiting for him. "I need to ask Merrick a few questions."

"It's been quiet in there for a while, no customers until that white SUV showed up. I'll be out here. If you need anything, give me a call."

"If I do, come running."

I ended the call and got out. Gray clouds hung low in the western sky, threatening an afternoon spring storm. However, at the moment it was warm, a little humidity in the air. I walked down the road and into the parking lot. When I walked into the shop, the employee who had been there the other day was again behind the counter. Merrick and the big man weren't around. The employee glanced up and gave me a funny look, not happy to see me.

"Where's Merrick?" I asked.

"He's not here right now."

I shook my head, letting him know I wasn't satisfied with that answer. I jerked a thumb toward the entrance. "His truck is parked out front."

He eyed the gun on my hip. "Um, he's ... not, uh, here." Apparently, he was having trouble speaking.

My phone rang. I ignored it. "Where is he?"

"Um," he repeated. His eyes went to the door that led to the back. Then Merrick appeared. The employee let out a breath, visibly relieved.

Merrick looked directly at me. "I told you all that I'm going to" He walked up to the counter and pointed toward the door. "You might as well head on out."

Where was the other guy? I gave him a friendly smile. "I just have a few questions, not a big deal."

Merrick tugged at his beard and glared at me. I recognized a Nirvana song playing from the stereo behind the counter. He hadn't insisted I leave, so I took that as a sign to continue.

"I'd like to clarify a few things, if you don't mind. First," before he could protest, I said, "You told me that you don't know Gary Pickett, just that he's a customer in here."

"I need a smoke," the employee said. He didn't wait for an okay, but came around the counter and quickly walked out the entrance.

Merrick was cautious and slow to answer. "Gary's a customer."

I nodded thoughtfully. "What's puzzling to me is that after you left here, you met with Gary and another man at a Thai restaurant on Broadway. The three of you had an animated conversation."

His lips twitched in a slight show of surprise, but he held himself well. Rather than asking if he'd been followed, he said, "There's no law against me talking to anybody. As I said, Gary is a customer." His words were measured.

"Are you in the habit of meeting customers at restaurants around town?"

"My habits are none of your business."

"Unless you've broken the law."

My phone vibrated in my pocket. I ignored it. Merrick stared at me and didn't answer. I went on.

"The next thing I'm trying to figure out is why there are so many phone calls between you and Gary. Not from this shop, but from your cell phone to his. That would seem unusual, don't you think? If you're conducting shop business, wouldn't you call a customer from your shop phone?"

"I can call customers from my cell phone."

"I'm sure that's true, but there are an awful lot of phone calls. What was Gary buying that you would need to have so many phone calls from him?"

"He has questions about the guns he's interested in. Again, no crime in that."

"Yes, but what about phone calls after hours? Are you in the habit of calling your customers in the evenings, even late at night?"

"How I conduct my business is my business."

"Fair enough," I said, still trying for friendly to keep him from shutting down completely. "Let's talk about last Saturday night."

"What about it?"

I leaned a hand on the counter. "Gary and you both said you hadn't talked to each other that night. But that's not the case. The phone records show that you did talk."

His eyes darted away as he tried to come up with an answer. "Last Saturday? Maybe I missed what day you meant. I guess we did talk. It would've been about a new gun that he was interested in."

Slick. A vague answer, could be a lie, possibly not. I didn't buy that. I changed subjects. "I noticed, too, that you rented a large SUV on Saturday morning, and you returned it Sunday morning. Then you rented another SUV on Tuesday morning. Again keeping it for twenty-four hours."

"So?"

"I'm curious why you would've rented SUVs if you have a truck of your own. What would you need the other vehicle for?"

He wiped his hands on his jeans. "I don't have to tell you anything."

Right at that moment, I wanted to slap the smug expression off his face. I resisted and found some level of politeness. "That's true, but you might want to. I'm puzzling over these odd series of coincidences around the time that Logan Pickett disappeared and then was found in a dumpster."

"You think I had something to do with that?"

I shrugged. "I have to look at all angles. One of those angles is you not telling me the truth about conversations with Gary." I ticked other things off on my fingers. "And you renting vehicles that you only need for a short amount of time. On top of that, I looked into your whereabouts Saturday evening, and then again on Tuesday. In both instances, you weren't where you said you were."

"I told you I was at the bowling alley on Saturday."

"Yes, and your pal, Bill, covered for you. However, I doubt Bill or you were counting on another worker at the bowling alley speaking up." He stared at me. "That person was certain that you weren't there last Saturday evening." His Adam's apple bobbed under his beard. "And as for Tuesday night, you don't have an alibi. You were here, and people can account for your whereabouts then, but when you left, you went home. Remember?"

He gazed at me, his expression neutral. Then his eyes flickered. "Will you excuse me for a second?"

Before I could say anything, he whirled around and went through the door to the back. The door swung slowly closed. I looked toward the entrance, then moved quickly to where I could glimpse down the hallway. I didn't see anyone. My nerves tingled, the hair on the back of my neck stood up. I waited and listened, but couldn't hear anything except the music on the stereo. I edged toward the entrance and looked out a window. Merrick's truck and the SUV were still in the lot, along with the 4x4. The employee was loitering nearby. He clearly wasn't coming back in the shop until I left.

I moved around the counter and to the door where Merrick had gone. I cracked it open, listened, heard nothing. "Hello?" I finally said.

No reply.

I called out again. When there was still no answer, I stepped through the doorway. I put my hand on my holster and walked quietly down the hall. The hair on my neck stood up. I took in a slow deep breath as I carefully entered the indoor target-practice area. It was dark. I let my eyes adjust and didn't see anyone. I had a fleeting thought I should've waited for Ernie, then dismissed it. I had to stay focused.

I slipped past the stalls, eyes wary, ears listening. It was quiet. When I reached the end of the target-practice area, I noticed a door I hadn't seen before. I put my hand on the knob and slowly turned it, my breath coming faster. I eased the door open and sunlight streamed in, illuminating the indoor target-practice range. I turned and peered into the shadows behind me and didn't see Merrick anywhere. I opened the door wider. I still didn't see him, so I exited the building.

Behind the shop, nestled into the hillside, was an outdoor skeet shooting area. Two houses with traps machines were off to the left and right, with shooting stations spaced around an arc path. I squinted against the sunlight and wished for sunglasses. The air smelled fresh, with a hint of pine. I took a few steps away from the building and a voice stopped me in my tracks.

"What do you think you're doing?"

I turned around and saw Merrick near a shed by the main building. Then the big man with the mustache appeared from around the shed. Both had guns in their hands, pointed down, but ready.

"Let's all take it easy," I said. My heart beat fast, and I took slow steadying breaths.

"I'll take it easy when you leave Merrick's shop," the big man said. His voice boomed in the open area.

"Who are you?" I asked.

"None of your business."

Clouds moved overhead and obscured the sun. "It'd be a lot easier if you help me out," I said. "I'm looking for some information."

He watched me closely. "Information about what?"

"All I'm trying to find out is why John," I indicated Merrick with my head, "doesn't want to tell me where he was last Saturday night. Why he doesn't have an alibi for that time? I've got a little boy who's dead, and I need to find a killer. You can help with that."

Merrick shifted from foot to foot, but he let the big man do his talking.

"I'm sorry about Logan Pickett," the big man said.

"Did you have anything to do with his kidnapping and murder?"

His eyes remained level on me. "Not in any way." Very cool in his reply. I looked toward Merrick, and the big man answered for him. "John didn't have anything to do with that either. He was here with me."

"That's interesting." I glanced at Merrick. He averted his eyes. "He said he was bowling all evening."

"I was with him at the bowling alley, and then we came here," the big man said.

"How late does this place stay open?"

"We were having a meeting."

"Of the Colorado Citizens Militia?" I asked.

He nodded his head appreciatively. "I see you've done your homework. I have nothing to hide. Yes, we're part of a patriot group. The Constitution gives us the right to assemble, and that's what we were doing. We weren't breaking any laws, and unless you have a warrant, you can't search this place."

"I can ask you questions."

"And we don't have to answer them." His eyes narrowed and his face took on a threatening look. "I've given you John's alibi, and that's all you need."

"Merrick," I called to him. "Where were you Tuesday when Logan's body was put in that dumpster?"

The big man answered again. "He was with me the entire time."

"You know Gary Pickett?"

He shook his head. "Never heard of him."

"Yes, you do," I said carefully. "If you're involved in Logan's death, just come clean. It'll go better for you."

"We're done here," he announced.

"Ivan Eklund?" I asked. "Know him?"

He shook his head. "We've told you all we're going to, all we need to."

"What's your name?" I tried for that again.

He evaded the answer again. "You can look into me as well, and you'll find out I'm telling the truth."

"I'll do just that."

"Yes, you do." He was daring me. He took a step forward.

I braced myself and stared at Merrick. "What about the SUVs you rented? Why do you need those, if you have your own vehicles?"

Merrick stayed silent, but I got the slightest hesitation from the big man. "There's nothing illegal about renting a car. We don't have to answer anything else." The gun moved slightly up in his hand, still not aimed at me, but coming closer. He pointed with his other hand at the door. "Now, we'd like you to leave."

"I'll be seeing you around," I said. "And I'll be checking you out, carefully." I locked eyes with him, making sure he knew that I wasn't frightened of him.

They both stared at me as I walked carefully back to the door, my eyes still on them. I quickly went inside, strode back down the hall past the indoor practice range, and into the main area of the shop. Merrick's employee stood behind the counter. His jaw dropped when he saw the gun in my hand. I didn't say a word as I left. It wasn't until I got outside that I holstered my weapon. I hurried back down the road to my car, angry. No one threatened me like that and got away with it. The big man had given Merrick his alibi, but the whole thing stank. And I was going to find out why.

CHAPTER TWENTY-EIGHT

It wasn't until I got back to my car that I relaxed. That was close, the situation much more tense than I would've preferred. I sat watching the gun range, waiting to see if Merrick or the big man would leave. If the latter did, I was going to follow him. My phone rang, and I yanked it out of my pocket, expecting Ernie.

"You okay?" Detective King asked. "I saw you walking back to your car. You looked like you were ready to take on a prize-fighter."

"I'm okay," I said. I realized I was breathing hard, so I held the phone away and took a few deep breaths. "A big man with a handlebar mustache went inside the shop earlier."

"Yeah, I saw him."

"I'm going to wait a while. If he leaves, I'm going to tail him. You stay with Merrick whenever he leaves."

"Okay."

I ended the call and stared at the shop. A while later, a Jeep Cherokee drove into the parking lot, and a man with blond hair got out and strolled inside. However, the big man didn't leave. I looked down the road and saw King's nondescript sedan. A few more minutes ticked by, and Ernie called me. I didn't want to talk to him right then and explain that I'd confronted Merrick without him. I let the call go to voice mail, then texted him.

I already talked to Merrick. I'll talk to you soon.

The clouds overhead darkened, and big rain drops pelted my car, the plinking sound a distraction. I flicked the windshield wipers on once, then gave up on having a good view as the rain came down in a rush. Then just as suddenly, the storm passed. The air was refreshing. I rubbed my neck, kneading out a tension knot. My phone buzzed with another text from Ernie.

Looking at Eklund's internet activity. He's been researching the Colorado Citizens Militia.

"I'll be damned." I stared at the shop for a second, decided I couldn't wait for the big man any longer, nor could I put off Ernie any longer. I called King to let him know I was leaving the scene, then drove downtown.

"I can't believe you went in there and confronted Merrick without me." Ernie swore and paced in front of his desk. He was as angry as I'd seen him in a long time. "I told you to wait for me, Sarah. We're dealing with a militia group, not a church social group. Surely you realize how they could be."

"I told you, I saw the big guy that I'd seen before with Merrick, and I couldn't wait for you any longer before I went in. I needed to know who he was."

Ernie swore again. "I know you can handle yourself, but this time, you should have had backup. Look how it turned out."

"I waited for you."

"I got tied up on a call with one of Eklund's friends." His surliness wasn't going away. "You should've waited for me."

"I didn't think I could wait for you."

Normally I might have been angry at Ernie for trying to tell me what to do, but in this case, of course, he was right. I'd been lucky that nothing had happened, that a more serious confrontation hadn't occurred. I didn't want to admit it, but I did like that Ernie had my back.

Captain Rizzo, who had been standing off to the side, raised a hand. "Ernie, take it easy. It's over now." Then he locked hard eyes on me. Tension hung thick in the air. "However, Sarah, be careful, huh? It could've gotten ugly."

"You know me," I said. "I can take care of myself."

"You always have," Rizzo said. "And you've gotten yourself out of some bad situations. But we don't know who we're dealing with." He wasn't going to dress me down in front of Ernie, but it was clear he wasn't too happy with me. He drew in a breath, let it out slowly. "The last thing I need is some militia group targeting the police because they think we're harassing them."

"I get it," I said, knowing I could've waited for backup. Then, more than ready to change the subject, I said, "We're missing something here."

"Then let's find that something before we hassle Merrick anymore," Rizzo said.

I ran a hand through my hair. "Ernie, will you sit down?" He glared at me, then sank into his chair. He grabbed an unlit cigar and jammed it in his mouth. That would keep him quiet. I went on. "Tell me about Ivan Eklund's internet activity."

He tapped his monitor. "Last week, he had a number of searches for militia groups, specifically ones in Colorado, including the Colorado Citizens Militia. It's only been in the last week or so. Nothing before that. I didn't find any activity on porn sites of any kind, let alone underground sites that specialize in kiddie porn. Nothing that would indicate we had a pedophile on our hands."

"Nothing?" Rizzo asked.

Ernie shook his head. "Not a thing."

I held up a hand. "Gary Pickett doesn't want to tell us about this militia group, but we know he's probably involved in it. Then we find out that Eklund–who lives close to where Logan Pickett's body was found–had a budding interest in militia groups. What's going on here? What's the connection?"

Rizzo stared at me. "Has this militia group, the Colorado Citizens Militia, been involved in illegal activities?"

I nodded. "According to Mike Crozier, the FBI agent I talked to, a couple of members are suspected of some theft, but other than that, nothing. Is it a stretch that the group might have kidnapped Logan Pickett to help his dad take him out of state? I don't know."

Rizzo leaned against the edge of Spats's desk and crossed his arms. "So this new guy that you saw at the gun range, the one that you met with Gary Pickett and Merrick, he provided an alibi for Merrick?"

"A new alibi," I said. "If they're all to be believed. The other guy said that Merrick was with him both on Saturday night, and on Tuesday night. But there's a problem with that." Rizzo looked at me, curious, and waited for me to go on. "Merrick said that he was bowling on Saturday night, and then he went home. So why would this new guy need to give a different alibi? Did Merrick lie to me before because he didn't want me to know about the militia group?"

"Probably." Rizzo rubbed his chin and thought about that. "Where was Gary at these times?"

"I can answer that," Spats said as he waltzed into the room. He looked around at us, sensing the tension in the room. "What's going on?"

Ernie pointed at me. "Sarah talked to Merrick, went into the gun range like Calamity-effing-Jane and she almost gets her ass blown off."

I rolled my eyes. "Don't be so dramatic, Ernie." I turned to Spats. "You know that guy that I'd seen Gary and Merrick with? He was at the gun range, and he gave Merrick his alibi, albeit a new one. They bowled, then were at the gun range Saturday night for a militia meeting."

Spats's gaze went between Ernie and me. "I know you can take care of yourself, Sarah, but I'd hate to see something happen to you." Amusement crept into his eyes. Ernie and I butted heads more, and Spats played the peacemaker.

"I'm fine," I said.

Rizzo turned to Spats. "What do you have on Gary?"

Spats moved toward his desk. Rizzo stepped aside, and Spats sat down. He held up a piece of paper. "I finally got the records from the phone company, pinging Gary's phone for his whereabouts. Gary was in Audra's neighborhood around the time Logan disappeared. Then he was at his house for less than an hour. After that he went to the Gold Creek Gun Range, and he stayed there for a couple of hours. After that, it appears he drove around, then went back to his house and was there the rest of the night." Spats glanced at us. "Or at least his phone was in those places."

"So he lied when he said that he searched for Logan, then was with his girlfriend, Kristi Arnott, the rest of the night?" I asked.

"He was with her, but only for a little while," Spats said. "I finally talked to Kristi, and she said she was at Gary's house Saturday evening. He, however, called her and said that his son was missing and he was looking for the kid. Then Gary came home for about a half-hour or so, around eight, then he was gone until about eleven. She dodged questions for a while, then finally admitted that Gary had wanted her to lie for him." He flashed a smile. "She didn't do a very good job. Apparently, when Gary came home, he'd told her he needed to go out. He never told her where, and she didn't ask." Spats leaned back. "According to his phone, Gary was at the gun range."

"What about the night Logan was murdered?"

"She wasn't with him then."

I thought about that. "What'd she say about Logan being missing?" I asked.

Spats shrugged. "She believed him. I didn't get the impression she was that close to Logan, or that upset about his being missing. And she didn't think Gary might've been lying to her about what had happened to Logan."

"So," Rizzo said. "This other guy, Gary, and Merrick, were all at the gun range last Saturday at a militia meeting."

"And they didn't want the police to know about that," I inferred. "What about the SUVs Merrick was renting? And I saw him buying fertilizer. Are they planning something?"

"What about our theory that they're all somehow involved in the kid's disappearance?" Spats asked. "Did Gary hire the militia to kidnap his kid? Did the group have the kid with them Saturday night at the gun range?"

"Where's the proof of that?" I asked. "I've never heard of a militia group kidnapping anybody, although there's a first time for everything."

Spats lifted his shoulders. "Are they a rogue element within the group?"

Rizzo impatiently tapped his thigh. "I don't know about that. From what I know, militia groups don't do crimes for money."

"Or maybe it's this guy Eklund," Ernie speculated.

"Except that so far we haven't found any reason to believe he took the kid," I pointed out.

Ernie jabbed his cigar at his monitor. "What about Eklund's

internet history, that shows his interest in the Colorado Citizen's Militia?"

"Is he a member of that group?" Rizzo asked.

"Not that I can find," Ernie said. "It's not like they keep a list of members anywhere. I asked Oakley if he'd heard about Eklund being in a militia from anyone his team interviewed, and no one mentioned it. I've been circling back to those people to specifically ask about that. So far, everyone says that doesn't sound like Eklund."

"Why's he looking at the same militia group that Gary seems to have a connection with?" I mused, not seeing the answer.

"Keep on that," Rizzo told Ernie. His eyes went to each of us. "A killer's still out there." He didn't need to say more about the urgency of the investigation. He snapped his fingers at me. "What's the name of that FBI agent? I've got to contact him right away."

"Crozier." I wrote down his name and number and handed it to Rizzo.

He rubbed his forehead. "All we need is for the FBI to believe that we suspected illegal militia activity and didn't notify them. I'll give Crozier a call." With that, he left the room.

Ernie leaned forward and gave me a hard look. I held up a hand. "Don't start with me."

"I know you think you've got it all under control ..." he began.

My desk phone rang. "It's Oakley," I said. I smiled sweetly at Ernie, but I was grateful for the interruption. "Hold that thought. Maybe forever."

He swore at me as I picked up the phone, but this time, at least, he had a twinkle in his eyes.

CHAPTER TWENTY-NINE

I picked up the phone. "Spillman."

"Hey," Oakley said. "I just got back from the school where that guy Eklund took school pictures. I thought you might like to hear this."

"What's that?"

"The school has a security guard working there, her name is Susan Palmer. I was asking her about Eklund, what she knew about him, how he acted around the kids, and it was interesting."

"Interesting how?"

He didn't answer for a second. He was in a noisy place, and the sounds of loud background conversations made it hard to hear him. "Tell you what, you go over to the school and talk to her. I'll tell her you're coming. After you do that, we'll talk."

He didn't want to prejudice me before I talked to her. "Okay, I'll head over there."

"Roosevelt Elementary. On Jackson Street." He disconnected, and I put my phone in my pocket.

"What was that about?" Ernie asked. His ire with me had evaporated.

I told him. "I guess I'll go to the school now. See what else you can find on Eklund's internet searches."

"I'm working on it."

"And I'll see what I can find on this gentleman with the handlebar mustache," Spats said.

"Gentleman. Right" Ernie rolled his eyes.

I could hear Spats and Ernie conversing as I walked down the hall.

When I arrived at Roosevelt Elementary School, the parking lots were almost empty. In the playground, a mother pushed her little girl on a swing. The same feeling that I'd had before, that remnant of sadness when I saw the playground swings, washed over me again, and I had to quickly tamp it down. I rubbed at the knot in my neck, drew in a breath to try to blow out some of the tautness I felt, and walked to the school entrance. No one else was around. I tried the door. Locked. I peeked through the window and into a reception area near the door. A desk sat empty. I tapped on the door and waited, then knocked louder. A woman with short curly hair finally came out of the office and gave me a small wave. She came to the door and unlocked it.

"Susan?" I asked.

She took in my badge and the gun on my hip. "Are you Detective Spillman?"

"I am."

She signaled for me to follow her into the reception area. The school was graveyard quiet. "Detective Oakley said you'd be coming. I'm not sure why he wants me to talk to you, too, but come on in."

We moved past a desk and into a smaller office. She was younger than I expected, with an athletic build and kind eyes.

She leaned against the side of a desk and pointed at a chair. "Have a seat. I was just about to leave, and I do have an appointment at the hairdresser, so if we could make this fast ..."

"Sure." A quick glance revealed all that was in the tiny office. A book case with a few notebooks on the shelves, a few plants on the desk. "You know that Logan Pickett was found dead yesterday?"

She fiddled with a watch on her wrist. "Yes, I did hear that. That's really upsetting." She glanced away. "You get to liking all the kids." She shook her head sadly.

"I get it. Ivan Eklund lived down the block from where Logan's body was found. You've heard about Eklund, that he's dead?"

"Yes." She nodded and drew in an unhappy breath. "It's a lot to take in. Detective Oakley said he's conducting the investigation on Ivan's death. He had some questions, said it's routine." She appraised me. "I heard from another teacher that Ivan may have committed suicide, but if you're asking questions as well, it makes me wonder, was it murder?"

"We have to look at everything."

She glanced at her watch. "So what do you want to ask me?"

"How well did you know Ivan?"

She exhaled through open lips, the sound loud in the quiet room. "As I told Detective Oakley, I didn't know Ivan very well. I'd see him around the school when he was taking portraits, and I'd say hello to him. He was here a month or so ago, and then he was back for retake day."

"Retake day?"

"Taking pictures for the kids that missed the first photo day."

"Oh, I see."

She smiled. "I tried to get to know him a little bit, you know, somebody coming in and out of the school, I need to keep an eye on them. He seemed like a nice guy, and he was really good with the kids. They seemed to like him. A lot of the teachers did too."

I shifted in the chair, the hard seat uncomfortable. "Did you ever hear that Ivan might've done anything inappropriate to the kids, anything suspicious?"

"Do you mean do I think he's a pedophile?" She didn't pull any punches. "Do I think he was doing things to kids that he shouldn't?" I nodded and waited. "Oakley asked the same thing, and I told him no." She kept her eyes on me. "I know, sometimes the nicest guys can be the predators, but I didn't see that in Ivan. I never saw him look at the kids funny, I never saw him acting like he was getting too close to any of them, that he was trying to manipulate them. And I never heard anyone else say that, either."

"In your interactions with him, did he ever act strange, depressed or anything like that?"

She shook her head. "The only thing that I thought was a little weird was that one time, he was asking me about some woman in the neighborhood, and then he also asked about a little boy, the one who liked comic books. At first I didn't know who he meant, but then he described the boy, and I realized it was Logan Pickett." She smiled warmly, thinking about Logan. "He was a sweet kid."

Now I knew why Oakley wanted me to hear this. "What woman did Eklund mean? One of the parents?"

"That's the weird part. I wasn't sure. He didn't have the name of the woman. And it didn't seem like he was asking about Logan's mom. He tried to describe her, but it basically sounded like half the mothers in this school. I wasn't able to help."

"And how did he describe this woman?"

She pursed her lips. "He just said that she was taller, with darker hair." She laughed. "See? That sounds like a bunch of the mothers here, don't you think?"

"Yes," I said, even though I really didn't know whether that was true or not. But it was a rather general description. "Why did he want to know about this particular woman?"

"He never said."

"What exactly did Ivan want to know about Logan?"

"I thought it was odd for him to be asking. He wanted to know where he lived, if I knew what his home situation was, was he by himself after school. If so, who was watching him if his parents were at work?"

I cleared my throat. "And didn't that make you suspicious?"

"Initially, yes. But when I asked Ivan why he was wondering, he said something vague about how Logan seemed to have an aura about him, that he thought Logan might be a great child model. And Ivan wanted to talk to the parents about that. I told him he would need to ask somebody at the school for the parents' contact information. I told the principal about it, but I don't know whether she talked to Ivan about his questions."

Susan may have bought Ivan's story, but I did not. "Did Ivan ever follow up on that?"

"I don't know." She pointed out the door. "I got busy with other things, and I didn't think about it. And since that conversation, I haven't seen Ivan at the school, so I don't know what he was doing." Then she paused. "Wait." Another pause as she lightly slapped her forehead. "Huh. I forgot this until just now. The other day–Friday– I saw him in the parking lot. He was sitting in his car, watching the kids come out of the school. I was going to go talk to him, and then I got distracted by some of the kids. I didn't see him after that."

"You'd never seen him watching the kids at other times?"

"No."

"Did Ivan ever express any interest in having other students be models for him?"

"No, at least not to me. Oakley might've heard differently

from some of the teachers, but I never heard that Ivan was interested in that."

"You never caught Ivan with a child alone, never saw him try to leave the school with a child?"

"No."

"Do you know of anyone else who was concerned about Ivan, anyone who questioned his behavior around children?"

She pursed her lips. "No." Another glance at the watch. I knew what was coming. "I'm sorry, but I do need to go," she said. "I told all this to Detective Oakley. Except for that part about Ivan being in the parking lot."

I stood up. "Thank you for your time. He and I talked, and he wanted me to hear for myself what you had to say."

She headed to the door, and waited until I went into the outer reception area. The quiet in the school was eerie. "I hope it was helpful. If I think of anything else, I'll call Detective Oakley."

She walked with me outside, and the door locked behind us. The mother and her girl were gone from the playground, and it was empty. I walked to my car, and Susan got into an older model Subaru. She waved at me as she drove out of the parking lot. I was about to leave when I got a text. I looked at it. Harry.

Meant to text earlier. Hang in there. I love you.

I stared at the screen for a minute. It was the perfect thing right at that moment, when I was irritated about how things had gone down at Merrick's gun shop and how unhappy Rizzo was with me. I texted Harry that I loved him, too, put my phone away, and then drove out of the parking lot.

CHAPTER THIRTY

I called Oakley from the car.

"What do you think?" he asked, a curious edge in his voice.

"I see why you wanted me to talk to Susan Palmer." He laughed. I told him about my conversation, and that Susan Palmer had remembered that Eklund had been at the school the previous Friday. "Eklund had a thing for Logan Pickett," I said. "But my questions are, did he have something for any other kids? From what I've heard, the answer is no. And was Eklund really just looking for a model, a subject for his art, as he said, or was he looking for a victim? The security officer, Susan, didn't think Eklund was asking about other kids, just Logan. What about any other teachers you talked to?"

"That's a dead end. We interviewed every teacher at that school that had dealings with Eklund, and none of them said he showed any unusual interest in the kids, or Logan, for that matter. When Eklund was around, things seemed on the up and up. He was nice to the kids, but nobody saw anything suspicious. We've also talked to several of the parents, and it's the same thing.

Those that met him say he seemed aboveboard in every single way. I had a lengthy conversation with the principal, and she said the photography firm they use does background checks, and I checked with that firm. Eklund passed the check. Everything with him looked good. I can't find anything screwy in his background or from checking with other people who knew him."

"Yeah, Ernie Moore has been going over the records you provided."

"There's a lot there. Moore told me that you noticed that Eklund was recently reading a militia group website. Does that pertain to your investigation?"

"It might. The boy's father may be involved in a militia group."

"You have any other possible suspects in the kid's death?" he asked.

I'd turned onto Broadway. I hadn't told Ernie, but I was going to talk to Gary Pickett again. There were a lot of things he needed to account for. "I'm still looking at the family. I've got some suspicions about his dad, but nothing concrete yet."

"If I find anything more on Eklund, I'll let you know."

Before he ended the call, I said, "Have you heard anything on Eklund's autopsy yet?"

"No. Jamison thought he might have it this afternoon or early tomorrow, but nothing yet. He said you were looking for a rush on it, and he's trying to get to it."

I laughed wryly. "Yeah, it's taking longer than I'd wish. We need to know whether Eklund committed suicide or not."

"I do too. If it's a suicide, I want to move on to other things."

It was a blunt statement, but true. He ended the call, and I drove in silence, my mind whirling on everything I had. Lots of pieces of information, but nothing yet that connected into a cohesive story about how and why Logan Pickett died.

It was almost five when I neared Gary's house. I parked in

front, knocked and rang the bell. He didn't answer, so I went back to my car and looked up his office address, then drove there. His silver Toyota Tacoma was parked in front. I parked next to it and walked inside. The reception counter was deserted, and seventies rock was playing on a radio. Beyond the counter was a short hallway and a door. I waited a moment, then heard Gary's voice. I moved around the counter and down the hall without announcing myself. I tiptoed around a corner and looked in a doorway. Gary was sitting behind a long oak desk, the phone to his ear. He was staring at a computer monitor, and then he looked up. Anger flashed across his face.

"Hey, I need to call you back," he snapped to whoever was on the other end of the line. He slammed the phone down and swore at me. "What the hell are you doing here?"

I was careful to remain neutral. "I won't take much of your time, but a few things have come up that I don't understand."

"I don't have to tell you anything."

I moved into the room without being asked and sat down in a chair across from him. "You're right, you don't have to tell me a thing. I'm not here to accuse you or cause problems, I'm here to fill in the blanks. I need everything I can get my hands on, and you answering my questions is helpful."

"I'm not guilty of anything." His words were clipped, angry.

I tried for calm, hoping it would de-escalate his anger. "Gary, some things aren't adding up." He started to protest, and I held up a hand. "You said that you hadn't called anybody last Saturday night except for your girlfriend, Kristi Arnott. But we know that's not true. You called John Merrick, the owner of Gold Creek Gun Range."

"I forgot, okay?" he blurted out. "There's nothing wrong with me talking to somebody else that night, is there?"

"Are you and Merrick friends?"

He hesitated. "I know him from the gun range. Is that a crime?"

"No, but things don't seem to be adding up."

"Like what?" He crossed his arms and leaned back in his chair, defiant.

"Merrick says that you're just a customer, that he doesn't know you that well. And you're saying the same thing."

"I don't have to tell you who I'm friends with."

"Fair enough. What do you know about the Colorado Citizens Militia?"

He gazed at me levelly. "I've heard of them."

"From what I understand, you've been spending time on their Facebook page. Looks to me like you have a big interest in militia groups, that maybe you're familiar with this one in particular." He didn't respond. "Are you a member of any militia group?"

"That's none of your business, and it doesn't have anything to do with Logan."

I made a show of pondering that. "It looks to me like the group might be heading out of state. I've heard that maybe their headquarters are shifting to Idaho."

"I don't know anything about that," he said sullenly.

"A lot of people that we've talked to think that you wanted full custody of Logan, that maybe you were upset that you have to share custody of him."

"Audra's a horrible parent. That judge wasn't seeing my side of things."

"We talked to a lot of people, and they say that Audra *is* a good mother, but you were pretty strict with Logan."

"So? A kid needs to be raised well. Audra was too soft on him. That doesn't mean that I hurt him, no matter what anyone says." A clear reference to what I'd heard about Logan's arm getting broken when they were in San Diego.

"Let me be blunt. Did you want to take Logan and leave the state?" He stared at me, and I went on. "Here's one of the things I'm wondering. Maybe you were frustrated with Audra, with how she was a bad parent, so you thought the best thing would be to kidnap Logan and hide him with you. Things went bad, and he was accidentally killed." I tilted my head. "You have a nice knife collection. Was Logan playing with one of them, and he cut himself?"

"I was looking for Logan Saturday night. How could I have kidnapped him?"

"You had help."

He looked me dead in the eyes. "I can assure you that that's not the case."

That sounded sincere, but he was a good liar. "Gary, why don't you level with me? It'd be a whole lot easier. Do you know more about your son's death than you're telling me?"

"No," he spat at me. "I didn't do anything to Logan."

"Okay, what about Merrick? I hate to keep bringing it up, but you seem more than just a customer at his shop. I saw him meet you at that Thai restaurant last night."

He rocked in his chair casually. "Why did you follow us?"

"I'm trying to find out what happened to your son. When people aren't upfront about what's going on, it makes my job harder."

"I met him for dinner, so what?"

"What about the big guy with the handlebar mustache. Who's he?"

"None of your business," he repeated. "He doesn't have anything to do with Logan's death."

"Give me the man's name, and we'll talk to him, clear this all up."

He shook his head.

"You were at Gold Creek Gun Range Saturday night with Merrick and that other guy. We pinged your phone location."

He flew to his feet and pointed at the door. "You're barking up the wrong tree. I didn't have anything to do with my son's death, and I ought to sue you for insinuating that. This is part of the problem with this country, our law enforcement isn't doing what they're supposed to be doing." He was growing more agitated, spittle on his lip. "I served my country, and I did things overseas that I never should've had to do. And what do I get for it? High taxes, the government spending money everywhere they shouldn't, telling us what to do, and all kinds of other problems. Do you understand what's happening to this country?" He shook his head in disgust. "Instead of looking at that, people turn a blind eye to it. And now that my son is dead, you want to accuse me of kidnapping and killing him? If you think somebody is capable of doing that, look at my wife. She was the bad mother. She didn't watch out for him. You want to ask me any more questions, we'll do it with my lawyer present. Now get the hell out of my office."

I stood up slowly. "I'm sorry for your loss, and that you feel we're not doing the best we can. I assure you we are. And I can also tell you that I will find out who kidnapped and killed your son."

I stepped backwards and went out the door. When I went by the front counter, the music still played softy, but it wasn't enough to dissipate the anger that emanated from Gary's office.

CHAPTER THIRTY-ONE

"What took you so long?" Ernie asked when I got back to my desk.

I took my time answering. He wasn't going to be happy with me. "I talked to Gary Pickett."

Ernie took just as much time contemplating me as I did in answering. His face twisted up as he went through a range of emotion. Then he took the cigar out of his mouth and slowly put it in the ashtray, deliberately letting me know he was calming himself. "Oh? How'd it go?"

Spats looked up from his desk, eyebrows arched, watching our exchange with amusement.

I told them the conversation. "Gary clammed up, so we won't get anything else out of him now."

Ernie folded his hands and put them on the desk. "What do your instincts tell you about Gary?"

"I'm not sure. I get the sense that his anger comes not as much from concern about his son as it does from concern about our prying into his personal life."

"We can't eliminate him as a suspect," Spats said.

"No."

Ernie seemed in a charitable mood, not picking at me for going to see Gary alone. "What did you learn from the security woman at the school?"

"Our man, Eklund, had an interest in Logan," I said as I sat down at my desk. I felt a pounding begin, the sure sign an exhaustion headache was coming on. "He'd been interested in Logan before he disappeared, wondering about Logan's family. Eklund also wanted to know if Logan could model for him."

"Model for him?"

"That's right. Eklund was only interested in Logan, though. He wasn't asking about any other kids. Not only that, he was asking about a woman in the neighborhood."

Ernie nodded thoughtfully. "Did he mean Audra?"

"Yeah, sounds like it. He was digging for information. Maybe he was trying to find out how easy or hard it would be to kidnap Logan. If he thinks he's dealing with a mom who isn't paying enough attention to her son, then he could go after him."

Ernie grunted. "I don't know. I still don't like the fact that we can't find any other indication that he might be into little kids. You'd think he'd have something on his laptop, or we'd find some pictures that he took of kids, something like that."

"Yeah," I said. "I keep coming back to that myself." I ran a hand through my hair, frustrated. "I wish we could get a break in this. I don't know what I'm missing."

"There's always a first time for a pedophile," Spats interjected. "But I agree with you. Long before somebody would resort to taking a kid, he'd likely have something in his history that would indicate he was on that path. That's always what I understood."

I nodded. "I'd like to know how this militia group ties into all these guys. I tried to give Gary an out, asking him if he'd kidnapped Logan, to take him out of state, and then Logan was accidentally killed. It's clear he wanted Logan away from Audra."

"He didn't bite?"

I shook my head. "No, he got angry."

Spats leaned to his left so he could see me sitting at my desk. "I feel like I'm getting more of an education on these militia groups than I want. I just watched a video on how a group from Colorado goes down to the Colorado-New Mexico border to help," he used rabbit ears to make quotation marks, "with the border patrol, trying to catch people coming across the border. It's a very interesting subculture that's been growing in the last several years. I looked at a bunch of these sites that Gary has been on, but so far I can't find hide nor hair of Merrick's buddy with the handlebar mustache."

I leaned forward and grabbed my mouse. "How much have you looked on Gary's Facebook page?"

"I poked around a little bit, but I got sidetracked. I'll get back to it."

"I'll give it a go." It took me a minute to get to Gary's Facebook page. I began scrolling through his posts. "A lot of them have to do with right wing politics, or anti-government sentiments. He also has a lot of stuff about the Marines."

"He's not too proud of that," Spats said. "The posts are about things that he wasn't happy about."

I scrolled, let the page load more posts, and looked more. Ernie typed, muttering under his breath. I heard Rizzo in another room talking to someone. I kept going through Gary's posts, and after quite a while, I was rewarded. A picture of Gary with the man with a handlebar mustache appeared on the screen. "There he is."

Spats came over and poked a finger at the monitor. "You found that on his Facebook page? Where?"

"Way back in the history."

"Oh yeah?" Spats studied the monitor curiously.

Ernie rolled his chair over and squinted at the screen. "Oh, he's a handsome fella."

I glanced at him with a grin. "Now we need to find his name."

Gary had a link in the post, but when I went to it, it had been removed. Then I clicked on the photo and got lucky. He had tagged the other man. His name was Dean Casper.

Ernie's eyebrows went up. "Casper?"

"Like the ghost?" This from Spats.

"He wasn't friendly," I said dryly.

Ernie studied the picture. "Let me see about a background search on him. Give me a little time."

I glanced at the computer clock. It was already eight o'clock. "I need to head home, talk to Harry, maybe get a little bit of sleep. You guys should do the same."

Spats yawned and stretched. "Yeah, I better get home. I'll do some work from home though."

I stood up. "Me too."

Ernie rolled back to his desk and nodded at his computer. "I found Casper's address." He frowned at me. "Before *we* go talk to him, let me find out what I can on him. We'll talk to him tomorrow, okay?"

I was too tired to argue. "Sure. See you guys in the morning. If you find anything noteworthy, call me."

He held up a hand, a small wave. "You do the same."

Weariness dragged on me as I parked my car in the garage and went inside. Fleetwood Mac played from the speakers in the living room. That meant Harry was in a mellow mood. If it was something harder, AC/DC, or some '80s hair bands, I knew he was in an energetic mood. An empty pizza box lay on the counter.

"Sarah?" he called out.

I kicked off my shoes and hauled myself into the living room. He had on shorts and a T-shirt, a glass of Scotch in his hand. "How was your day?"

I went over and sat down next to him. I let out a sigh. "Right at the moment, I feel like I'm spinning my wheels. I hope something breaks soon."

He put his arm around me. "I put some leftover pizza in the fridge."

"Maybe later."

He surveyed me. "Want to talk about it?"

I shook my head. He held the glass to me, and I took a sip. The burning feel of the alcohol felt good, soothing. I wasn't a big drinker, not wanting to dull my senses, but a little right at that moment was nice.

I put the cool glass to my forehead and rubbed it around. "That feels good. I've had a headache for the last little while."

He gnawed his lower lip. "You're not going to like this."

I exhaled. "What?"

"Your sister dropped by. She wanted to talk to you about your mother's sixtieth birthday party this Sunday."

I swore under my breath. I had forgotten about it. I didn't have time to think about it, and yet I knew I needed to be there. I handed the glass back to Harry a little too forcefully. Some spilled on his hand. He laughed and licked the liquid off his finger. "What's with you two?"

"You know how it is. Diane and I have never gotten along."

"I know. You got her out of a jam when you were in college, and she wasn't grateful enough. Maybe it's time to let it go?"

There was more to it than that. I'd not shared it with Harry, and wasn't sure I would. "Diane has never seen me as an equal. I was just there to clean up whatever mess she made. You wouldn't understand."

He finished the Scotch and set the glass on the coffee table. "Maybe I would. Try me."

I stood up and began pacing, my mind briefly returning to the girl in the playground swing. "Diane was always the perfect one, at least that's what Mom and Dad thought." I exhaled. "They still think that. She has the perfect career, the perfect husband, the perfect children, and all that. I'm the one who barely made it out of school. And for some reason, I never felt like they thought police work was quite the right career choice for me. A little too blue-collar for them, you know? "

"You're not 'just a cop,' you're a lead homicide detective. And you're a damn good one."

I stopped and put my hands on my hips. "Harry, I appreciate your saying that. I really do. But sometimes those words can't erase the past."

He leaned back against the couch, his dark eyes full of sorrow, with a hint of his own ache from my refusal to let him in. "I know she hurt you."

A mix of emotions swelled within me, pain, weariness, anger. It was too much to deal with now. I sat down next to him again. "I don't want to talk about it."

He wrapped his arms around me again and kissed the top of my head. "You have to call your sister. She's still going to need an answer about Sunday."

I shook my head vehemently. "Not now, okay?"

"You can call her about the party tomorrow." I could tell he was smiling. "You'll deal with your sister when you're ready to."

"Yeah."

"Hold on." He got up, went into the kitchen, and returned with a slice of pizza on a plate. "Eat."

"Oh, that tastes good," I said as I took a bite.

He sat down next to me and waited while I ate. My mind was still on Diane.

"She doesn't get me," I muttered. "She never did."

He put a hand on my knee. "Seriously. Try me," he repeated. "Tell me about it."

I nodded and put the plate down. I didn't like talking about this part of my past–this thing wrapped in shame–even with Harry. Maybe it was time to start to trust him, even if just a little bit. I drew in a breath. "A long time ago I made a mistake. I was a sophomore in college, and Diane messed up, did something she shouldn't have. She was terrified it would screw things up for her, that she'd get kicked out of med school. I stepped in to help." I frowned. "Turns out, she got off scot-free, but what I did could've got me into trouble. I suppose it still could."

Harry thought about that. "You didn't have to help her?"

"She was my big sister," I snapped, "and all I ever wanted was her approval."

"I know," he said softly. "You thought this ... mistake ... would get that for you?"

I laughed derisively. "Yes. Of course it didn't. And you know Diane. She was, and is, completely oblivious. She's never acknowledged the risk I took, or that it could've cost me the career I wanted. But ...." I gnawed my lip. "I guess, in the end, it was my choice to help her."

He reached over and turned my head toward him, to look me in the eye. "You don't have to tell me what you did if you don't want to. You know I love you no matter what."

"Oh, Harry."

"Don't worry about Diane right now." He kissed me. "Relax."

I sighed heavily and returned the kiss, then held out a hand.

He used the remote control to turn off the music, then took my hand, and we went into the bedroom. We crawled under the covers, and he held me. Eventually he fell asleep. I lay awake for a long time, but I wasn't thinking of Diane. I couldn't get rid of the images of Logan Pickett lying in the dumpster.

CHAPTER THIRTY-TWO

The next morning, I was up early, having slept fitfully for only a couple of hours. A headache lingered at the base of my skull, and I took aspirin that finally took the edge off. After poring over case notes in the living room, I showered and dressed quietly while Harry slept. I checked my Glock, put it in my hip holster, and went into the kitchen. I fixed coffee and sat on the back porch with a blanket around me. The black night morphed into deep blue, then the sky turned pink and purple as the sun rose. I yawned and went back inside, threw a breakfast burrito into the microwave and turned on the television. I sat and mulled over the investigation as I ate and drank more coffee, the TV droning on in the background with the weather and traffic. Then something caught my ear, a story about a little boy. I almost dropped my coffee cup when the words filtered into my brain.

"... boy was last seen near his mother's house. If you have any information, please call the Denver Police Department."

I grabbed the remote and backed up the newsfeed.

"In other news, nine-year-old Samuel Quigley went missing from his home in the Cherry Creek neighborhood last night. His mother, Laurel Quigley, said that he was in the front yard playing when he disappeared. The police haven't named any suspects at the moment. Samuel was wearing blue jeans and a red T-shirt." A picture of Samuel appeared on the screen. He had brown hair and eyes, and a cute face. "If you have any information," the reporter continued, "call the Denver Police Department." She put on a friendly smile, as if what she'd just reported was meaningless. "Now let's turn to the weather ..."

I tuned out the rest. Samuel Quigley lived in the same neighborhood as Audra Pickett. Another boy missing near there? My cell phone rang. I didn't immediately recognize the number. I snatched it up. "Spillman."

"It's Oakley," his nasally voice said. "I got the autopsy results last night on Eklund. It doesn't look like a suicide to me. He didn't have enough gunshot residue on his hand. It doesn't add up, so I'm treating it as a murder."

I muted the TV. "Do you have any clues to who would've killed him?"

"Have you been going through the documentation I gave you? You'd think we'd find something in all of it, but there's nothing suspicious. Except that he was asking about that kid."

"I know. We've been pouring over everything you gave us, and I don't see anything there. Have you uncovered any enemies, any money trouble?"

"Nope. We're still talking to people who knew him, but so far this guy is about as clean as you can get. I can't find anything in his past, nobody says anything bad about him. He doesn't have a record, and he's not hanging around any kiddie porn websites. Nothing like that. Oh, did you hear about another kid going missing in that same neighborhood?"

"Yeah, I just saw it on the news."

"That means Eklund couldn't have taken that kid, what's his name?" he said matter-of-factly.

"Samuel Quigley. Do we have two kidnappers on our hands, or one that tried to set Eklund up?" I asked. "The first kidnapping goes bad, so the kidnapper makes Eklund look guilty."

"By murdering him," he mused. "That's a thought, but who?"

"That's the question of the hour."

"I've got to go," he said. "If you find anything to shed light on my investigation, I'd appreciate a call."

"Right back at you."

He disconnected, and I unmuted the TV. I watched for a bit, but they didn't say anything more about the missing boy. I turned it off and called the police station. I got routed until I was connected to the detective who had the Quigley case. I identified myself, then said, "Tell me what happened."

"Pretty basic," he said. "The kid was outside playing, the mom was making dinner. When she went out to get him for dinner, he was gone. She ran around the neighborhood looking for him, then called all her friends to help, but he was gone."

"What about the dad?"

"They're divorced. He lives in Ohio."

"Any clues?"

"Not a one, but we're still canvassing the neighborhood to see what people saw or heard. From what I can tell, the kid and his mom got along, and nobody sensed that there was any trouble. And nobody saw anything unusual in the neighborhood."

"I want to talk to the mother, if it's okay." I told him about my investigation.

"Sure thing, here's her address. Report back to me, okay? She might remember something else when she talks to you."

"I will." I wrote down the Quigley address, thanked him, and ended the call.

I reached for my coffee, then felt a sinking feeling in my stomach. Was there a serial kidnapper on the loose? Was it Gary Pickett? I got up and put my coffee cup in the sink, then heard the shower going. I went back into the master bath and called out to Harry, "Hey, I've got new developments on my case. I need to head out."

He stuck his head out the shower door. "Have a good day."

I walked over and kissed him.

"When this is finished, I want a little of your time."

I glanced down. "I could arrest you for indecent exposure."

He burst out laughing, then grinned at me lasciviously. "Tonight? Bring your handcuffs?"

I kissed him again. "You got it." I wiped the moisture from my face, gave him a shameless look as my eyes roved over his body, and walked out.

Laurel Quigley lived a few blocks from Audra Pickett in an older red-brick ranch. She answered the door, her face drawn, her eyes puffy. She hadn't slept at all. When I identified myself, she led me into a small living room that looked as if it had been decorated from an IKEA catalog. I took a seat at a couch with large cushions and she sat on a similar loveseat. I could smell the roses in a vase on a coffee table, the aroma not erasing the strained feel in the room.

"Did you know another little boy, Logan Pickett, who disappeared from his house last Saturday night?" I began.

She nodded. "Yes, I'd heard something on the news, and some of the mothers that I know said something. Since then, I've been watching Samuel more closely, and I just don't understand it." She dropped her head and wept. "I was fixing dinner and he went out front. I wasn't even gone that long," she said through sobs. "How could I be so stupid?" she chided herself.

"Don't be hard on yourself. It could happen to anybody. It takes no time at all for somebody to make a move."

"I know, but I should've done better."

"Tell me about Samuel."

She sniffed a few times, grabbed a Kleenex from an end table and blew her nose. "He's a good kid. We've had the talk about not going with strangers." She hesitated. "At least I did when he was younger. I thought he'd be more careful. I don't think he would've gone with a stranger, but I guess you never know"

"Would he run away?"

"I don't think so. He's a pretty happy boy, and no matter what anybody believes, I'm a good mom. There wouldn't be any reason for him to run."

"He's a good student?"

"He works hard. He struggles some, and I have him working with a reading tutor. I started him with some comics to help with that, then simpler reading. He's getting better. He loves baseball, and we go to the Rockies games when we can. When he's in Ohio, his dad takes him to the Cleveland Indians games. Other than that, it's not been too bad. He spends part of the summer with his dad. That does give me a break, but truthfully, I miss Sam when he's gone." She sighed. "I don't know what else to tell you."

He sounded a bit like Logan, I thought. "Do you have other children?"

She shook her head. "Samuel's an only child."

"Is your husband in Ohio now?"

"Yes, the police there went to talk to him."

That eliminated him as a suspect, I thought. "Have you seen anybody suspicious in the neighborhood lately?"

Another shake of her head. "Not that I recall. I drove all around last night, looking for him, and I didn't see anybody that I didn't know. The neighbors helped as well." She dabbed her eyes. "Samuel was gone."

"Are you familiar with a man named Ivan Eklund?"

She thought about that. "No, I don't think so."

"He takes pictures of the students at Roosevelt Elementary."

"Samuel goes there, but I didn't know who took the school pictures."

"Have you seen a silver Toyota Tacoma truck or a blue Honda Pilot around the neighborhood?" I asked, thinking about the vehicles Gary Pickett and Ivan Eklund drove.

"It doesn't sound like anybody I know."

"Have you seen anything different from the norm recently?"

She pushed a strand of hair from her face. "No, nothing has seemed out of the ordinary."

"Would you mind if I looked in his bedroom?"

"Of course not. The officer who came over already did, but you can look as well."

I followed her to a small bedroom at the back of the house. It was cozy, with a small bed with a Rockies comforter on it, pictures of the Colorado Rockies teams on the walls, a desk, and a dresser. Two baseball trophies sat on the windowsill.

"He's on a little league team," she said when I noticed the trophies. "He's really good."

Sitting on the desk was a picture of Samuel in his baseball uniform, holding a bat. The typical pose of a kid in baseball. He was cute. It reminded me of a similar picture I'd seen of Logan on Audra's Facebook page.

"Nothing seems out of place," she said. She watched me closely. "Will you be looking for Samuel?"

I shook my head. "I'm working on a different investigation, but if my case overlaps with your son's disappearance, I'll let the investigators who are working on his kidnapping know. I'm sure the other detectives are doing what they can." I didn't have the heart to tell her that at this point, there wasn't a lot the police could do. "I would continue to look for him. Maybe somebody saw or heard something."

"I will," she said. "I already told my work I wouldn't be in."

"What do you do?"

"I'm in software development." She threw up her hands. "How could I work with this?"

"I understand."

I followed her back to the front door and thanked her for her time. I went outside and as I walked to my car, I called the detective in charge of the Quigley kidnapping, and gave him a rundown of my conversation with Laurel. She hadn't given me any information that he didn't have, and he sounded disappointed. He thanked me and I swiped over to a call from Ernie.

"You need to get back to the office."

I opened my car door and slid behind the wheel. "Why?"

"Ivan Eklund has a connection with Dean Casper."

CHAPTER THIRTY-THREE

Time was short and things needed to happen fast. People were asking questions, and soon someone would know.

What about the new boy? Would he listen, would he obey? If so, then everything would be okay. And the agonizing pain would stop.

Calling from outside the door, "Turn out the light."

After a moment, the sliver of light underneath the door vanished.

Making sure the hood was down, then opening the door.

"Are you hungry?"

The little boy on the bed nodded.

"You're being good?"

His voice quivered. "Yes."

"What do you want?"

"To ... stay here," he answered in a tiny, halting voice.

"Do you think you could like it here?" He didn't answer. "Tell me you want to stay here."

"I want to stay," he finally said.

Ah, yes.

CHAPTER THIRTY-FOUR

"What do you have?" I said as I walked into the room.

Ernie glanced over his shoulder. "Where have you been?" His cigar bobbed as he talked. He saw my look, knowing how much I hated that habit, and he put the cigar into an ashtray.

"Did you watch the news this morning?" He shook his head. "Another little boy was kidnapped." Ernie grunted, and Spats muttered something under his breath. I filled them in. "I talked to the boy's mom. The pattern's similar to what happened to Logan. The child's name is Samuel Quigley. He was playing out front, and his mom was getting dinner ready. She says Samuel wasn't out front for very long, and when she went to get him, he'd vanished. Seems to me that maybe he knew his kidnapper because nobody saw or heard anything. The kid seemingly didn't scream for help, nothing."

"And here's an odd thing: Logan and Samuel look a lot alike. Both have brown hair and eyes. Both play baseball. I saw a photo of Samuel in his baseball uniform, and I saw the same kind of picture of Logan when I went through Audra's Facebook page."

Ernie drummed his fingers on the desk. "Somebody's kidnapping kids that look the same? That's a pattern, all right."

"A kidnapper wanting a certain type of kid?" Spats asked, then swiveled in his chair. "Obviously Ivan Eklund couldn't have kidnapped Samuel."

"A copycat?" I wondered aloud.

"Are there two kidnappers, or is there just one who killed Logan, then tried to make Eklund look guilty? Then he offs Eklund and makes it look like a suicide?" Spats asked. "And now the kidnapper grabs a second kid?"

"I asked Oakley the same thing." I rubbed my neck. "I hope to God the boy's found alive."

Ernie sucked in a breath and swore. "If there's a serial kidnapper and killer out there, good Lord, how are you ever going to protect every little kid that fits that description?" He swore again.

"We're running out of time," I muttered.

"Maybe I have something," Ernie said. "Take a look at this." He waved for me to come over to his desk. I looked over his shoulder. "Eklund was searching on militia groups, that kind of thing." He tapped the monitor, leaving a fingerprint. "He was looking at the Colorado Citizens Militia as well. And," he drew the word out, "he called Dean Casper, Mr. Handlebar Mustache himself." He looked at me triumphantly.

I took a deep breath. "You're kidding."

"Nope. I'll show you" Ernie grabbed a notebook sitting on the corner of his desk. "Check this out." He opened the notebook to a marked page of phone numbers. Then he ran his finger down the page. "See this number? It's Casper's home phone."

I glanced over at Spats. "What have you found out about Casper?" I leaned on the edge of his desk while he talked.

He perused some notes. "Casper works for a trucking company, so he's on the road quite a bit. He's worked at the same company for ten years. He's forty-two, never been to college, and he's an ex-Marine."

"Just like Gary Pickett and John Merrick," I observed.

"Yep. I ran a background check, and he had a little trouble with the law when he was younger, disturbing the peace. Other than that, his record's clean. No financial trouble that I could find. A little credit card debt, but nothing out of hand. He's been married for thirteen years, and he's been living here in Colorado for about that long."

"What's the wife's name?"

"Mallory. Oh, a Ford SUV is registered to him."

I nodded. "Yeah I saw him in that."

"He also owns a Hyundai Sonata."

"Where's he from?" Ernie asked.

Spats consulted his notes again. "Idaho."

Ernie glanced at me. "Isn't that where that FBI agent, Crozier, said the militia group was heading?"

"Yes."

"What else do you have on Casper?" I asked Spats.

"I've got some searches running, and I'll have the results in a while."

"Why would Eklund be talking to Casper?" I mused.

"And what are they hiding?" Spats put in.

I narrowed my eyes. "I think it's time to talk to Dean Casper."

Ernie sat back and crossed his arm. "And I think I should go with you."

I knew not to argue with him this time.

I turned to Spats. "See what else you can dig up on Casper, and if it'll be helpful, give me a call." Then I tipped my head at Ernie.

He grabbed the cigar and clamped it in the side of his mouth. "Let's go."

The Casper residence was a ranch house surrounded by tall trees on Monroe Street, not too far from Roosevelt Elementary School. As Ernie and I walked up the sidewalk, we heard the sounds of kids playing outside. We stood on the porch, and Ernie gave me a "Here goes" look and then rang the bell. We waited a moment, but no one answered.

"No one's home?" he asked. We both glanced at a red Hyundai Sonata that sat in the driveway.

He rang the bell again, and still no answer. He sighed impatiently, leaned off the porch and tried to look in a front window. "Too much glare," he muttered.

"Let's try this." I opened the screen door and knocked. A couple of times of that, and I concluded, "There's no one home. Or Casper sees us, and he's not going to answer."

"He better be smart enough not to try that."

"Or what?"

Ernie shrugged. "What do we do now?"

"How about trying Casper's work? Spats has the info," I said. "And I want to talk to Latoya Anderson again. She never called me back. I want to know whether she or Terrell saw Eklund's car."

"Yeah, okay. This guy Casper can't dodge us forever. I've got a lot of questions for him, and he better have some good answers."

"Let me drop you back at the office," I said as I started down the sidewalk.

Ernie followed, his quick movements showing his agitation. He got in. "Do me a favor."

"What?"

He pointed at the house. "The garage is detached."

He was correct. A single-car garage with a short driveway faced the street. "So?"

"Drive around to the alley so I can approach from the back of the house. I want to see if a car's in their garage."

I looked at him askance. "I don't know."

"What, it's no big deal."

"Uh-huh."

I started the car and drove around to the alley. As I neared the back of the Casper garage, Ernie held up a hand for me to stop.

"Wait here."

He got out, and he was surprisingly stealthy as he moved up to the detached garage behind the Casper house. He glanced into the backyard, then slipped around the side of the garage. He reappeared moments later and hurried back to my car.

"I looked in a side window, and the garage is empty," he said.

"So they're gone."

With that pronouncement, I drove out of the alley, drove to the station, and dropped him off. Then I drove to Latoya Anderson's house. I didn't have a chance to knock before the door opened.

"Detective Spillman," Latoya said. "I happened to look out and saw you. I'm so sorry for not calling you back."

I held my irritation in check. "That's all right. Another question came up."

She stepped onto the porch and pulled the door shut. "I don't want Terrell to hear," she said in a low voice. "He's having a hard time with Logan's death."

"That's understandable," I said. "My partner, Ernie Moore, talked to you about Ivan Eklund's death."

She looked puzzled. "Ivan? Oh, the photographer who died. Yes, I remember now."

"Eklund drove a light blue Honda Pilot SUV, and he took some pictures of Logan and Terrell riding their bikes."

"Oh?" Concern in her voice.

"Do you recall seeing that car in the neighborhood recently?"

"It doesn't sound familiar."

"What about a white SUV or a red Hyundai?"

She shook her head. "I don't pay that much attention to the cars around here. Neither sound familiar to me. Let me check with Terrell. He stayed home from school today." She hesitated. "Would you mind staying out here?"

I would've preferred to talk to Terrell myself, but she disappeared inside before I could ask. It was quiet as I waited, no one outside. Latoya returned a few minutes later.

"I asked him if he saw any of those cars recently, and he doesn't remember seeing any of them around."

"That's okay."

"I heard another boy is missing."

I frowned. "That's right."

She looked past me and shuddered. "It's scary."

"It is." What else could I say?

I thanked her for her time and walked back to my car. I drove away and initially was going to head back to the office, but I couldn't resist driving back by the Casper house. I parked, walked up the porch, rang and knocked again. Still no answer. I went back to my car, drove down the block and studied the house. The lawn was not nearly as manicured as some of the others in the neighborhood. It needed mowing, but it also had dry spots. Some of the bushes were dying as well. A rake and shovel leaned against the side of the house near a flower bed with dead plants in it, and it appeared someone was trying to clean things up. The Caspers didn't seem to care about their yard nearly as much as others in the neighborhood. Was that because they were leaving the state soon? The Hyundai Sonata was still in the driveway. I looked at the sky to the west. Dark clouds were creeping eastward. A good rain would help the Caspers' lawn. The time ticked by.

I was about to leave when a tall woman with dark hair walked out the front door and got into the Hyundai. Casper's wife? I felt like I'd seen her somewhere, but couldn't place her at the moment. She glanced around, and I ducked down, then peeked over the dash. She backed the Hyundai out of the driveway and went in the opposite direction. I waited until she'd turned the corner, then started my car and followed.

When I got to the corner, the Hyundai was a few blocks ahead. She got onto East First Avenue and went east. There was enough traffic near the Cherry Creek Mall that I could keep a good distance between her and me. She drove to Colorado Boulevard and stopped at a Target. I quickly pulled into a space down the next aisle and followed her into the store. She picked up bread and milk, then went to the checkout. I watched her pay, then was back in my car by the time she reached hers. She drove west, stopped at a gas station. I watched her pump gas, then she drove through the car wash. The car was already clean as far as I could tell, but it had been in an accident, the front bumper slightly scratched. After she pulled away from the station, I was disappointed when she went directly home from there.

I watched her get out of the car and stroll into the house. I waited a while, but she didn't come back out, and I never saw Dean's SUV. I got out and went up the walk again, rang the bell and waited.

No answer.

I knocked hard, but the woman didn't come to the door. Was she in the basement, or was music playing that drowned out the bell and my knocking? I put my ear close to the door, heard nothing. I hurried back to my car and stared at the house and the woman's car. Where was she? Finally, frustrated, I started the car, flipped a U-turn, and drove away.

CHAPTER THIRTY-FIVE

When I got back to the office, Spats and Ernie weren't there. Someone was talking in another room, but I tuned it out as I sat down at my desk and logged onto my computer, then reached in the drawer for some Tylenol. The headache had returned, a pounding at the back of my eyes.

I began a more in-depth search on Dean Casper, trying to find anything that we might have missed, when my phone rang.

"It's Spats," he said. "I'm with Ernie at Dean Casper's work. Ernie's speaking to some of the people Casper works with. I had a chat with his boss. Turns out the truckers are on the road a couple of weeks at a time, then they have several days off."

"Since I just saw him yesterday, I'll bet he's still in town."

"That'd be my guess, but he hasn't been seen by anybody from work."

"He hasn't been home, either." I told him about going back to the Casper house.

"Who was the woman?"

"Probably his wife. I'm going to see if I can find a picture of her. If we don't find Casper soon, I may stake out his house until he comes home."

He laughed. "Be careful, huh? My gut says Casper is dangerous."

"Don't worry."

"I'll call you if I get any more information."

"Thanks."

I went back to work. Tara had sent me all her research on Ivan Eklund's laptop, and I tackled all that as well. Did Ernie miss anything? He had a sharp eye, but there was so much information, it was possible. I swore under my breath. I knew *I* was missing something. That piece, that *something*, was there, at the base of my mind, just out of reach. I poured over all the research and notes I had, but didn't see anything new, and I couldn't see anything differently.

I got up and stretched, then sat back down and got on the internet. I looked up Dean's wife, Mallory. I found a Facebook page for her. It was the woman I'd seen at the Casper house, and I felt as if I'd seen her somewhere else. As I looked at her page, I noticed she hadn't posted anything recently, but starting about a year before, she'd shared a lot of pictures of her and a little boy with dark eyes and brown hair. She was a proud mother, and she commented frequently on her son, how he was doing in school and sports.

My cell phone rang and I hoped it was Ernie or Spats with a report on Dean Casper. Instead, it was my sister. I let out a breath that carried with it all the frustration and irritation that was so much a part of our relationship. I was tempted not to answer. But, no point in putting it off. I knew her. She would keep bugging me until I answered. I swiped at the screen.

"Hey, Diane," I said. "I'm kind of busy right now."

"You're always busy."

What is it about her tone that always gets under my skin?

She, in fact, has a pleasant voice, or so others tell me. But it grates on me, a screeching bird.

"What do you want?" I asked.

"We're getting together at Mom and Dad's on Sunday. You haven't forgotten, have you?"

"No."

Even though Harry had mentioned the party last night, I had forgotten again. Just like I do with Harry, I tend to forget family things. And I'd often had to miss get-togethers, canceling at the last moment because I was in the middle of an investigation. My parents begrudgingly understood because they knew the work I was doing was important. Even so, they weren't thrilled that I'd become a homicide detective rather than some more noble profession. However, Diane never let me forget that my job seemed to take priority over family.

"It's Mom's birthday. She's going to be sixty."

"I know how old she is," I muttered.

"We've been planning this party for months, and you said that no matter what, you'd be there."

I stared at the mountain of papers before me, wondering if I'd still be looking for Logan Pickett's killer on Sunday. I loved my mom, though, and I wouldn't miss her party. Besides, I'd get to see my little brother, Hunter. He's three years younger than me, and he's sweet and kind. A lot like Harry. And Hunter thinks Diane is a pain too. "I'll make sure I'm there."

"You and Harry are bringing the salad."

"Yes, we'll bring the salad."

She made an exasperated sound at me. "Why is it that every time I talk to you it seems like you're frustrated with me?"

My blood boiled. I stared at my monitor, thinking, "Because I always am." I stayed silent.

"You always blame me for everything," she went on. "I swear, even starting way back there when you blamed me for Uncle Brad's death."

"That's not true." Why was she bringing this up now? I didn't need it. "Diane, I really need to go."

"Yeah, you always do." She let out a heavy sigh, similar to mine. She was as annoyed with me as I was with her. We were equally talented at goading each other. "I guess we'll see you on Sunday. I hope you're in a better mood."

With as much politeness as I could muster, I told her goodbye and ended the call. I turned back to the computer and continued going through all the information I had. But I couldn't focus. My mind was on the conversation with Diane. There was so much there, so much that she didn't acknowledge. Old memories boiled to the surface, ones of her in college, of her getting into a bad situation and me helping her. At a cost to me. But did she remember that I'd come to her rescue? *No*, I thought. All she remembered was that ultimately I'd taken the blame for her mistake. That seemed to be the way it always was. Even Uncle Brad knew that, knew that she would often get in trouble and manage to make it look like my fault. My parents never seemed to see that, and in their eyes, I was the troublemaker. But Uncle Brad knew. He saw what went on.

I pulled opened a desk drawer and pulled out a framed photo of me with Brad. I didn't keep it on my desk, I didn't want anyone to ask questions about Brad and me. But I often pulled out the photo because it gave me a sense of peace in times of chaos.

I stared at the photo. Uncle Brad had wavy brown hair, broad shoulders, and muscular arms. When he sensed I wasn't okay, he would wrap me in a huge comforting hug. In the photo, he was leaning against the front of a black Dodge Charger, me beside him. We both had big smiles on our faces. That had been a good day, in part because Diane had been at summer camp. Those times when she was gone were always easier for me.

I smiled, remembering Brad and the Charger. He loved that car, the sleek lines, the front grill, the shiny bumper. Then something occurred to me. I stared at the photo and the front of the car, then set the photo aside. I got on the computer and went to the pictures that Ivan Eklund had taken of Logan Pickett. I scrolled through them until I found the ones of Logan that Eklund had taken from afar. I quickly clicked through them until I found the one where Logan was on his bike, looking off into the distance. In that photo was the partial view of a car that Ernie and I had noticed the other day. The front end of the car had a unique grill and the bumper was slightly scraped. The damage looked similar to the Hyundai that I'd seen Mallory Casper driving.

She'd been around Logan at the same time that Ivan Eklund had been taking pictures of the boy. She must've been visiting Latoya Anderson. Had she seen Eklund around? I needed to talk to her, now. I logged off my computer and hurried out of the room.

CHAPTER THIRTY-SIX

No one answered when I rang the bell at the Casper house, but I wasn't easily giving up. I opened the screen door and knocked hard on the wood door. The sunlight dimmed, and I glanced up. Dark clouds obscured the sun. I rapped a third time, and Mallory Casper finally answered.

"Yes?" she asked. Her eyes darted to my badge and gun. "Can I help you?"

I nodded. "I'm sorry to bother you." I introduced myself. "I'm a homicide detective with the Denver Police Department."

"Is there something wrong?"

I gestured at her car in the driveway. "I was here earlier. I rang the bell and knocked, and you didn't answer. I could've sworn you were here." I didn't want to tell her I'd followed her.

"I'm sorry. I was in the basement for a while, and I must not have heard you. What do you need?"

"I'm looking into the death of Logan Pickett. Have you heard about that?"

She glanced past me. "Um, I think so. Was that on the news?"

"It might have been." Then I remembered where I'd seen her. "Or you might've heard about it from Latoya Anderson."

"How do you know that I know her?"

"I visited Latoya the other day, and you were coming out of her house. I recognize you. You were at a book club?"

"Oh yes, that's right." She looked past me to the street again. "Would you like to come inside?"

"Thank you."

I followed her into a small foyer, then she went into a living room. It was all white walls, a tan couch and chairs, and glass coffee and end tables. Very neutral, very uninviting, especially gloomy with the dark clouds outside obscuring the sun. She sat down on a chair and indicated for me to take the couch. She ran a hand along her jeans, then looked me square in the eyes. "What can I do for you?"

"Do you know a man named Ivan Eklund?"

She ran her tongue over her lips and thought about that. "No, why?"

"He's a person of interest, and as we were going through his phone records, we noticed that he called your house."

Her eyebrows pinched. "That's strange. Maybe he knows my husband. I can't keep track of all of his friends," she said with a small laugh.

I nodded. "That makes sense. Is your husband around? I'd like to talk to him about Eklund."

She shook her head. "He's out and about. He's a trucker, and he's out of town a lot. When he's home, he has a lot of catching up to do, errands to run." She glanced out the front window. "I'm not sure when he'll be home. I don't know if you'd want to wait. It could be a long time."

"Will he be home for dinner?"

"He might be out with friends tonight."

"Was your husband home this previous weekend?"

"He was out of town."

"I thought he was in town, and that he visited the Gold Creek Gun Range Saturday night."

"Yes, that's right. He got into town that afternoon, but he didn't come to the house. I was in bed when he finally came home late, and he was gone early Sunday, so it felt like he was still out of town."

"I'll definitely want to talk to him."

"Of course."

"Have you seen anybody strange in the neighborhood in the last week or two?"

"No. I'm a bit of a homebody, though. I don't go out much."

"Have you ever heard other parents at the school talking about Ivan Eklund?"

A head shake. Her eyes darted away from me. "Is that all?"

I leaned forward and put my hands on my knees. "No, there's one other thing. Eklund was a photographer. He took school pictures at Roosevelt Elementary. We have reason to believe he might have been taking pictures of other children, and that might be where he first took an interest in Logan Pickett. And I have one of Eklund's pictures of Logan riding his bike near Latoya's house. I noticed your car in that picture, with the flared grill and scratched bumper."

"I don't know much about Logan."

"Yes, but it appears your car was close to Latoya Anderson's house, parked on Third Avenue, near Cook Street. Were you visiting her, and if so, did you see Ivan Eklund? He was thinner, with short blond hair and blue eyes."

She sat back in the chair and crossed one leg over the other. "I don't think so. I don't even remember the last time I was at Latoya's house."

"Besides the day before yesterday, for your book club?"

"Oh yes, that's right. Before that, I don't know when it would've been."

I thought back to Eklund's photos on his laptop. "I believe the picture was dated about a week ago."

She mulled that over as a flash of lightning lit the room. "I must've been visiting Latoya." She let out a nervous laugh. "I'm sorry, I just don't remember. I've been a little stressed lately."

"When you were there, do you recall seeing a blue Honda Pilot?"

"I'm sorry, Detective, but I just don't remember."

"Do you recall seeing Logan talking to any strangers?"

She cracked her knuckles. "I saw Logan playing with Terrell. That's about the extent of it."

Thunder clapped loudly and we both glanced out the window.

"Could be a big storm," she observed.

I nodded and scanned the room, my gaze stopping on glass shelves on one wall. There were several framed photos of a little boy in a baseball uniform. I pointed at them. "It looks like you have a son about Logan's age."

"Yes, that's true." She hesitated. "I think he's a year younger than Logan. They don't play together."

I stood up. "Do you mind?" Before she could answer, I moved to the shelves and studied the photos. Her son had brown hair and eyes. "What's his name?"

"Curtis."

"He's a nice looking young man." I looked over my shoulder at her.

"Thank you," she said, something akin to melancholy on her face. Just as quickly, it vanished.

"Does your son go to Roosevelt Elementary?"

"Uh, yes."

The house was quiet, no TV on, no sounds of children. "Is your son here now? He might know something about Eklund."

"He's playing at a friend's house, and I'm not sure that I'd want you questioning him." She balked. "He's pretty shy, and it might scare him."

I glanced at her. "I might need to talk to him."

She drew in a breath. "If you feel that's absolutely necessary, but I'd want my husband to okay it."

"Fair enough. Do you have other children?"

"No, just Curtis."

I looked at other pictures of her son. "Did Eklund take pictures of your son at the school?"

She shrugged. "I have no idea who actually takes the pictures." She stood up. "I hope I'm not being rude, but I need to take care of some things. Do you have any other questions?"

"I do have one more thing."

"You just said that." She laughed, but she didn't mean it to be funny.

I smiled. "Eklund might've been interested or involved in a militia group."

"Oh?" She moved over by me.

"Is your husband a member of a militia group? Might Eklund be contacting your husband because of their mutual connection to this militia group?"

"No and no." She was impatient for me to leave now.

Lightning flashed again. I turned and glanced into a dining room. A partially finished puzzle lay on a table, along with a stack of comic books and a little Batman figurine. Mallory stepped in front of me, blocking my view. She held up a hand, indicating I should go to the door. As I went into the foyer, I studied her face. Her eyes were blank.

"If you'd like to come back later, maybe my husband will be home," she said.

"I appreciate your time." I stepped out onto the porch.

"I hope you find what happened to that little boy," she said. Then the door quickly shut.

As I walked back to my car I felt Mallory's eyes on me. I glanced over my shoulder to see her peeking out the front window.

CHAPTER THIRTY-SEVEN

Thunder rumbled, and heavy clouds made the day dark and ominous. I got back to my car and just sat there, thinking. Something wasn't right with my conversation with Mallory Casper. My phone rang, sidetracking my thoughts.

"Sarah, I've got something." Ernie was talking so fast he was stumbling over his words. "I haven't have a chance to talk to Dean Casper yet, but get this. They lost a kid about a year ago. His name was Curtis. He died in a boating accident, and according to people that know the family, the wife was especially devastated. Dean has been telling people at work that he's almost glad to be on the road because she's so depressed and not herself. He says that she puts on a good front for other people, but behind the scenes, it's terrible. He even told his friends before this last trip that he was worried about her, that he thought she might do something crazy. They assumed he might've meant suicide, but what if it was something else?"

I gripped the wheel and all the pieces started falling into place. I stared at Mallory's house. I didn't see any movement, and it appeared she was no longer at the window.

"Sarah? Are you there?"

"I just talked to Mallory," I said slowly. "She made it sound as if her son was still alive."

"He's not. I even looked up the record. They were at a lake near Estes Park. It's all there. The kid's dead. And Dean has been hinting about moving out of state."

"We've been looking at this the wrong way. What if Eklund called *Mallory*, not Dean?" Now I was talking fast. "Eklund had been asking the security guard at the school about a woman in the neighborhood, and both the security guard and I assumed he was interested in Audra Pickett because he was asking about Logan. But Mallory fits the description that Susan gave me. Is it possible he was trying to figure out what Mallory was up to? Maybe he had some suspicions? He saw her watching the boys? And Mallory's car was in that picture." I then told him what I'd seen in the photo. "I assumed she was at Latoya's house, and maybe *she* had spotted Eklund. Could it be the other way around? Could it be that he had seen *her*, and he wondered what she was doing in his neighborhood, if she was watching Logan? And was he looking at militia groups because he was trying to find out about the Caspers? I'll bet if we look closer at some of those photos in the neighborhood, we might see Mallory in them." I hit the wheel. "And she has the Batman figurine."

"What?"

"Audra Pickett said a Batman figurine was missing from Logan's room. I just saw one at the Casper house."

"Where are you?"

I started the car and drove down the street.

"Where are you?" he repeated.

I parked around the corner and got out of the car. "Ernie, there's something I want to check."

"You be careful, Sarah. Spats and I are headed over there right now."

"You're a ways away, right? I want to look around the house."

He cursed. "Wait for me before you talk to Mallory again."

By now I had trotted down the street. I went up the neighbor's drive and crossed their front lawn, then went around the corner of their house. "If Mallory kidnapped a child, she could have him right here in the house."

"What are you doing?"

I lowered my voice. "Looking for signs of Samuel Quigley."

"You think she kidnapped him too?"

"It's a possibility." I edged along the neighbor's house, careful not to step onto Mallory's property. I couldn't be tampering with a potential crime scene. I passed by the flower bed and the rake and shovel that leaned against the side of the house. I moved toward the back of the house and saw a basement window.

"A basement window has been broken. I can see cardboard taped on the inside."

"Hang up the phone," came a voice from behind me.

My back went rigid. I slowly turned around to see Mallory with a small gun in her hand. It was aimed at my chest. She held it well, no trembling. She knew how to use a gun.

"Sarah?" Ernie yelled. "What's going on? Sarah?" He sounded frantic now.

"Show me the phone and hang it up," Mallory said more forcefully. Lightning lit the sky, giving her a quick ghostly glow.

I carefully held the phone out away from my ear.

"Let me see you disconnect it." I showed her the screen and carefully ended the call as Ernie continued to shout at me. "Throw it over here."

I did as instructed, and tossed the phone on the lawn. I held my hands away from my sides, away from my Glock. I was hoping she wouldn't notice the gun, but I wasn't that lucky.

"Take the gun out, carefully, and toss it over here. Don't try anything stupid. I know how to use this gun." She gave her gun a little wiggle. "No tricks."

I slowly unholstered my gun, bent slightly, and tossed the gun near my phone. "When I talked to you, you acted as if your son was alive, but he's dead."

"That's true." Her lip trembled. "Curtis was such a good boy." She stared at me. "Do you have children?"

I shook my head. "No, I can't imagine what you've gone through, losing your son." *Keep her talking*, I thought. My gaze darted behind her. Where were the neighbors?

"You're right. You have no idea what it's like. It ripped my heart out. I wasn't sure how I could go on. Days and days of crying, not being able to get out of bed." She let out a burdened sigh. "Dean worried about me at first, thought I should see a therapist and get on medication. I tried that, and it didn't really help. Eventually he stayed on the road more, far away from me. I know he thinks our problems are just about me, but I know he misses our son as much as I do. I know he's suffering too. Then I realized something." She got a faraway look in her eyes. I glanced behind her again, wishing a car would come by, wishing a neighbor would see us. "If we could get another little boy, someone just like our Curtis, it would be just like before."

I shifted on my feet, edging closer to her house. She didn't notice. I glanced toward the basement window, wondering if Samuel Quigley was down there.

"So you kidnapped Logan Pickett," I said. "He looks a lot like Curtis, and like Samuel Quigley, another boy who was kidnapped last night."

"If I was going to replace Curtis, I needed a boy that looked like him." Her eyes seemed lost, disconnected. Blank. Whatever temporary grip she'd had on reality had vanished. "It would've been just fine. Logan was well fed here, and I would've taken good care of him."

"In Idaho?"

Her eyes widened in surprise. "Yes. It wouldn't matter where we go. I'd have loved him. How do you know about Idaho?"

I nodded. "I know a lot." I sidled a little closer to her house. Closer to the rake leaning against the wall. "You were watching Logan when you were hanging around over near Latoya's house, right? You weren't at Latoya's those times. How long had you been watching him before you took him?" She didn't answer. "And Ivan Eklund saw you, didn't he?" I shook my head. "All along I've assumed Eklund had some connection to your husband. You're the one that Eklund was asking about at the school."

Rage leaped into her eyes. "If he had only left things alone. He'd seen me watching Logan, and then he started asking around about me."

"How do you know that?"

She shook her head in disgust. Lightning flashed. "I talked to him about it."

I remembered Ernie's report from Eklund's neighbor. "People also saw you arguing at his house." She didn't reply. "You didn't have to kill him."

"He would be alive today if he had left things alone," she snarled. "He messed everything up."

"Why did Eklund even suspect you? He didn't know you, did he?"

"No, but he said he saw me talking to another boy in the neighborhood and trying to get him into my car."

"You mean, another boy *before* Logan?"

"Yeah. That one wouldn't come with me." She paused, then continued. "Then Ivan started asking questions, poking around my business. He found out Dean is in a militia." Another pause. "He shouldn't have confronted me. It was none of his business. I had to do something." Another clap of thunder punctuated her words. "He made choices, and he had to pay."

"How did that happen?"

"It was easy. I went over to Ivan's house, and I came through the back. It was late, but he let me inside." She held up her gun. "He didn't want to argue with a gun pointed at him."

I glanced at the gun she was holding. "What about the gun left at Eklund's house?"

"I had two guns. The one that killed Eklund is one of Dean's. It's unregistered, part of his militia stuff."

"Slick. How'd you get him into the bedroom?"

She laughed at that. "People will do a lot of things when a loaded gun is pointed at them." She cocked an eyebrow at me. "He was pathetic, begging me to let him live. But I knew that he would tell people about Logan. He'd figured it all out. He knew when he heard that Logan was missing that I'd kidnapped the boy." She shrugged her shoulders. "Ivan had to go. He would've told. So I ordered him to go back to the bedroom and sit on the bed." She seemed to be picturing it.

Something occurred to me. "Did you have Ivan delete photos he'd taken Saturday afternoon?" She nodded. "You didn't realize he had photos of Logan from another day that had your car in them."

"It doesn't matter now. I took care of Ivan."

"You tried to make it look like a suicide."

"I made him take the Sig Sauer while I kept my gun on him. He was scared, so I had to help him pull the trigger."

My stomach roiled. She'd been cold and cruel beyond measure, and my heart broke for Eklund, for his last moments. Mallory seemed oblivious to that.

"Where are you parked?" she asked.

"I parked around the corner. No one saw me."

"Good."

I gestured toward the broken basement window. "Was Logan down there?"

Her eyes didn't leave me. "I kept him down there. He was learning to obey."

"Why'd you kill him?" I knew that wasn't likely true, but I wanted to keep her talking.

"No!" The same fury that she'd unleashed when discussing Eklund poured forth again. "Logan wouldn't listen. I told him he needed to obey, but he got scared, said he was missing his mom. I was going to be his mom," she insisted. "He didn't understand that, and he tried to get away. He bashed the window and tried to climb out, and when I went to grab him, he cut his arm. It was his own fault." Her mouth contorted in a mix of rage and pain. "I couldn't do anything about it. I tried to cover his arm, to stop the bleeding, but I couldn't. And I couldn't take him anywhere, either. He just shouldn't have broken that window."

"He bled out in the basement."

She nodded. "Well, then I had to do something with the body, so I waited until night, and then drove him over by Ivan's house."

"And you put that poor little boy in the dumpster," I said, not able to conceal my own disgust.

Her eyes narrowed. "I couldn't leave him in the basement. Dean was going to be home."

"So you set up Ivan." I'd been right in that deduction. "If Logan's body was found near the house of a man who'd apparently committed suicide, it might look as if that man were guilty. And by that time the police figured any different, you'd be out of state."

I thought I saw movement in a window in the neighbor's house. I glanced over, but couldn't see anyone. Why was it that when you needed a nosy neighbor out and about, everybody was minding their own business?

"Dean and I are going to Idaho. We'll rent this house for now."

"After Logan died, you couldn't stand it, could you? You take another boy, figuring you'll go out of state, making him that much harder to find. How'd you kidnap them? Neither boy yelled for help."

"The boys know me because they saw me when Curtis was alive," she said simply. "I was in the neighborhood and saw Logan walking home. I asked him if he knew where another neighbor lived. I told him if he could show me, then I'd drive him home. He believed me and got in the car."

"What about Samuel Quigley?"

"I asked him to help me find my dog. He was a little more hesitant, but I said I'd pay him and that I had comic books to give him, and he got in the car."

"And no one saw you."

She tipped her head. "Apparently not."

"How is Dean helping you?"

"He doesn't know anything. I'll tell him when the time is right." She took a step toward me. "I have to deal with you first." She snarled again. "You saw the Batman figurine."

I nodded. "Did Logan have that with him the day you took him?"

"Yes, in his pocket. I didn't know. I found it in the basement. I should've thrown it out, but I just couldn't." She nodded her head at me. "Seeing it was your mistake."

"Yes, but keeping it was *yours*."

She gripped the gun a little tighter. "It will be my last one."

Lightning crossed the sky again, and a horrendous clap of thunder hit. Mallory jumped and turned slightly, giving me my opening. I dived left, grabbed the rake, and lifted it as Mallory turned back to me. I swung fast and slammed the rake end down on her arm. The gun went off, the bullet hitting the ground.

Mallory screamed as her arm snapped. The gun dropped from her hand, and I quickly kicked it away as I snatched up my own gun.

"Don't move!" I said. I was breathing hard, feeling the blood pounding in my ears.

Just then, a woman with an umbrella came around the corner. Finally, a neighbor. "Mallory? What's going on?" Her gaze went from Mallory to me.

I glanced at her. "Call 911. Tell them to get someone here fast."

Mallory was weeping now. "You've ruined everything. It would've all been fine this time."

The woman in the umbrella whirled around and ran back to her house. I glared at Mallory.

"You talk about the pain you suffered, but what about Logan's parents? Think about his mother and father, what they're feeling now."

Mallory hung her head and sobbed. "I just wanted the pain to end. I wanted my family back."

"A kidnapped boy isn't family," I said.

I reached down for my phone and called for backup. Mallory was on her knees, her broken arm cradled to her chest. I felt my body slow to normal. I kept the gun on Mallory as sirens approached.

CHAPTER THIRTY-EIGHT

A moment later, two uniformed officers ran up. I pointed at Mallory, who was now sitting cross-legged on the ground, still clutching her broken arm.

"Watch her," I ordered one of them. "And call an ambulance." I gestured at the other. "We're going in the house. There may be a kidnapped child inside." He followed me around to the front. I opened the door and hollered "Hello?"

No one responded, and I glanced at the officer. He nodded, and we went inside, guns drawn. We quickly walked through the living room, kitchen, and two bedrooms and bathroom down the hall. No one was around.

"The basement," I said. The officer nodded again, and we found a door that led downstairs. I opened it and flipped on the light. Then I called out.

"I don't hear anything," he murmured.

I took a breath, my nerves tingling, and we went downstairs. It was dark, so I turned on a light at the bottom of the stairs, which illuminated a large room with a pool table and a gun safe in the corner. I noticed a short hallway and another door. I walked up to it, the officer behind me. A shiny new sliding-bolt lock was installed high up on the door, and it was bolted shut. I reached up, slid the bolt, and opened the door. Light from the hallway spilled into the room, and I saw a futon in the corner, a little body on it. My heart raced. Was he dead? Then a boy with brown hair rolled over and blinked at me. I gave the room a quick glance to determine no one else was in it. Then I holstered my gun. He sat up.

"Who're you?" His voice trembled.

As gently as I could, I said, "I'm a police detective. I'm here to help you. Are you Samuel Quigley?"

He rolled his legs off the bed. "Yes." He stared at me, then at the officer behind me. "Where's that person?"

I got down on one knee. "We took her away. She's not going to hurt you."

He stood up, unsure at first what to do. "I want my mommy."

"We're going to take you to her," I said.

He hesitated a second longer, and his lower lip trembled.

"It's okay." I went over and held out a hand. "It's going to be okay," I said. He nodded his head and took my hand. "Are you hurt?"

He shook his head. "I'm hungry."

I smiled at that. "We'll get you something to eat. Come on, let's go."

The officer went first, and Samuel and I walked upstairs. When we went outside, another squad car pulled up. Two officers got out, and I took charge.

"One of you go around back, make sure no one enters the house." He nodded and headed around the side of the house. I still held Samuel's hand. I jerked my head at some of the neighbors who were congregating, wondering what was going on. "You keep everyone back," I said to the other officer. "This is a crime scene."

"Okay," she said and walked toward the crowd of onlookers.

Spats and Ernie drove up, tires screeching. They hustled up the walk to me.

"What the hell happened here?" Ernie asked. He looked at Samuel and his face immediately softened. Whatever anger he and Spats might've felt about my acting alone vanished.

Ernie bent down to look Samuel in the eye. "Hey there. I'm Detective Moore. How're you doing?"

Samuel leaned against me. "Where's my mom?"

"We'll get her as soon as we can." Ernie glanced up at me, knowing what needed to happen.

"He's okay, just hungry," I whispered.

He smiled at Samuel. "How about you ride with me? We'll get you something to eat, and we'll take you to the station, where your mom can come pick you up. You're not in any trouble, and I would love to hear how brave you've been. I'll bet you have quite a story to tell. Sound okay?"

Samuel glanced at me, then nodded. "Can I have a hamburger?"

Ernie smiled. "You bet." He straightened up and took Samuel's hand. "We'll catch up soon," he said to me.

I leaned over and spoke in his ear. "Mallory's sitting around the corner. Don't let the kid see her."

He nodded. "Come on," he said to Samuel, using his body to block the boy from Mallory's view.

Spats and I waited until they'd gotten in Ernie's car. The car drove away, and Spats turned to me. "I want to hear what happened. You had us scared to death."

"I want to hear too," Rizzo said as he walked up. A few big raindrops pelted us, and he glanced up. "I hope this damn storm holds off until we can get finished here," he said. "What went on here?"

I went through everything that had occurred from the time I'd watched Mallory drive to Target to going down in the basement and rescuing Samuel Quigley. When I got to the last part, Spats shook his head at me. Rizzo gave him a look that said to be quiet for the moment.

I glanced at Spats. "I had to act. If the Quigley boy was in there, and if he was hurt, I had to get to him."

He nodded begrudgingly. "I'm glad you got him out alive."

We edged toward the side of the house, where an officer was still guarding Mallory.

"She confessed, huh?" Spats asked.

I nodded. "Logan, and then Samuel, were supposed to be replacements for her own son."

Rizzo and Spats both studied her, then simultaneously shook their heads. If Mallory heard them, she didn't show it. An ambulance drove up, and two EMT's got out.

"She's over there," I said to them. We followed the EMTs.

"Hey," Mallory looked up at me. "Where's Curtis? Is he still in the basement? He'll want some dinner." Her tenuous hold on reality was gone.

"Get her out of here," I said to the EMTs. They nodded at me and set to work stabilizing her broken arm. Then they put her on a stretcher and loaded her into the back of the ambulance.

"You go with her," I said to Spats.

"Yep, I got this. Should be an interesting interview," he said as he got into the ambulance. The door closed, and he gave us a small wave through the back window. Then the vehicle drove off.

Rizzo turned to me. "It's going to be a long night for you. Once you're finished, you go home and get some rest. You need it." A CSI team drove up just as the rain began, tiny droplets. Rizzo spoke briefly to the team, then said to me, "Let's go inside."

It started raining more heavily, and we followed the team inside. I gave them a briefing on the case and what had happened at the house so that they'd know what to look for. They would methodically take pictures of the crime scene, take measurements of the rooms, use 3D cameras to document the crime scene, and collect evidence. They started working, and after watching them for a while, I went outside for some fresh air. As suddenly as the rain had begun, it had stopped, and the air smelled clean, pure, and untainted by the horrors that had happened in the Casper house. I drew in a few deep breaths, but the calm moment didn't last. A white SUV drove down the block and parked, then Dean Casper got out. He approached the house, and the uniformed officer stopped him. He swore at her, gesticulating at the house.

"I'll handle this," I called to the officer.

She let him past her, and I stepped off the porch.

"What the hell's going on here?" he said, his eyes wide with surprise and fear. "What happened?"

"Your wife is on the way to the hospital, and then we'll detain her for questioning."

"For what?"

"We've just begun an investigation, and I'd like to ask you a few questions." I formally introduced myself. "I'd like to ask you some questions about Samuel Quigley."

"Who's that?" He appeared genuinely surprised by the name.

"Your wife is a suspect in Samuel Quigley's kidnapping, and for the kidnapping and death of Logan Pickett."

His mouth fell open, and he had a hard time finding words. "What?" He tugged at his baseball cap and muttered, "Mallory, what did you do?"

"What did you know about this?"

His eyes were wide. "I don't understand what you mean. I don't know a thing about any kidnappings or death. I was on the road until this last Saturday. I got back into town, met some friends, and then I was at the gun range till late."

"What about since Saturday? You didn't see or hear anything unusual in your own home?"

He shook his head. Pain filled his eyes. He ran a hand over his face. "You don't understand. Since our son died it's been really hard. Mallory hasn't been herself, and when I'm home I haven't known what to do with her. I guess maybe ..." his voice trailed off. He took a big breath, then went on. "It's been hard as hell. She's been distant, and it just seems like we can't hardly talk anymore. I tried to get her to get some help, but she didn't want to listen. I didn't know what to do. Most days when I'm home, I just go somewhere else because it's too uncomfortable to be around her. I come home, and I go to bed. Hell, I don't even try to eat around here." He didn't seem to have a lot of sympathy left for his wife, and he also didn't seem to know a thing about her kidnapping spree.

"When you are at home, where do you hang out?"

"In the kitchen, the living room to watch TV, or the bedroom. Like I said, I'm not around that much."

"You don't go in the basement?"

He shook his head. "Of course not. Hardly ever."

"How has Mallory acted the last week or so?"

"When I talked to her on the phone, I guess she seemed a little more upbeat. I figured maybe she was excited about our move, that she thought the change would do her good."

"Your militia is going out of state?"

Now I got a hint of anger. "That's none of your business."

He was right, and I moved on. "Mallory gave you no hints of what she was going to do?"

He shook his head. "I didn't have any idea. When we talk on the phone, she doesn't tell me much. If you want to know the truth, we've been drifting apart since our son died."

"What did you discuss when you got home this last time?"

"I called to let her know I was in town, but that I wouldn't be at the house until late. When I got up Sunday morning, I guess she was a little nervous. I just figured that was Mallory being Mallory. We didn't talk much then, and I left the house for the day." Some of his blusteriness was gone. He glanced past me. "When can I go inside?"

"It's a crime scene, and we'll be here for quite a while. And if you don't mind, I'd like to talk to you some more, down at the station."

"Why?"

"This is a serious situation, and I need all the information I can get from you."

He grimaced, but then agreed.

"If you'll wait a moment." I found another officer, and instructed him to transport Casper to the station. "Tell him I'll be with him soon."

The officer walked over to Dean. They went to a squad car, got in, and left. I went back up on the front porch, but before I entered the house, I drew in a deep breath and let it out slowly. It had been a long forty-eight hours. Even so, I felt the tension release from my body. I hoped I would sleep well that night. As Rizzo had said, I needed it.

"Are you ready for this?" Harry asked as we parked in front of my parents' house. It was a beautiful Sunday afternoon, temperature in the seventies, not a cloud in the sky.

"Yeah, let's go inside." I was in shorts and a pullover, wearing my peppiest attitude.

We got out of the car, and Harry took a big salad bowl from me. We strolled up the walk of the two-story house that I'd grown up in. When we entered the foyer, we heard voices in the kitchen. Something was baking, a cinnamon smell that made my mouth water.

"They've already started," Harry said in a low voice. He looked sexy in khaki shorts and a denim shirt.

I smiled, and we strolled into the kitchen. My sister Diane was adding cut veggies to a plate of appetizers, and when she saw me, her look said that it was a good thing I'd showed up.

"Well, I'm glad to see you," she said.

"I told you I'd be here."

Harry smiled. "Diane, how are you?" He set the salad bowl on the counter and gave her a kiss on the cheek. *Bless him*, I thought. He's always so nice to her.

"Harry, how are you?" And Diane was always nice to him.

"Couldn't be better," he said. "I'm happy to be here celebrating your mom's birthday."

Diane glanced at me. "Yes, it's important."

I resisted shaking my head. She couldn't help but dig at me any way she could. She eyed me again and went back to the veggie tray. Before she could say more, my brother Hunter came through the back door. He's tall, with a shock of blond hair and the brightest bluest eyes. Quite the lady-killer. He saw me and smiled.

"Sarah! I'm so glad you made it. I've missed seeing you." He walked over and gave me a big bear hug. He always knows how to make me feel welcome.

"It's been crazy lately."

"I knew you'd make it for this," he said. "I know your work is important to you, but family is too. And you've never forgotten that."

I gave him a hug and looked over his shoulder at Diane. I smiled and said, "Yes, family is everything. Right, Diane?"

The killer has chosen his next target. Can Sarah stop him in time?

Get Deadly Invasion
The next book in the Detective Sarah Spillman Mystery Series!

Turn the page for a Sneak Peek.

DEADLY INVASION

CHAPTER ONE

He stood in the doorway, peering into the darkness. Over the sound of his own shallow breathing, he heard the slow, steady rhythm of the woman's breaths. He listened for a moment and watched the form on the bed. Rays of moonlight cascaded over her long blonde hair and gave her cheeks a soft glow. His nerves tingled in anticipation.

The bedroom window was open, and he heard a dog bark. Then silence. She stirred and mumbled something. He froze, then took a quiet step back and waited. Her breathing evened again. He slipped stealthily into the room, his footfalls silent on the carpet. He moved to the window, quietly closed it, then shut the blinds. The square of moonlight on the bed vanished. He gazed at the woman for a moment longer. His heart sped up, his palms began to sweat inside his gloves. He gripped the knife tighter and stepped over to the edge of the bed. The woman's mouth was slightly open, as if she were about to say something. He put the knife blade to her face, ran the edge of the blade along her lips, then up to her cheek, not enough to cut the skin, but enough that the cold metal woke her. She blinked a couple of times, then her eyes flew open. She started to sit up. He pressed one hand to her mouth, and pushed the blade against her neck. She sank back into the mattress, her body trembling.

"It's okay," he said softly. "Do what I say, and you won't get hurt."

She nodded slowly, but the terror in her eyes betrayed her. She knew everything would not be okay.

CHAPTER TWO

The sound of the 1940's-style jazz quartet greeted me with gusto as I walked into the banquet hall of the Westin Hotel near the Sixteenth Street Mall. The upbeat tune was familiar. Then I placed it. "Who Can It Be Now" by the Australian band Men at Work.

"You've got to be kidding me," I muttered under my breath. It was bad enough I had to come to this event, but to have a cheesy jazz quartet softening up a great 80s tune, that was too much.

I scanned the dimly lit room, searching for Harry Sousen in the throng of guests. Practically every man in the room was wearing a dark suit. I had no doubt Harry would be similarly dressed, which made finding him even harder. I walked between round tables covered in neatly pressed white tablecloths and scanned faces. I recognized a few by name only. This wasn't my crowd. Truthfully, it wasn't Harry's either, but being the president of his own computer consulting company, he had to rub elbows with many of these people; it was good for business.

The band finished "Who Can It Be Now" and I listened to the next tune. This one I didn't recognize, but it, too, had a familiar ring. I looked to the stage. Above it hung a large banner with blue lettering: "Denver Small Business Association." A podium sat centered on the stage, surrounded by chairs, ready for the awards presentation. I shouldn't have been so down on the event, but in my mind, Harry should've been receiving the award for Business Person of the Year, not Darren Barnes. I frowned. I'd met Darren a few times at this type of event. He was smug and arrogant, and he always left me feeling as if I needed to wash away his presence. Seeming to know I was thinking about him, Darren materialized in front of me.

"Sarah Spillman." He flashed a set of gleaming white teeth at me, his salesman smile in excellent form. He moved smoothly between people and approached me, took my hand, and pecked my cheek. "You look lovely this evening."

I resisted the urge to wipe away the subtle kiss. "Darren, it's nice to see you. Congratulations on your award." I was as sweet as I could be, which wasn't much, I admit.

The smile remained plastered on his face. "I suppose you're looking for Harry."

He wasn't faking the smile very well, showing too many teeth, keeping his brown eyes open. With a real smile, the eyes tend to close as the cheeks enlarge, forming the classic crow's feet around the eyes. None of that from Darren.

I nodded. "I got tied up at work and got here as soon as I could." I didn't know why I was explaining things to him. He made me feel as if I had to, which was part of what I didn't like about him. Among his many negative qualities, he'd made blatant comments in the past about the police, and how he didn't think my profession as a homicide detective was commendable. In some ways he reminded me of my sister, Diane, who often implied the same. A psychologist would say I was transferring some of my frustration with her to him. Possibly. Or maybe Darren just wasn't a nice guy.

"Well," Darren said, his smile intact but his eyes cold, "a woman like you shouldn't be left alone." He appraised me. "You know, you may be a homicide detective, but that would be fine with me."

I gritted my teeth and forced a laugh. That was another thing I didn't like about Darren. He joked about my relationship with Harry. I wasn't sure whether Darren was kidding about his interest in me or not. Regardless, I would never be interested in him.

"Darren–"

"Don't say a word." He stepped back and surveyed me again. "You do look ravishing. That blue dress does wonders for your eyes."

I didn't reply to that. "Have you seen Harry?" I said. Try as I might, I couldn't keep my smile.

"I just bought a Corvette. It's spectacular. Black. Sleek lines. We could take it out for a spin."

"What, are we in high school?"

He ran a hand over his brown hair. "Trust me, I'm better than any high schooler."

Was his act all in jest? I didn't want to make an enemy, but I wanted to take my handbag and smack the slimy look off his face. Instead, I made a show of rummaging in the bag so I wouldn't have to look at him. "So ... have you seen Harry?" I asked again.

"I'll give you a call." Before I could protest, he went on. "I believe he's talking to the mayor." He was tall and could look over the crowed. He reached for my elbow to escort me to Harry, then someone called his name. He glanced over his shoulder, disappointment in his eyes. His gaze fell back to me and lingered, an uncomfortable moment. "That dress does look good on you." The voice called again. Darren's eyes flashed hot. "Excuse me, please. I do hope to see you after the ceremony."

"Of course." It was insincere, but I don't think he caught it.

He smiled again, pointed toward Harry, and brushed against me as he stepped by.

"What a douchebag," I muttered under my breath. I smoothed my dress, wishing Darren hadn't made the comment about my eyes. I took a deep breath and squared my shoulders, then made my way across the hall. Of all the people to run into the second I walked through the door, it had to be Darren Barnes. I was still silently grousing about him when I saw a tall, handsome man with steel-gray hair and dark eyes. His dark suit and yellow tie fit him perfectly, enhancing his sleek physique. He turned, saw me, and his eyes lit up. All thoughts of Darren slipped away.

"Sarah."

With that one word, Harry made me feel like a queen. He held out a hand, *his* smile warm and genuine. I reached out and his hand enveloped mine, that small gesture a reassurance of my love for him. Harry, ever the gentleman, introduced me to the man he was chatting with. "I'd like you to meet Mayor Carlson."

I'd been in the same room as Mayor Carlson a few times, but the circumstances had been different, dealing with a homicide investigation. This time, it was much more pleasant.

Carlson obviously remembered me, and he smiled. "It's so nice to see you, Detective Spillman. We've never met formally. I'm Boyd." He held out a hand and I shook it.

"Sarah," I said.

"I sure appreciate your hard work."

I murmured a thank-you, and he gestured at Harry. "Harry and I were discussing the upcoming elections. In general terms, I assure you. I'm not pounding the pavement for votes." Harry and I laughed. Carlson waved a hand in the air. "Boring stuff. But it's what I have to do." He smiled, as practiced as Darren Barnes in that art. And yet I didn't feel the slime as I had with Darren. "If you'll forgive me," Boyd said. "I do need to mingle. Part of the job."

"It was good to see you again," Harry said.

Carlson nodded, and we watched him move away and greet other people with precision. He knew how to make people feel comfortable, eliciting genuine smiles and laughs from everyone he spoke to.

"He's a nice enough man," Harry said in a low voice, "but I don't agree much with his politics."

"I could never rub elbows and schmooze people like that," I said. "I'm too blunt."

Harry put his arm around my shoulder. "Yes you are. And I love you for it."

I squeezed his hand. "Sorry I'm late."

"No worries. Would you like a drink?" Harry took in my dress. "You look stunning. I love that blue. What it does to your eyes."

"Thanks." I frowned.

"What?"

"Darren Barnes just said the same thing. Then he asked me out for a drive in his new car."

He tipped his head, bemused. "He did? You think he was kidding?"

"I would like to think so," I said. "I've never liked the guy. He's ... smarmy."

"In what way?"

I mulled on it for a moment. "I can't put my finger on it. His words are nice ..."

"Well, he'll be busy schmoozing with other people the rest of the night. And if he comes by, we'll dodge him."

I smiled. "I like the sound of that."

"Now let's enjoy the party."

"Right."

He caught the sarcasm. "Thanks for coming. I know you don't like these events."

"Anything for you." I meant that.

He kissed my cheek, and *that* I didn't mind. "How about that drink?"

I nodded toward the bar behind him. "I would love a martini."

He took my hand. "You got it."

We made our way to the bar, got drinks, and went to a table with several other guests. Soon everyone was taking their seats. Harry introduced me to a few people, and I played the chit-chat game. Finally a prime rib dinner was served. I had to admit, it was delicious. Unfortunately, it came with a side of awards, and that meant having to listen to Darren give a speech. He was good, though. He had a way of working the crowd, punctuating his speech with well-timed jokes that elicited plenty of laughter. At one point, Harry leaned over and whispered in my ear. "He aspires to politics."

"That explains why I don't like him."

"Yeah, I don't much care for him either." Harry caught a whiff of my perfume and whispered, "I can't wait to get out of here and take you home."

He put his hand under the table and squeezed my knee. I wanted nothing more than to go home with him right then. Instead, we suffered through more speeches. Finally, the award ceremony was over. Harry stood up.

"Let's go home."

We said polite good-byes to the others at the table and turned to go. Out of the corner of my eye, I saw Darren Barnes making his way toward us.

"Harry," I murmured.

He glanced over my shoulder and saw Darren. "Let's get out of here. I'll talk to him later."

Darren was too quick for us. "How about this?" he said, holding up a plaque with his name on it.

"Congratulations," Harry said. He put an arm around my waist, pulling me close. "If you'll excuse us, Sarah and I need to go."

"Sure," Darren said.

We turned and hurried for the door. I felt Darren's eyes on me. Harry held me close as if to shield me from Darren. We went outside and the valet brought our car around.

"What is it with Darren?" I said as I slid into the passenger seat.

"I've never really liked him, but he throws a lot of business my way." Harry pulled onto the street.

"I know." It was part of why I was trying not to make too big a deal about Darren. "You know how he is about the police." I thought about my encounter with him. "It's like I'm somehow not worthy."

"Of being a cop? You're a great homicide detective, and you know it."

I thought about that, trying to pull together what I felt. "It's more than that."

"Wait. He thinks you're not worthy of me?"

I stared out the windshield. "Maybe."

He rested his hand on my leg. "You know that's not the case. Sarah, you're beautiful, smart, and I love you."

I dismissed that with a wave of my hand. "It reminds me of Diane."

He drew in a breath, looked over, then back at the street. "What's going on here? Is this about Darren, or about you?"

"What?" I snapped. "You should've heard him."

"I'm sorry I missed it."

"Me too."

He glanced over his shoulder, then suddenly pulled over and

put the car in park. He drummed the steering wheel, and I stayed silent. He finally spoke. "Sarah, I don't know what happened between you and Diane when you were in college, but you can't continue to let it overshadow things now."

"I'm not."

He twisted in his seat to lock eyes with me. "Are you sure? I get that Darren isn't a great guy, but he's not Diane."

"No," I said slowly. "He's not."

"And maybe it's time to talk to Diane, to tell her how you feel about what happened to you in college."

A long time ago I made a mistake. A big mistake. I was a sophomore in college. Diane was in med school, and she messed up, did something she shouldn't have. She was terrified it would screw things up for her, that she'd get kicked out of med school. I stepped in to help her, and I worried then that what I did could cost me my career in law enforcement that I'd dreamed of since I was a teenager. The whole incident has been eating at me ever since.

"Maybe," I said.

"Hey." He leaned over and kissed me, long and lingering. "Let's go home and forget about both of them."

I put a hand on his chest and felt his heart thumping. "That sounds good."

He kissed me again, then forced himself back to the wheel. He pulled into the street and we drove home. And I didn't think about Diane or Darren for the rest of the night. However, I would have to deal with both sooner than I realized.

DEADLY INVASION

Detective Sarah Spillman Mystery Series Book 2

is available on Amazon

AUTHOR'S NOTE

Dear Reader,

If you enjoyed *Deadly Christmas*, would you please write an honest review? You have no idea how much it warms my heart to get a new review. And this isn't just for me. Think of all the people out there who need reviews to make decisions, and you would be helping them.

You are awesome for doing so, and I am grateful to you!

ABOUT THE AUTHOR

Renée's early career as a counselor gives her a unique ability to write characters with depth and personality, and she now works as a business analyst. She lives in the mountains west of Denver, Colorado and enjoys hiking, cycling, and reading when she's not busy writing her next novel.

Renée loves to travel and has visited numerous countries around the world. She has also spent many summer days at her parents' cabin in the hills outside of Boulder, Colorado, which was the inspiration for the setting of Taylor Crossing in her novel *Nephilim*.

She is the author of the Reed Ferguson mysteries, the Dewey Webb historical mysteries, and the Sarah Spillman police procedurals. She also wrote the standalone suspense novels *The Girl in the Window* and *What's Yours is Mine*, *Nephilim: Genesis of Evil*, a supernatural thriller, along with children's novels and other short stories.

Visit Renée at www.reneepawlish.com.

RENÉE'S BOOKSHELF

The Sarah Spillman Mysteries:

Deadly Connections

Deadly Invasion

Deadly Guild

Deadly Revenge

Deadly Judgment

Deadly Target

Deadly Past

Deadly Premonition

Deadly Price

Deadly Christmas

The Sarah Spillman Mysteries Boxsets:

Sarah Spillman Mysteries Books 1-3

Jo Gunning Thrillers:

Gunning for Trouble

Gunning for Truth

Gunning for Hire

Standalone Psychological Suspense:

The Girl in the Window

What's Yours Is Mine

Reed Ferguson Mysteries:

This Doesn't Happen In The Movies

Reel Estate Rip-Off

The Maltese Felon

Farewell, My Deuce

Out Of The Past

Torch Scene

The Lady Who Sang High

Sweet Smell Of Sucrets

The Third Fan

Back Story

Night of the Hunted

The Postman Always Brings Dice

Road Blocked

Small Town Focus

Nightmare Sally

The Damned Don't Die

Double Iniquity

The Lady Rambles

A Killing

Dangers on a Train

In a Lowly Place

Shadow of a Snout

Ace in the Hole

Walk Softly, Danger

Elvis And The Sports Card Cheat

A Gun For Hire

Cool Alibi

The Big Steal

The Wrong Woman

Reed Ferguson Mysteries Boxsets:

The Reed Ferguson Series: Box Set 1-3

The Reed Ferguson Series: Books 4-6

The Reed Ferguson Series: Books 7-9

The Reed Ferguson Series: Books 10-12

The Reed Ferguson Series: Books 13-15

The Reed Ferguson Series: Books 16-18

Reed Ferguson Stories: Five Mystery Short Tales

The Reed Ferguson Series Boxset Collection

Dewey Webb Historical Mystery Series:

Web of Deceit

Murder In Fashion

Secrets and Lies

Honor Among Thieves

Trouble Finds Her

Mob Rule

Murder At Eight

Second Chance

Double Cross

Dewey Webb Historical Mystery Series Boxsets:

The Dewey Webb Series: Box Set 1-3

The Dewey Webb Series: Box Set 4-6

The Noah Winter Adventure

(A Young Adult Mystery Series)

The Emerald Quest

Dive into Danger

Terror On Lake Huron

Take Five Collection (Mystery Anthology)

Nephilim Genesis of Evil (Supernatural Mystery)

Codename Richard: A Ghost Story

The Taste of Blood: A Vampire Story

This War We're In (Middle-grade Historical Fiction)

Nonfiction:

The Sallie House: Exposing the Beast Within

AFTERWORD

A long time ago, I wrote three Sarah Spillman short stories, but I never fully developed her character.

Then I moved on to the Reed Ferguson series, but by book four (*Farewell, My Deuce*), I thought it would be fun to bring Sarah, Ernie, and Spats into the Reed series.

She has appeared in every Reed book since then.

For a long time, I thought Sarah's character could be expanded, and I finally did so with *Deadly Connections*.

It has been a lot of fun to see her grow into her own, along with the other characters in the series.

I now have ideas to spin off some of those characters into their own series.

We'll see. I have so many ideas and so little time!

ACKNOWLEDGMENTS

The author gratefully acknowledges all those who helped in the writing of this book, especially: Beth Treat and Beth Higgins. Thanks again to Randy Powers, retired, Chief Deputy. He continues to answer my questions, no matter how trivial, and any mistakes in police procedure are mine.
If I've forgotten anyone, please accept my apologies.

To all my beta readers: I am in your debt!

Dianne Biscoe, Brenda Enkhaus, Tracy Gestewitz, Sherry Ito, Becky Neilsen, Becky Serna, Lynn Short, Peg Smith, Albert Stevens, Joyce Stumpff, Marlene Van Matre

Deadly Connections

Published by Creative Cat Press

Printed in Great Britain
by Amazon